Churchill's Gold:

the Ripples of War

by

Robert D. Hubble

Copyright © 2012 Robert D. Hubble.

All rights reserved.

ISBN-10: 1479388998
ISBN-13: 978-1479388998

DEDICATION

To the man in the park,
Who told a tale of mystery, with hope of fortune.
That led to misery and loss, and a life,
Forever after, fighting demons in the dark.

Cover design by Christina Voyles

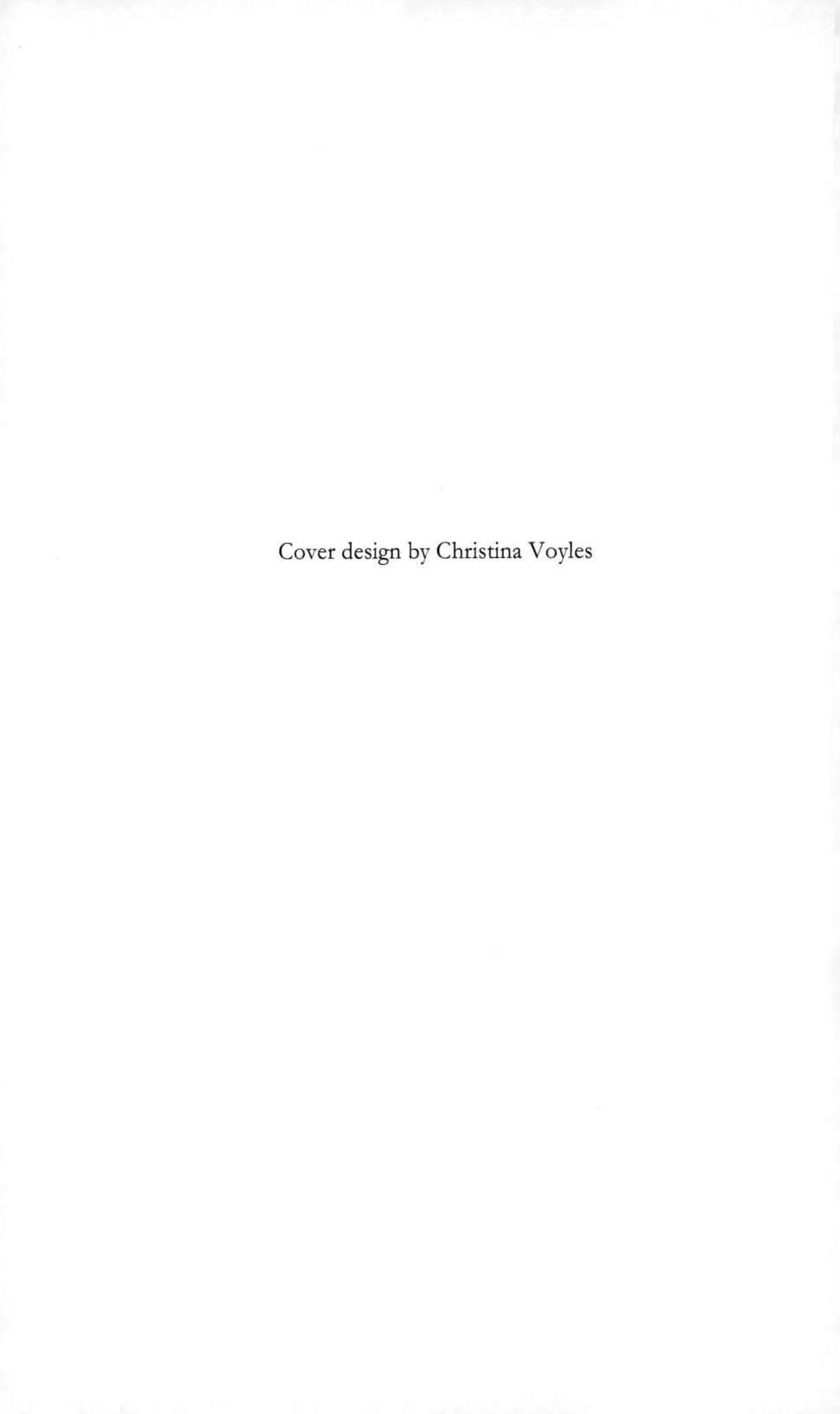

Preface

The man in the park, London, England / October 2004

Love… is the principal means of escape from the loneliness which afflicts most men and women throughout the greater part of their lives.
– Bertrand Russell

IT WAS SUNDAY MORNING. London was at ease. The park in which he sat was quiet, surprisingly peaceful even, given that it was situated in the midst of one of the world's great cities. The distant noise softly enough for him to enjoy the sound of crisp autumn leaves rustling as they rolled across the white-tipped autumn lawn in the breeze, mustering themselves in piles beneath the earthward branches of the evergreens.

Squirrels made industrious use of the time, empty of hordes of rushing humans and rambunctious dogs, to collect and bury scores of the thousands of acorns littering the ground. An occasional pigeon fluttered noisily from its lofty oak perch, adding to the desiccated mess congregating on the stone steps below. Rain had been a long time coming this year and everything was dusty and brittle. So dusty that flocks of sparrows had wiggled small scrape holes in patches of bare earth, flapping a bath for themselves in the dry dirt.

The morning began frosty and his old naval greatcoat guarded him against the chill wind blowing down the great river. But the early sun, appearing above the meandering river in the distance, was now pleasantly warming and cast a reassuring orange glow on the surroundings. It was a soothing morning and in another time he would have enjoyed the peace and quiet, the solitude. Inhaled the briefness of tranquility before the bustle, and let the troubles of the world float away on the breeze, if only for a few moments. But this was not another time.

Sitting on the green park bench the rather pleasant, though melancholy, looking gentleman didn't yet know how his morning would end, or that he would even see it end. But it was a choice in which he was steadfastly resigned and, once made, a strange uncluttered calmness seemed to engulf him. He thought he could live only if she lived, and was happy for this life to finish if she didn't. At this moment he didn't know one way or the other, every day was a struggle. But he would know shortly. In that he was relieved. It had been a long time, half a lifetime almost. And much of it wasted on secrets that were not secret, truths surpassed by time, and lies, lots of lies; designed by zealots and woven by experts unbeholden to national or moral boundaries.

To him now they were all meaningless, insignificant: Insignificant lies. Insignificant truths. Insignificant secrets. That insignificance born from the realization of what really mattered, what was of value and what was not: Living a life with someone, living it alone, or not living it at all. One had not been a choice, the other two were.

How everything became so cloudy, cluttered and confusing he couldn't remember. It had, as I have mentioned, and as he told me later that morning, been half a lifetime. Long enough to purge the reasons for it all, but enough, also, to recover the purpose. Being engulfed in a longstanding, unflinching, chase for truth had cloaked the original purpose for life, cocooned it, retreated it into the deep recesses of his subconscious. Strange that now it was so clear, so apparent, the mistakes so obvious, the reason so lost.

Strange also, that a perceived irretrievable subconscious can suddenly evoke such vibrant perspective and consciousness when snapped back to reality. Almost as if regaining the thoughts of childhood, full of lost innocence and honesty.

People had died for it, for the truth, or what they thought was the truth, for the secret created that was for years protected and that which was abused. Some were remembered too late for their efforts. Others forgotten altogether. On a still autumn morning the wheel had turned full circle, it was clicking into position and maybe it was now his turn. Could he forget? Would others forget? Or would he finish at only half a life?

A life for which he hadn't even been a pawn, just an entity to be kicked around; drawn in first by choice, then by guilt, and finally by design. Events hadn't always included him at all and yet they affected him at every turn. He'd been swept along with it, often ignorant that the game was even being played in distant fields. How is it that some people can float through life with no conscious navigation at all, getting everything they want with little effort? While others, equally talented and ambitious, eager to do what is right, and willing stand up for it, are forestalled at every turn, with no fault? Why is it they who pay the price?

The hue of sunlight slowly brightened from deep orange to yellow and stirred the sleeping city awake. There wasn't long to wait, even if the journey had been long, half a lifetime long, and more for some; spanning two generations, several wars, hot and cold, and a life he allowed to pass him by. And for what?

A train clattered and squealed as it traversed over complex points on the bridge and working tugs on the river below blew their deep bellowing foghorns in unison; the sound of industry, old fashioned industry. Then, between the glint of the sun off the water and the rolling leaves he remembered a long forgotten conversation, and slipped into imagination, watching, in his mind's eye, a hulking great battleship enter a distant port in time of war. A monster creeping silently into berth to be victualed. The ship not yet scarred by war, only by salt water, but prepared to unleash its formidable power to do war's bidding nonetheless.

War. It always starts with war. Wars are the ripples of life: Starting as tiny drops of misery that spread ever outward, growing, multiplying, absorbing everything in their path; the hurdles we must breach to push humanity forward in its endless quest for a better future, a more peaceful existence, a righteous and more truthful world. He was never able to breach that wave, but carried forever along on its tip, involuntarily, from one event to another, unable to break the cycle.

Awake he dozed, his mind carrying him from his troubles as the tidal Thames washed against the stone...

Chapter One

U.S.S. Phoenix, Simon's Town, South Africa / March 1941

Silver and gold are not the only coin; virtue too passes current all over the world.

– Euripides

THE GREAT WARSHIP GENTLY SLIPPING alongside the pier caused quite a stir among the small group of onlookers. Not for her size, though she was large for a light cruiser, at 608-feet and 10,000-tons, and not for the unusual designation on her bow. But because of the red, white and blue flag flying proudly from her stern. The stars and stripes waving in the southern breeze were easily identifiable, but since the start of the war had been an infrequent sight in the Cape Town port. The United States Ship *Phoenix* was being tugged into position at the secure berthing area on the edge of the Simon's Town naval base at False Bay. Her crew standing rigidly side-by-side in neat white rows along her decks, watching the intricate procedure of docking the massive rust stained vessel after her transatlantic crossing. She was only two years old and yet her structure already bore the appearance of a much older ship, the natural wear and tear of a long sea voyage, having recently come from the Pacific for a quick modification to her armaments. Along the pier, dock workers, although not attended in such neat lines, also stood rigid and stationary, gazing up in wonder at the formidable black and grey behemoth towering high above them. They were accustomed to seeing large merchant vessels but this was clearly not one of them. The *Phoenix's*[*] array of fifteen six-inch guns protruding from her deck portrayed a magnificent military presence, and the unusual color scheme, made up of abstract drab blocks of color, designed to obscure her shape and size and make it difficult for marauding submarines to gauge her speed and range, just compounded the collective awe. Nevertheless, this *Brooklyn*-class cruiser appeared as a colossus next to the other vessels in port and no curious color scheme could hide the fact.

Few people knew the real purpose of the 'Phoo-bird's' visit and everyone that did were keeping it very quiet, not least the Americans for sending her. If people outside the privileged few had known, things might have been very different for the following five war-torn years, and possibly more.

The *Phoenix's* covert task was to pick up gold bullion as the last 'cash and carry' payment before America would release fifty rusting hulks that were purported to be seaworthy destroyers, which, twenty-five years previous during the First World War, they might have been. Since then, though, these clunky 314-foot, 1,200-ton, four-stacker, flush-deck rust buckets had been mothballed, their empty shells creaking and groaning the approach of their death knell even while in dock. In reality, they were not far from the knackers yard, thanks to being improperly preserved prior to being deactivated twenty years before. The embattled engineers attempting to maintain the antiquated engines were resorting, ironically, to jerry-built tactics just to make steam. Once running

---

[*] While *Phoenix* was the name given to me, there is no record of it being in the Atlantic during this time. The ship was most probably the *USS Vincennes*, a *New Orleans*-class Heavy Cruiser. This miscommunication might simply be due to sailors transferring from *Vincennes* after she was sunk in August 1942. However, *Phoenix*'s presence at False Bay is not beyond the scope of WWII subterfuge, therefore the name remains because it is integral to the story as described to me.

their four funnels often spewed huge clouds of smoke that could be seen along the horizon for miles. Admiral Lord Ramsey called them "the worst destroyers I had ever seen... The price paid for them was scandalous."

Later, however, after Royal Navy crews had time to become familiar with their many awkward idiosyncrasies, some of them performed with distinction in the convoy role for which they were assigned, with their superior speed enabling them to at least keep up with the slower transports they were tasked with protecting, though due credit should be paid to naval skill rather than steel. Their maneuverability, however, was somewhat questionable; their turning circle so huge that twelve ended up colliding with friendly ships. The sailors also generally hated them; with cramped damp quarters and a rough ride they surely must have thought they had stepped back in time. Not one of them survived beyond 1947, most of those surviving the war being broken up between 1944 and 1945. This desperate deal, which demanded the transfer of bases for American use, was, in the long term, far more advantageous to the Americans, but it was trying times.

This, then, was the purpose behind this recently commissioned warship's arrival; to protect the last of the British Empire's gold bullion while on its way to the United States before initiating the transfer of fifty aging destroyers under the Destroyers for Bases Agreement.* Those destroyers so urgently needed, even in their current dilapidated state, to safeguard Britain's beleaguered lifeline during the Battle of the Atlantic.

Despite the largely one-sided deal, the British Parliament really had no choice in the matter, they were at the end of the rope, as it

---

* This agreement was a loose precursor to the Lend-Lease Act which effectively ended American neutrality by providing the Allied nations with war matériel from March 1941 onwards. The Lend-Lease Act being a much more favorable deal, much of it being written off after the war when replaced with the Anglo-American Loan Agreement that Britain finished repaying 60 years later in December 2006.

were, and about to fall into the abyss. Every member of the age-old parliament knew it was the New World gouging the Old in an obvious attempt to end, once and for all, what America saw as an outdated imperialistic empire. Before the Americans got their way, however, there was a diminutive deluded Austrian corporal staking a claim to a new empire, and squeezing the Home of the British Empire so that he could be leader of the next Reich. The New World knew that if they could bleed the Old dry, use its manpower and drain its resources in fighting this Nazi tyrant and his hordes, they could pick up the pieces as the spoils of victory. They, however, like Hitler, didn't fully appreciate the practiced shrewdness and determination of Britain's new wartime leader and its new Prime Minister, Winston Churchill.

Churchill had been long behind the scenes of government and largely forgotten for ten years, from 1929 to 1939, known as his 'wilderness years.' This had infused many foreign leaders into the mistaken assumption that if Churchill was of no value to Britain then he was no threat to anyone else. Indeed, even the respected British Broadcasting Corporation (BBC), under its founder John Reith, who absolutely loathed Churchill,[*] went to extraordinary lengths to limit Churchill's exposure to the public by denying him (and also David Lloyd George) access to the radio – such is the political sway that one vindictive man in power can wield. Churchill said that for eleven years "they kept me off the air... prevented me from expressing views that proved to be right."[†] But the pugnacious bulldog was born to this role; his Parliamentary speeches were his teeth, and once in his grasp his bite inescapable.

---

[*] Reith hated Churchill so much that he would not even walk past Churchill's commemorative plaque in the floor of Westminster Abbey after Churchill was dead.

[†] Churchill once explained to a producer that he was constantly being "muzzled" by the BBC, having been on 'air' only 10 times in 10 years. But was informed that the BBC was in no way biased. The producer's name, Guy Burgess, of the infamous 'Cambridge Five.' The treacherous dealings of which will become apparent later.

He was, then, perhaps Arthur, King of the Britons, as in legend, returned to protect Britain in its moment of greatest despair. It was the role for which he had been born and, moreover, he well knew it and thoroughly relished the thought of it. Fortunately for him, and the country, and despite his initial unpopularity and the BBC's "tyrannical" intransigence, he regained his seat in government at exactly the right moment, immediately shrugging off any soft talk of appeasement in exchange for untold toil and violence.

Churchill had risen to almost instant national notoriety while a Boer War correspondent for the London *Morning Post*. Becoming somewhat of a hero after being captured for playing too big a role in a skirmish when an armored train he was traveling on was ambushed and derailed, and then later escaping to freedom. War reporting being the only way he could get into the fray in order to make the name for himself for which he was so desperate, in order to follow in his overbearing father's footsteps. "It is astonishing how we have underrated these people," he wrote prophetically only few days before his capture… "The contribution of mounted infantry and heavy guns is extremely effective." On his return he was commissioned into the South African Light Horse, acting as courier between General Buller's HQ and the battle at Spion Kop. Where, in another of life's stranger coincidences, he very likely rode right past a little known, and yet already politically active, Indian stretcher bearer who was to become a thorn in his side for much of his political career; Mohandas Gandhi.

Churchill had previously fought in India and North Africa and knew well what was needed to fight. But the feeble bloodstained foothold on Gallipoli during the Great War, the great debacle for which he was solely blamed, being First Lord of the Admiralty, leaving untold French, British, Canadian, Indian and Anzac bodies littering the bloody hills around the Dardanelles, abruptly ended any political aspirations in the immediate future. But the failure of

Gallipoli cannot entirely be laid at Churchill's feet. Incompetence among high-ranking aristocratic officers, which was so prevalent as to be almost endemic during the Great War, hadn't provided the required forces to complete the mission, nor had they taken full advantage of favorable events elsewhere, all of which inevitably caused the catastrophe.*

Such is the nature of war; bold chances have to be taken to seize initiative, seize the day, and more often than not, even during the seemingly endless gloom and misery of an army shattered on the morbid sands of Dunkirk, his stoicism behind a few stalwart military minds, surprisingly brilliant on occasion, would win the day and steer Britain inexorably towards its 'Finest Hour.'

While 'The Few' gained deserved immortality, many difficult decisions were being made. Not least among them giving up the last of the empire's gold. Churchill was deeply hurt by the request from Roosevelt and said that it "was not fitting that one nation put itself wholly in the hands of another." But that is exactly what the American government was demanding. The American people, and Congress in particular, were unprepared for the looming cataclysm and in no hurry to get embroiled in another European war; even accusing President Roosevelt's circumvention of Congress, in agreeing to the destroyer deal, of being akin to "an act of war."

America knew Britain was on her knees. London was being systematically blown asunder during the blitz and crucial men and cargos being sent to the bottom of the Atlantic in ever increasing numbers by German U-boats. Britain had manpower to fight and, with Churchill's determination, was willing to fight, but it badly

---

* Such was the loss of life among Australian and New Zealand troops during their first major action, horrifying people at home, that April 25th is now annually remembered as Anzac Day, even surpassing Remembrance Day (11hr/11d/11m). Red Poppies, reminding Commonwealth Countries of the battles in Flanders' fields, arriving too late for Remembrance Day in New Zealand in 1921 were, instead, used the following Anzac Day, starting a tradition that remains to this day. "They shall grow not old, as we that are left grow old." — Laurence Binyon (p. 279).

needed the matériel with which to fight. That matériel could only come from the great untapped resources and industry of America. Churchill's dilemma, then, was to fight the good fight alone, hoping that the empire would, one day, be able to provide the modern tools with which to fight, or sell the empire's very soul in guarantee to save it, and be beholden to another sovereign nation. For the man who said he did not "become the King's First Minister in order to preside over the liquidation of the British Empire," it was a considerable choice.

Two things made the decision especially difficult: Admitting to being wholly indebted to one country, with all that that entails was bad enough; but to know that the gold America had come to collect was no longer available was worse, if not downright embarrassing. Only a handful of people apparently knew of this conundrum and most of them were already dead. Churchill reportedly knew, however, and he was very much alive, and more than willing to keep it a secret for as long as necessary to save his country and precious empire. Churchill was, no doubt, aware because of the time he had spent in South Africa, which provided him a network of friends on both sides, including Jan Smuts, one of the Boers' great guerilla leaders and, later, Prime Minister of the Union of South Africa. Churchill, like others before him, discovered that the gold had been locked up and held as collateral against reconstruction loans needed to repatriate the thousands of Boers who had been interned during the War. Interned in shocking conditions against the wishes of the vast majority of British people. For one reason or another the bullion had then remained on the books, just waiting for someone bold enough to tell parliament and the country of the deal. But so far no one had. Elections, strikes and the Great Depression always managing to get in the way of its disclosure and inevitable outrage.

Initially, by aiding the Boers, someone had attempted to do the honorable thing, but many British pro-colonialists saw it as a guilt payment to placate and keep released internees quiet from future claims against the Government. Despite this, Louis Botha, then Prime Minister of the Union of South Africa,[*] was clearly happy to accept the loans for which he had fought so hard and share them among Paul Kruger's tough old Boers so that they could rebuild the devastated farmsteads that were necessary to feed the country.

Now, forty years on, the gold was still on the books, and too late to change the fact for fear of financially devastating an already indebted country. As embarrassing as it was for the gold not to be available, Churchill was glad it had been used as it had, for it went some way to heal the deep rifts between the two nations after the expensive bloody war against the Boers ended. In effect, enabling Britain to later count on South African troops in the Desert War against the Italians in North Africa, to great advantage. However, all the advantages that the bullion initially bought were now being offset by the problem of its absence.

Thus, all those nice neat white rows of sailors and awestruck dock workers appeared to be witnessing a great lie. Was the ship's arrival, then, nothing more than an elaborate ploy, where, "In wartime, truth is so precious that she should always be attended by a bodyguard of lies," with Churchill, as usual, the puppet master?

The British War Room, consisting of those people in the loop and privy to sensitive information, decided not to divulge the lack of gold and apparently provided a load of gold plated lead instead, securely contained inside welded steel crates lest inquisitive eyes should notice the discrepancy. The *Phoenix's* formidable clusters of six-inch guns were, therefore; to be transporting both a great

---

[*] General Botha was also the Afrikaner who captured Churchill during the war, and met Churchill once again in London in 1902 while arranging for his country's reconstruction loans. He became the first Prime Minister of the Union in 1910, the precursor to the present Republic of South Africa.

weight of lead, valued at virtually nothing; and the great weighty conscience of an entire empire, the value of which was priceless. No one else would know. Certainly not the captain of the vessel who was anxiously overseeing the loading of the worthless cargo for which he had just signed. After all, who would not trust Britain's claim that the heavy steel crates did not, in fact, contain what they should?

Roosevelt had originally requested that the cargo be delivered. But this was impossible due to the workload of both the Merchant Navy and Royal Navy, in convoying matériel from the Americas to sustain Britain and its colonies in the war effort, much of it being transferred immediately to the active campaign in North Africa. London and its docklands had been bombed for weeks, ever since Germany lost its fight for air superiority over the Royal Air Force during the Battle of Britain in September 1940.[*] Many other ports around the country had also been severely damaged, straining to breaking point the reserves of the Merchant Navy and general transportation system. Guns and ammunition of all types were needed desperately, as was antiaircraft artillery to avert the air menace and instill the embattled populace with confidence that the government was doing its very best to protect them, even if it couldn't. The British Army in the desert had shown their bayonets and provided some tremendous and sorely needed morale-boosting victories, pushing the Italians back over two hundred miles in five weeks during the first of the great sea-saw battles of North Africa. However, a lack of supplies, and Rommel's arrival in February – to be immortalized as the Desert Fox – slowed the British advance after they had captured 113,000 Italian prisoners. There was only one country in which this replaceable matériel could be produced

---

[*] A pivotal point during the Second World War which directly prevented Hitler's Germany from fulfilling his plan, Operation *Sea Lion*, to invade Britain. Equivalent, in many respects perhaps, to Nelson's victory at Trafalgar.

in large enough quantities and be supplied in a timely manner; the United States. And there was only one navy, apart from valiant Canadian assistance, that was powerful enough, and available, for the protection of that matériel since neither the Royal Navy nor the Merchant Navy had ships or time to transport gold, and Churchill said as much in his frequent correspondence to the United States President, Franklin D. Roosevelt.

By this time Roosevelt was used to getting such frank letters from the 'Former Naval Person,' as Churchill referred to himself, and accepted them with candid politeness, knowing full well the strains under which the Prime Minister was working. Roosevelt was more aware than most in the United States Government about Britain's situation and he fully understood the New World would eventually be drawn into the conflict sooner or later, by choice or otherwise. Infamy later that year meant that it was to be otherwise. In the meantime, however, an isolationist American Government was happy to see khaki-clad Tommies use American manufactured equipment, especially since it was now understood England would not give up the fight, as had been earlier expected.

With Winston at the helm, Britain was not going to fall prey to the Germans as easy as the French. Or not, at least, until they had given it their all and had nothing more with which to fight but their wits – although the 22 mile stretch of English Channel also helped, much as the mud at Agincourt had hindered French knights five centuries before. Two things changed the minds of the pessimistic American Government and its politically powerful media on that account: The sinking of the French fleet at Oran and Mers-el-Kebir, to prevent the Germans from taking control of the superior French ships; and the Battle of Britain, when American newspaper reporters, such as the evolutionary Edgar R. Murrow, sat above the White Cliffs of Dover watching the daily aerial spectacle between the youthful beleaguered 'Few' of the Royal Air Force, who were becoming fewer by the day, and the overwhelming might of the Luftwaffe. Prior to these two significant events, world opinion had largely predicted that Britain would succumb to the inevitable. But Britain's audacity was now cemented in the eyes of the world, thanks, in no small part, to the likes of Murrow, whose efforts altered the attitudes of world leaders, especially the Americans, causing everything to change quite considerably in Britain's favor.

However, this still didn't prevent the New World from wanting to dissolve the Old, even if Britain and its empire were willing to fight on alone to save the world from domination by Hitler's arrogant Aryan masses and Mussolini's pompous, Romanic delusions. America had successfully stayed out of the war for almost a year and a half, forced to do so mainly by its traditional isolationist policies that Roosevelt was slowly but steadily eroding, to the vocal consternation of many powerful and highly influential senators. A few of whom were still actively doing business with both German and Italian companies and reaping tremendous rewards, albeit indirectly in most cases. Even the more legitimate, and one could attempt to say moral, businesses within the United States were garnering huge profits from the production of war matériel in ever growing proportions, until, that is, the government was forced to cap such exploitive gains once it realized that it also would have to pay the same exorbitant prices.

Meanwhile, as all the political wrangling and soul searching was underway in London and Washington, the South Atlantic was about to be host, once again, to the *Phoenix*. The great ship slid quietly from its moorings in total darkness, ready to negotiate the dangerous U-boat infested waters of the frigid Atlantic Ocean. America was not yet at war and so far no United States Navy vessel had been attacked, although some United States Merchant ships had. But the *Phoenix's* captain didn't want to be the first to chance a U-boat encounter before hostilities had been declared, because the current rules of engagement gave complete advantage to the attacker, which he wasn't allowed to be.

While slipping quietly out into the murky depths they didn't go completely unseen, however. On shore someone was watching the whole affair. Not for the cargo as much as for the vessel itself. The spy's information was transmitted to the Japanese High Command, which immediately sent orders to one of their active submarines rendezvousing with a German counterpart to exchange sensitive coding materials. The German submarine, finished with its Far East exchange, and armed with this new information, was on the surface and speeding toward the expected path of the warship. Although no one aboard the submarine knew what they were going to do if they made contact. All but the most ignorant knew that a shooting war with America was inevitable, but no one knew who would be allowed to fire that first fatal shot.

Unknown to the submarine's captain, the Americans had successfully broken the Japanese naval code in 1939, and long before the information had been decoded on the surfaced Japanese submarine it had already been read in plain text by the Americans. The *Phoenix,* therefore, knew well of the submarine's whereabouts and avoided the area, successfully evading the unwanted rendezvous without the Japanese being any the wiser to their signal being deciphered. Once past danger the *Phoenix* steamed toward the eastern seaboard far faster than any submarine could match. The German U-boat captain, unaware of why he hadn't made contact with the battleship, passed the information to the German Naval High Command who then alerted their patrolling U-boats in mid-Atlantic. It seemed as though all the active U-boats wanted to be first in line to have a potshot at this American vessel and be first to sink her should the situation arise after orders were changed. One or two ambitious captains knew that even without orders they could always later say they had thought she was British, as they had done a few weeks earlier when sinking an American merchant vessel with all hands off the Azores. So the Germans had many practiced veteran U-boat captains either in the vicinity or in the *Phoenix's* expected route just waiting for a glorious opportunity to serve the Fuhrer.

With increasing risk of attack, American Naval Headquarters changed plans for the shipment immediately. This was no time to lose a major warship in a fight in which they were not yet a combatant. The ship would be too valuable later when they most assuredly would be. The cargo was then arranged to be transferred to a small ballast only merchant ship on its way back to the United States, while the *Phoenix* was ordered on to the Pacific to join the Seventh Fleet, much to the pleasure of the crew who were already tired of the Atlantic weather. The British naval officer portraying himself as a spy on Table Mountain above Cape Town had made everyone very happy.

The transfer occurred without a hitch a few hundred miles west of the African coast, well away from the U-boat's prime hunting ground around Sierra Leone. *Phoenix*, happy to be away, steamed for the Scotia Sea and Drake's Passage and later found her place in history in the midst of the Pacific War. She was fondly known as a lucky ship and survived Pearl Harbor and the whole Pacific Naval War. Ironically, she was eventually sunk during another war, by a British nuclear submarine forty years later in the South Atlantic, when she was called the *General Belgrano*. In that, she found herself yet another place in history; being the first ship ever sunk in conflict by a nuclear submarine. The merchant ship, *Albatross*, meanwhile, empty except for ballast and a few extremely heavy crates, steered north by east toward the eastern seaboard for her new destination, Portsmouth, Virginia.

Churchill had apparently already devised a suitable plan in the event that the *Albatross* actually made it to port, which was not thought likely. That plan was reported to have real bullion coming from Russia shipped onboard the *Duke of York*, currently engaged in escort duties and shipping Italian prisoners of war to captivity in Canada. In the unlikely event the *Albatross* did make landfall, Churchill would indulge Roosevelt into his obscure 'bodyguard of lies,' scenario, in which the *Phoenix* had been nothing more than a lavish decoy. It was, after all, the last of the empire's gold and should be protected as such.

The likelihood of the dilapidated old rust bucket *Albatross* reaching Portsmouth was remote, however. Her reduced crew were Royal Navy volunteers, instrumental to yet another of Churchill's ploys; an exercise in coastal safety and an attempt to get the United States into the war by having her sunk by a submarine just as she reached the apparent safety of the U.S. coast. A British submarine was already laying in wait for her arrival should the Germans fail. The ship would sink to the deepest depths, with no possibility of salvage. With her would disappear the 40-year secret and the lies which had kept it. Yet with her loss would also come hope in the form of destroyers, and possibly the eventual entry of the United States into World War Two. The latter of which Churchill knew would guarantee victory to the 'Grand Alliance.' The Old World and the New locked together in battle against the tyranny of fascism to save the world.

Once within sight of the eastern seaboard the skeleton crew of the *Albatross* disembarked and boarded the surfaced Royal Navy submarine, while commandos placed onboard a few deceased Germans they had picked up from a destroyed U-boat and attached some strategically placed explosives. Transfers completed, the captain of the submarine unleashed four torpedoes from four hundred yards. Three fired straight and true and hit the *Albatross* broadside, obliterating everything in a great fireball that could be seen for miles along the shores of numerous, still well-illuminated, small towns up and down the coast. The next day all the coastal inhabitants knew of the ship that had gone down with all hands. She had probably exploded and disappeared so quickly because her empty tanks hadn't been vented, a fatal error on behalf of her inexperienced crew. Rather unexpectedly, but to make it even more believable, a U-boat patrolling unusually near the area actually claimed her loss to make up tonnage in order for her captain to receive a much prized *Ritterkreuz*[*] – for sinking 100,000 tons of allied shipping. The captain had seen the ship blow up, apparently all by herself, and added her to his already numerable sinking tonnage. No one ever thought differently because soon after documenting the claim his U-boat was itself sunk with all hands on its way home a week later, by a patrolling RAF Coastal Command Sunderland flying boat during standard antisubmarine operations off the south coast of England.

The Royal Navy's submarine crew would never say a word, even if they were fortunate enough to survive the war. The British Government's wartime secrets made available thirty years hence never mentioned any part of Operation *Burden*, and no one at the time was overly worried about the lost bullion; such cargos were being sunk with alarming regularity in the north Atlantic.

It was total war. People were dying of starvation and being murdered by the millions. No one was going to worry about a few bits of gold. Moreover, the British would finally be released from years of subterfuge. For another 40 years anyway, by which time everyone directly associated with it was dead and buried.

---

[*] The Knights Cross of the Iron Cross — introduced in 1939 as an addition to the Iron Cross family. A highly respected decoration awarded for bravery on the battlefield. A total of 144 were awarded to U-boat men.

Chapter Two

Sean O'Connor, Eastern Seaboard, United States / May 1982

Ocean: A body of water occupying about two-thirds of a world made for man - who has no gills.
– Ambrose Bierce

THE LARGEST NAVAL CONVOY SINCE World War Two had been scraped together and was underway, and heading in all haste to the South Atlantic in response to Argentina's aggression in invading the Falkland Islands on April 2, 1982. The task force had been organized remarkably quickly – sailing on April 5 and 6 – surprising many and shocking skeptics who thought the Royal Navy incapable of such a daunting task in the aftermath of major defense cuts. Yet they had, and a few weeks later a convoy of commandeered troopships would catch up and rendezvous with the fleet at Ascension. There, men would train, ships would be revictualed, aircraft would ferry more men and matériel, and the country would see if the Argentines would either rethink their position or believe that Britain's first woman Prime Minister, Maggie Thatcher, was bluffing, and would wobble. They should have known that she wouldn't. She had already shown her mettle against the Soviets and the European Union, earning her the nickname 'Iron Lady.' To the majority of the British public and government there was no doubt whatsoever what would happen if the Argentines[*] were still on the islands when the green of the Royal Marines and the maroon of the Parachute Regiment arrived; they would kick them off the island in the manner to which they deserved. Although few were fully prepared for, or could properly comprehend, the true nature and ferocity of the bloody conflict that was about to erupt on these sparsely populated, barren islands deep in the South Atlantic Ocean. People and politicians languishing in luxurious ignorance in a time of lasting peace had all but forgotten the brutality of war. It was to hit them like a brick, brought on a wing by a French jet carrying new technology. Again, Britain was unprepared for war and again troopers would have to win the day, slog by long bloody slog, and divested of the technology that was supposed to save them.

The world had seen newsreel footage of jubilant Argentinean youth going ashore on their self-proclaimed Malvinas, after having first sent a covert salvage team to South Georgia to raise their flag. The only news coming out of the islands was Argentinean, and it would soon tell the world how the Argentines had sunk the Royal Navy's prize aircraft carrier, *Invincible*, not once, but twice. Before that, however, they had been held offshore by a small detachment of Royal Marines from Naval Party 8901, fortunately in double strength (67 marines) but still completely outgunned. While fully prepared to continue the fight, their defense would have meant needless civilian casualties around the town of Stanley and Rex Hunt, Governor of the islands, ordered the marines to surrender. The marines were then transported by C-130 to Montevideo, Uruguay, and released, whence they returned home to board one of the first troopships to head south. On leaving the islands one of the Royal Marines was heard to say: "Don't make yourself too comfy

---

[*] Throughout I use both 'Argentinean' and 'Argentine', for no other reason than I grew up with both and interchange them freely as I see fit.

mate, we'll be back." They were, 76 days later, this time on the winning side, still outgunned, outnumbered, but not out-manned.

Rumors circulated about which side the great superpowers were on. It was assumed the United States would be on Britain's side and that the Soviets would aid the Argentineans. Although it took persuasion by Prime Minister Thatcher before the American Government would allow the Royal Air Force to use the U.S. airfield on Ascension Island, even though the island is, itself, British overseas territory! There was also speculation about the Soviets providing the Argentines satellite data on the whereabouts of the British task force. If so, this could prove devastating, and two nuclear powered submarines were patrolling the total exclusion zone looking for the existence of the Argentine fleet, which, until it was later kept in port for its own safety, was a major threat to the under-protected task force, especially the all-important troopships. The French President, François Mitterrand, meanwhile, ordered an immediate arms embargo, forbidding anyone in France to give assistance to the Argentines. French intelligence also tipped off MI6 who were then able to carry out covert sting operations, on French soil, that prevented Argentinean agents from buying further Exocet missiles on the black market. This was all well and good, except for a small group of French technicians already in South America helping to repair and fine-tune missiles the Argentines had already purchased.[*] Israel, on the other hand, with Menachem Begin as leader, who vehemently hated the British with a passion, actively transported all the arms and equipment to Argentina they could muster. While Britain's old, twice wartime, European ally,

---

[*] These were technicians provided by the manufacturer, a company 51% owned by the French Government. There is also evidence suggesting that at least one of the group was a member of France's Direction Générale de la Sécurité Extérieure (DGSE), or France's version of MI6. The same evidence also states that had the technicians not repaired the missiles they would have likely been duds — from a BBC Radio 4 documentary broadcast on March 5th, 2012.

Belgium, steadfastly refused to supply Britain with any artillery or small arms ammunition.

With friends like these who needs enemies, one may ask.

#   #   #

WATCHING THESE EVENTS UNFOLD in the safety of the western North Atlantic were a group of marine experts onboard the salvage ship *Ulysses*, comprising three Britons and five Americans. The Brits were paying special attention to the goings on in the South Atlantic because had they not just recently finished their active service in the Royal Marines, they would be in the South and not the North Atlantic, where they were now using the skills gained in the marines for their current role as advisors to the team's deep-sea divers. The Americans were providing technical expertise and camera work while looking for a particular World War Two U-boat that was thought to have sunk along the eastern seaboard in 1941. Someone had discovered an engraved German naval knife on a diving expedition around the area, sparking an interest because it had belonged to a captain of a U-boat that was reported to have been in the Bay of Biscay, and was thought to have perished there. Now, however, with this new find, U-boat records were being checked against Allied naval logs because there were some discrepancies. If they could find the remains of the U-boat in these waters then there was a story in it, and the cameras were here to record it for National Geographic on Assignment.

Ulysses had been here for two months and no one had seen anything except for a few rusting hulks of old coastal tankers that had been torpedoed by lone German submarines and wolf packs between 1942 and 1945. Interesting as they were for history's sake, they were of no use to them in their present task, because they couldn't sell advertising on a program based on a few sunken coastal tankers, of which there were so many. At the time they didn't realize how wrong they were. The convoluted string of events that had brought them here might later alter history, so long as they realized what they were looking at one and a half miles below them in the great abyss off the eastern seaboard.

It was Sean's turn to watch the monitor of the deep sea rover. He was drinking cup after cup of coffee to keep himself awake in the gently rolling cabin. High above where the rover crept slowly along the ocean floor, its incredibly bright lights only managing to penetrate a few feet in front of its path in the gloomy, greatly pressured, depths below. When he needed to go to the bathroom to relieve himself he taped the rover's progress and rewound it on his return. It was his responsibility to see something, since no one else would likely bother watching the tape later if nothing happened. Returning to his post after his second bathroom visit he watched both the taped portion and the live version. If he had looked at the monitor as he walked through the small cabin door he would have just seen a strange rusty steel box sliding out of view beneath the rover. He didn't, however, he was too tired after three hours on shift and it was four o'clock in the morning. Neither did he bother to rewind the tape because there was nothing down there but endless stretches of boring sand. Besides, today was May 2. It was his birthday.

# # #

THAT SAME DAY IN THE SOUTH ATLANTIC the old 'Phoo-bird,' now the *General Belgrano*, was taking up patrolling duties with two destroyer escorts just outside of the British assigned total exclusion zone, inside which anything hostile could be attacked under the rules of engagement specified by the British Government. One of the Royal Navy's nuclear submarines in the waters around the islands, *HMS Conqueror*,[*] had made contact with this force earlier, while searching for the Argentinean carrier *Veinticino de Mayo*, and was now trailing it. The Argentine ships were a distinct threat to the task force because the Royal Navy couldn't afford to lose either of its two carriers, which together provided the fleet's only air support and which were also needed for air cover during the land operations. So after discussion with the Cabinet the Prime Minister gave orders for *Conqueror* to engage. She fired two Mark VIII torpedoes that sank the *General Belgrano* in forty minutes. Her escorts then either fled or left the area unaware of her sinking, leaving 368 of her crew to perish in the sea. With the *Belgrano* sinking, the 'Phoo-bird's' luck finally ran out and, contrary to her name, would never rise again. The sinking gave credence to the submariner ethos: there are only two types of naval vessels; submarines and targets. Following the controversial sinking the Argentinean Navy never ventured from port again, resulting in their air force having to fly 425 miles to attack the myriad of targets in the task force now awaiting them. Had the Argentine Navy stayed at sea the outcome might well have been different. So in retrospect, to the British at least, the 'Phoo-bird's' eventual demise was fortunate.[†]

\#   \#   \#

---

[*] Commissioned in 1971, the *Conqueror* ('Conks') was a *Churchill*-class submarine specifically designed to attack and spy on nuclear-armed Soviet submarines.

[†] Two months after the Falklands the *Conqueror* was again in action. This time in Soviet waters of the Barents Sea, at the request of the U.S. Navy, for a high risk, very secretive operation to steal a brand new towed-array sonar from, literally, right under the bow of a Soviet spy ship sailing amongst the Soviet Fleet. Operation *Barmaid* is now considered to be the reason why *Conqueror's* logs were shredded, inevitably further adding to the controversy over the sinking of the *Belgrano*.

BACK ONBOARD *ULYSSES* THEY had just heard news of the sinking of the *Belgrano*. Sean let out a cheer.

"Sinking a ship is nothing to cheer about. I don't care what side you're on," said Peter, the American technical wizard.

"Wasn't cheering at that," Sean said, pointing to the monitor. "Look there mate. What do you think those are?"

"Rewind that," Peter said excitedly.

They had been examining tape from the previous days, fast-forwarding through the boring parts but studying anything looking remotely interesting. It was tedious work but they badly needed to find something in order to justify their role and the camera crew's existence before they were all pulled from the operation.

"Steel boxes of some kind laying in a debris field. What ship went down here? Can you look in the records Sean?" Peter asked.

"There were several. That's why there's such a massive debris field. All of them tankers or merchant ships working the eastern seaboard," Sean replied.

"Yeah, I get that, but this one was obliterated. There has to be some record."

With that conversation under way the ship's skipper entered the cabin with the unexpected news that they needed to head back to port because the National Geographic crew were being pulled off the project. Money was tight and there were plenty of other more enlightening projects with which to be associated.

The crew showed their annoyance but they'd been expecting it. They marked the location of the boxes for future reference just in case they found additional investment, which wasn't considered likely, and glumly headed back to port.

Pulling into the small harbor the old dockhand glibly pointed out that they obviously hadn't found what they were looking for. Their long faces told the story.

"Just what we need," Peter said, "an old smart bastard."

"Well, I know what I need to forget this crap; a decent beer. *Albatross* then?" Sean said.

"We'll be up for that," Peter said, speaking for the remainder of the crew as well.

"Let's get cleaned up and meet at the bar," Sean suggested.

After checking into the hotel they made their way in ones and twos to the small bar which the older locals frequented and had kept going since the forties, when it had been started by a D-day veteran after his return home. The food was traditional seaside fare: Boiled fish, fried fish, baked fish, fish as cakes, and fish battered, all served up with a variety of potatoes, or grits if preferred. The beer wasn't too special for Sean's crowd, who were more used to the upcoming micro-brews on the west coast. Here the choice was Budweiser. But after days onboard a dry vessel anything was welcome and they soon relaxed in the comfortable environment, quickly becoming the topic of conversation among the regulars and answering numerous questions as to what they were looking for, where and why. They were also provided plenty of advice as to where they should have been looking instead, from hearing stories the local fishermen had told after dredging up an assortment of wartime relics over the previous forty years.

The old dockhand entered later and Sean had to move from his stool after the barman explained that it was his seat, literally. He had bought it years ago because it formed to his rather large posterior and its higher position gave him a commanding look over the whole bar, which in normal life he wasn't used to, being little over five feet tall.

After Sean had politely moved the man said: "Yer must have run into a debris field out where you were?"

"Well, we did find something, but not what we were looking for," Sean replied.

"Aye. I'll suppose you're after that German submarine folks have been talking about. Let me introduce m'self to you lad, Larry. 'Short' Larry they call me."

"Nice to meet you Larry. Sean. Sean O'Connor. And that's Pete. The other limey over there is Dave," Sean said, shaking the man's rough old hand vigorously.

"Cheers lads. But yer knows there's no submarine out there. Never was," Larry said, raising a glass of dark rum to his lips.

"Oh come on now Larry, give them a break, we've heard your long winded stories before," the landlord cut in. "Let them alone."

"Aye, but these lads haven't," Larry said, smiling at the opportunity to go over his tale again to a new captive audience.

"What's this Larry? You've got a theory about this U-boat?"

"No theory lad. Gospel truth. I've lived my whole life on this patch of ocean and I guess I know as much, if not more, than the next man about what it contains, and what it doesn't."

"So what doesn't it contain?" Sean asked, with everyone else leaning in to hear.

"There's no German submarine out there. I know that much. The only thing everyone has been going on is a blade, supposedly belonging to a U-boat captain and found in these waters by a hobby diver a while back. There were some sunk further up the coast much later in the war, but you won't find one here, and not this close to the coastline, the waters are too shallow."

"Yes, and the fact that they can't find the wreckage of the U-boat where it was supposed to have been sunk, in the Bay of Biscay," Sean explained. "That pretty much started the rumors."

"What about the ship that was attacked and blown up by the supposed U-boat back in '41?" Larry said. "There were no U-boats working the coast then. America wasn't at war and most of the subs were in the Arctic. They didn't get here 'til later."

"So what sank the ship you're talking about? I heard it was quite the explosion, it was seen for miles," Sean said.

"Aye. It was. I remember it though it were yesterday. My old man was on a coast guard cutter at the time and he was called out to pick up survivors. They found nothing but a patch of oil. Blown to smithereens it was."

"For a tanker that generally means a submarine, right?"

"Yes, it does. But why does it have to have been a U-boat?"

"Okay, Larry, that's enough. You lads want to order food before the tales get any taller?" The landlord asked.

Sean looked hard at Larry. There was something in Larry's eyes and his manner that interested him. He'd seen the look before, in someone trying desperately to get the truth out but without having anyone believing. Consequently falling inward, resolved to despair, cynicism and booze. Larry knew something. Sean would eat and finish the conversation later, when the others had gone to bed. He would give Larry his undivided attention. Besides, he liked the old guy. Larry was quite the character, born from years of hard graft and more than a little of life's hardship.

The landlord brought out a selection of plates and plopped them on the table for the men to help themselves. "Here you go. This'll take your mind off water for a while. You do know, of course, that this bar is named after the ship you're talking about?"

"Really. Why is that?" Sean asked.

"The *Albatross*. My father named it. He came back wounded from Normandy in '44 and his father kept telling him of the ship that had blown up with all hands, so in sort of respect he named his bar after it. No other reason really," said the landlord.

"Seems like there's an interesting history around these parts, and with the people still here to tell about it," Sean said.

"Suppose you're right. Being here all the time we don't think much about it. We just get on with our lives, each day as it comes, you know," the landlord said, returning to the kitchen.

"You're mining for something Sean," Peter said.

"Yeah. There's something out there, I know it. I just don't know what it is. I'll bet Larry has an idea though," Sean replied, digging into his freshly caught cod and chips, the best on the coast.

Chapter Three

James Devlin, Admiralty, London, England / May 1982

There is a tide in the affairs of men, Which taken at the flood, leads on to fortune. Omitted, all the voyage of their life is bound in shallows and in miseries. On such a full sea are we now afloat. And we must take the current when it serves, or lose our ventures.
– William Shakespeare

THE WALL INSIDE ONE OF THE SMALLER rooms in the admiralty was covered by a large world map, which contained a variety of colored pins, hundreds of them, each corresponding to a ship lost during World War Two. Around Arctic waters were numerous markers ranging from Iceland to Murmansk, where ships had met their end at the hand of U-boats or surface vessels brave enough to risk competing with the Royal Navy's protective force during the perilous Russian convoys. The few red markers denoted bullion or valuable metals; blue marked loss of information, or secrets; the greater number of green denoted major armaments, which may remain an environmental problem, especially if disturbed. No matter what their color, though, all were considered war graves and, as such, permission was required from the government of the day and the War Graves Commission before any exploration of these wrecks was allowed.

On the map there was also a single unmarked pinhole with a circle around it, just off the eastern seaboard of the United States, for which no record could be found to its meaning. All marks on the map had to be explained in the map's log. If someone inadvertently made a mark, in error either by pencil or pin, then they were obliged to initial the error and follow it up with an explanation in the log. Most people had thought this mark a simple unlogged mistake, and yet there had never been a meaningful examination in 40 years. Somewhere there would have to be a record if this was where a ship had gone down, if there was indeed a ship at all. In the sixties many a subaltern had casually delved into countless old ledgers and log books, but come up empty after hours of fruitless searching. So, for the past few years no one had even bothered with it. It remained nothing more than a legend, a mystery. Since man ventured onto the oceans the seas have been littered with them.

Lately, however, there had been a salvage ship in the area. Although no one particularly worried about them finding anything worthwhile, there was, nevertheless, the usual bureaucratic nonchalant interest in covering your ass just in case. The salvage company hadn't requested permission to search the area – not unusual these days with so many hobby divers freely roaming the oceans – even though it was clearly in United States territorial waters. Apart from naval records people rarely knew where the old wrecks were anyway, they were so numerous and usually too deep to disturb. The navy was adamant that the submarine everyone was searching for off the eastern seaboard was nothing more than a wild goose chase. Records had it sunk with all hands in the Bay of Biscay by a patrolling aircraft on antisubmarine duty, destroyed by the latest and more powerful depth charge being tested by the Air Force before entering regular service in 1941. The aircraft's crew had reported seeing the vessel literally blown apart in the blast, lifting its middle right out of the water and breaking its back before sending each half plummeting to the ocean floor. There had been no survivors, though a nearby frigate picked up a few oil soaked bodies in surface wreckage a few hours later.

Admiralty records mentioned no warships in the area of the mark either since they were all on convoy duty elsewhere. The United States was responsible for the safety of merchant ships along its seaboard to the mid-point in the North Atlantic, from where the Royal Navy took over sole responsibility for convoy protection. The only ships known to have been destroyed so near the coastline were merchant ships, and those being predominantly light tankers ferrying oil up and down the eastern seaboard after 1941. The Germans hadn't officially sent any U-boats on active patrol until Operation *Drumbeat*[*] in January the following year. There seemed to be no good reason for either a salvage team or an inadvertent hole in the map, though stranger things had happened in the past and it would be nice to finally put it to rest. An injured admiralty subaltern was tasked to do just that. Or rather he tasked himself to do it out of sheer boredom.

James Devlin had been in the navy for four years, lately as a lieutenant attached to the admiralty after injuring himself in a diving accident a year earlier while onboard his first ship, one which he would never see again. He was now just biding his time before discharge and more than agreeable to get out of the secretarial coffee making role he'd had for the past few weeks. His commanding officer also needed to get this short-timer out of the way because the Falklands were taking up much of his time and over-stressing his normally quiet temperament. This simple task seemed a good way to accomplish what was good for everyone.

---

[*] Operation *Drumbeat*: the plan by Admiral Dönitz to deliver a surprise attack against merchant shipping along the eastern seaboard, in which German U-boats sank 25 ships (156,939 tons) within three weeks, and which was the first in a series of coordinated 'wave' attacks that became the 'Second Happy Time' for submarine commanders.

The last words from Rear Admiral Fletcher, his CO, were: "Don't go looking too hard Devlin. There's nowt to find." James had thought as much also, realizing it was a ploy to get him away from the office since naval short-timers had a Jonah quality.

James researched much the same information as many had before him in the early sixties; wartime maritime charts, ship's log books, wartime records, newspaper reports, merchant shipping records, personal diaries, and anything else he could lay his hands on. In the space provided, which, in reality, was no more than an oversized janitor's closet in the basement, complete with the dank smell of mildew, he laid out all the papers in order by date. Then, of course, the first time the door opened the draft blew pieces of paper to the four walls. To fix the problem, James placed stones on the piles, the stones having been collected from all the corners of the world by a previous subaltern no doubt doing the same endless thankless task.

Going through the papers there was nothing that immediately stood out and the words of his CO began to make more sense: "There's nowt to find," so why look. The BBC World Service was on the radio and the reporter was talking about the sinking of the Argentinean ship the *General Belgrano*. The reporter went on to mention the cruiser's previous history with the United States Navy, when it had been the *Phoenix*. The name sparked something in his mind. He was sure he'd seen that name somewhere in the reams of papers he had been going through for the past few hours. It was in the 1940s pile somewhere.

"*Albatross*: Rendezvous with *Phoenix* 02:30, 300 miles west Sierra Leone. Loaded cargo, heading to United States, Portsmouth, Virginia," the declassified report ran.

There was nothing more on the scrap of paper that was all that remained of an obviously much larger piece, but which had been torn years ago. What was the *Phoenix* doing in those waters? She had been assigned to the Pacific Fleet. James now looked for information on the American ship, but could find none in his collection of predominantly British registered shipping. He called a friend in an upstairs office to see where he could find more. The friend upstairs, Jeremy, was a faucet of knowledge and seemed to immediately know what the ship had been doing in the South Atlantic, and explained as much to James, who was surprised he had never heard of it. James went to the library and picked up a couple of volumes of Martin Gilbert's Churchill biography but unfortunately found nothing to corroborate Jeremy's story. So he surmised that *Albatross* must have taken possession of the cargo before *Phoenix* was ordered to the Pacific, where it later witnessed firsthand the full onslaught of Japanese aggression at Pearl Harbor.* But what then happened to the *Albatross*?

There were no ships lost due to U-boat activity along the eastern seaboard in 1940 or early 1941, most were lost much later, during and after January 1942, when Hitler ordered major U-boat attacks against the Americas from being pressured to declare war on the United States after Pearl Harbor. Hitler really had his hands full with the Russians at this time, but had been convinced of the need to destroy England's lifeline, and by that token, American merchant ships, by Admiral Dönitz. According to the few Kriegsmarine records James had access to the *Albatross*, however, was sunk in March 1941, even though the British records showed the ship was just listed as lost, without any U-boat contact. James seemed to remember something going on with people looking for a lost German submarine in the same waters. Though he later

---

* On the morning of December 7th, 1941, the *USS Phoenix* was anchored southeast of Ford Island, in Pearl Harbor, but escaped damage. Her crew were one of the first to engage the attacking Japanese planes and immediately afterwards joined a task force searching for the enemy carriers, but was unsuccessful.

discovered that this particular submarine hadn't been destroyed until two years afterwards.*

James then found an interesting record of a British submarine, *HMS Sturgeon,*† which had been used to ferry commandos to various clandestine operations up and down the North Sea coast of occupied Europe. In this particular record, however, she was not positioned in her usual area of operations in the North Sea, but was instead placed to the side of the map, indicating that she was maneuvering somewhere in the North Atlantic, probably just a few hundred miles from the American coastline. James could find no information on what she had been doing there, even though her manifest stated she was still carrying her normal complement of marine commandos. Then, just a week later, she was back to her normal covert activities; creating havoc against the coastal forces of occupied Holland, Belgium and France. Looking at the manifest of the Commando he cross-checked names against the deceased list. All but one had been killed during the war. The only surviving member of the original Commando was a John 'Stinger' Sprite, forced out of the war after being wounded on a beach in Belgium. James surmised he would be about 65 and retired.

There were a few Sprites in the phone book, in all parts of the country; eight Johns, with three in Cornwall alone. James started calling and found Stinger at the third attempt. He was still living in Plymouth, a few hundred yards from the Royal Marine barracks on

---

* Possibly in May 1943 when 25 percent of the U-boat operational fleet was destroyed, thanks to technical advances in radar, communications, land-based aircraft and Enigma cryptanalysis, thereafter making U-boat attacks on Atlantic convoys almost suicidal.

† An S-class submarine that had an inauspicious beginning to the war when on September 14th, 1939, she attacked her own sister ship *HMS Swordfish* with three torpedoes (which fortunately missed) off the Norwegian coast. She was later used by Combined Operations to deliver Commandos onto occupied territory, and acted as a navigation beacon directing the attacking convoy up the Loire estuary during the famous St Nazaire Raid in March 1942: Operation *Chariot*.

the Hoe. His wife said he would be back later in the afternoon after finishing a shift at the fisherman's dock.

James gathered all his information and placed it in his leather issue attaché case. He called British Rail and booked a return seat on the two o'clock train to Plymouth. He would arrive in a little over three hours, by which time Stinger should be on his way home. James was excited, he had found something new, something that no one else had either thought of or looked for. He just knew this would lead somewhere and was anxious to get going, and couldn't wait for the train journey to be over, no matter how scenic was the view on the way down or his exhilaration at being out of the oppressive admiralty building.

He had visited Plymouth numerous times, and had even been inside the barracks when visiting the marines to explain to new recruits the logistics and requirements of deployment on one of Her Majesty's warships. He had always found the new marines incredibly well motivated and totally professional in all aspects of his dealings with them. They weren't like typical soldiers. They were marines. Elite troops of the Royal Marine Commando would be considered a special force in most navies of the world, but not in Britain. Such was the intensity of professionalism and training in service life in the early eighties, having improved dramatically since the relatively somber years of the seventies. Despite the improvements, the Falklands conflict had still been a wake up call. Many marines moved on after a few years of regular Royal Marine service to become members of the Special Boat Service (SBS) or to join the Arctic Warfare Cadre. These were the true Special Forces in the eyes of the British Army. James had had the pleasure of working with many of them in his short stint while onboard ship and had always walked away impressed, supremely grateful that they were on the same side as he.

An early member of one of these groups was Mr. John 'Stinger' Sprite, an unassuming gentleman now well into his sixties who would never normally have received a second glance. Many assumed he had just worked the fishing docks all his life and never gave him another thought, but one look into his eyes showed something was lurking. James had seen it before, in the men of the SBS; a glint of knowledge mixed with the uncanny ability to do anything, supreme confidence. Stinger had tired, rough old hands, but they grabbed hold of James's like they could tear his off at the wrist. He was obviously still tough and quite agile for his age. Meeting up with Stinger after work they walked together toward the local bar, and James noticed that he didn't just step up each curb, but hopped, and James had trouble keeping up with his brisk military pace, even though James was a good four inches taller than this older ex-marine.

"Your shout I think," Stinger said, smiling as they arrived.

"A pleasure, sir. What'll it be?" James asked, just as a pint of dark fluid was plopped down on the bar in front of Stinger without any other conversation having taken place.

"So, Stinger. Got some other poor punter to buy yer beers tonight then," the barkeep said, smiling at James with an 'I've seen this too many times before look.'

"Pint of Oak please. Come here often do you Mr. Sprite?"

"Oh, once in a wee while, after a day's work on the pier and before having to go home to the blunderbuss. But call me Stinger, laddie, everyone else does." He said, grinning again and soaking up half the glass in one enormous satisfying gulp.

To James it seemed as though this charade must go on each evening, just with a different host. But it was fun to be with such down to earth people after spending the previous months stuck in the admiralty offices in central London, dealing with all the bullshit, frustrations and pitfalls of city life. These men were the salt of the earth, no different to those his father had described all those years ago. And to see it, all he had to do was come to this one pub. Looking over to the old commando, who was already giving the barkeep the eye for a refill, he saw Stinger rubbing his thigh and resting it on the barstool.

Stinger saw James was stifling the question: "German bullet. Caught a Spandau blast off the coast of Belgium in '42. Shattered my leg completely. And back then they didn't use pins to put you back together. Doctors wanted to take it off, but my wife wouldn't let 'em. So at least I have the leg, but it gives me gyp once in a while. Although a few pints of this usually takes the edge off," Stinger said, as if the pain was still an everyday occurrence.

"Sounds like your wife did you a favor," James remarked.

"Aye, now and again I get lucky and she does right by me."

"Com'on Stinger, you've got a terrific woman. Don't tell fibs out of school," the barkeep interrupted, giving James the upturned eyes before walking away and shaking his head in disbelief.

"So lad, what on earth makes you come all the way from the big smoke just to see me? Come to pay me the back wages they stole from me after getting shot?" Stinger said sarcastically.

"Well no. Sorry. More mundane stuff. I'd just like to know what was happening when you were onboard the *Sturgeon* in 1941. Specifically while you were off the American coast," James said.

Almost spitting out his beer, Stinger sent James a sideward glance that would have cowered lesser men. "Don't beat about the bush do you lad? Get right stuck in there. Christ! Ah well, to be honest, I don't remember much about times on the sub. We just got moved around until we did a job here and there. Then got picked up again. Not being an officer I never even really knew where we were most of the time, except for home waters, of course. Never had a need," Stinger responded, obviously taken aback by the question, and then asking: "Is this official like?"

"Well, yes it is. We're researching a vessel that went down off the eastern seaboard. The Germans said they sank it, but they didn't have submarines working that area at the time. The U-boat that claimed the kill was sunk a week later, but shouldn't have been in the area. There's a salvage team working the vicinity now, and we just want to make sure the wreck isn't a hazard or a war grave if it's disturbed. Lawsuits, insurance and all," James lied.

"Aye, well, I suppose it's been a long time now. That'll be the *Albatross*," Stinger said. "Everyone knows about that."

"The ship carrying gold bullion from South Africa. Sunk with all hands in a mysterious explosion. Yes. But what were you doing in the area at the time?" James asked.

"Oh we was just training, nothing special," Stinger responded, looking to the bottom of his empty glass as if he was staring into the black murky depths of the Atlantic, and having seen something he'd rather not.

"Long way to go for training. Especially as you were already actively engaged up and down the North Sea coast?"

"Aye well, there's no sense sometimes in what they make you do. You've done your time, you know that. Hell, even though we were at war we still had to paint coal white one day just to give some Rupert a kick, to make him look good an' all."

"That's true, there being no sense sometimes, but rather a coincidence wouldn't you say? Besides, it's been a while now, all the secrets are out and you're probably no longer covered under the Official Secrets Act anymore," James said, not really knowing whether Stinger was still obliged or not.[*]

"We did some nasty things back then. Had to be done though, but lots of folk died because of our work, we didn't abide much by

---

[*] He was obliged. The Official Secrets Act is a law, and as such does not need signing to be effective. Signing is simply a subtle though strong reminder of a person's lifelong obligation, especially to anyone involved with national secrets.

the convention either. But just the same as would have happened to us. We'd have been shot as spies after countless days of torture, even though we always wore our uniforms."

Staring into the thick foam on top of his new pint Stinger lapsed into thought as he started to remember some of the things he had done whilst an early marine commando in his twenties…

Chapter Four

'Stinger' Sprite, North Sea Coast, Holland / November 1940

It is well that war is so terrible. We should grow too fond of it.
– Robert E. Lee

SPENDING COUNTLESS DAYS COUPED UP inside the cramped space of the submarine, with the evaporating body sweat of every man dripping from every nook and cranny of the dank steel tube, was uncomfortable to say the least. The relentless bashing from the heavy swells of the North Sea shook the boat to and fro as it cruised near the surface to replenish air, and being a marine didn't guarantee anything against the onset of sea sickness. Many of the commandos were puking all over the insides of what could very quickly become their communal coffin.

Submariners are renowned for being a special breed; readily accustomed to the great abyss to which commandos are not. Commandos prefer the surface, where they excel in the fresh night air, usually to the detriment of others. The submariners wondered how on earth these men could carry out their land missions in such a state of sickness. But once away from the dank confines of the submarine, to their immense relief, the commandos soon recovered and relished being in their new environment.

As the submarine positioned itself a short distance offshore in total darkness the twelve men clambered into three small rubber rafts, their assortment of weapons carefully wrapped in waxed cloth to protect them from the corrosive qualities of the salt water. Their faces were blackened and they each wore the traditional woolen cap comforter. Once in the small boats they were already soaked through to the skin, and cold. But they were still greatly relieved to be away from the stench onboard that tiny black tube.

Paddling to shore they could just see the dark outline of the coast a few hundred yards away. Behind them the submarine slid silently beneath the waves where it would lay hidden for two hours before emerging again to retrieve what was left of the group and any captives they brought with them. German patrols were common, both onshore and on the sea. These men, and more like them, had dramatically increased the German war machine's need for resources in protecting the coastline. And any splitting of the enemy's forces was providing a valuable function to all the other operational theaters of war.

Most of Stinger's group had been among the first volunteers in Churchill's experiment to organize the Special Services Group, later known as Commandos.[*] After seeing the effectiveness of guerrilla operations in the Boer War,[†] Churchill decided Britain needed to use similar styles of operations, and earnestly set about organizing these men in such a way as to cause as much havoc and aggravation to the Germans as possible; sneaking in, hitting them hard, and bolting away unscathed.

John 'Stinger' Sprite was just shy of twenty-three, an above average soldier in 1940, as fit and agile as any athlete of the day, only a lot more dangerous. Enduring the harsh commando training course in Scotland had toughened them far beyond what any of

---

[*] Originating from an Afrikaans word, Kommando, which translates roughly to 'mobile infantry regiment', originally used to describe a body of men, or a unit, and not a single soldier. South African Kommando guerilla tactics, and superior marksmanship, rained havoc on the conventional 'in-line' forces of the British, successfully expelling them during the First Boer War, 1880-1881.

[†] Also known as The Second Boer War, The Anglo-Boer War or The South African War, 1899-1902.

them had heretofore thought possible. They had learnt to kill in a myriad of horrible ways, and kill effectively, without thought. Their preferred close quarter weapon of choice was the Sykes Fairburn; a long double bladed stiletto knife used for murdering their victims quickly and quietly if presented in the correct manner, and after hours of training that manner was so well practiced that it became second nature.

They also carried British Sten guns; a light rapid-fire, 9mm automatic machine gun, excellent for close quarter battle but questionable at a distance. Rumor had it that a wet blanket at thirty yards would protect you from the rounds a Sten would spit out, but no one had yet volunteered to test the theory. However, a number of Germans had once thought upturned tables would protect them, to their ultimate demise. Two Brens were also taken for covering fire. These were incredibly accurate fast firing machine guns when used with the attached tripod, although being magazine fed they tended to jam at times, always at the most inopportune moments.

Explosives were used to demolish everything they saw fit. The new more powerful explosives designed in the last couple of years could be carried with relative ease and positioned quickly for maximum destruction. Explosives were also used to great effect during the escape and evasion procedure, after the initial mission had been accomplished, to slow down the larger number of Germans that would inevitably be sent after them. The Germans gave out rewards for capturing live commandos; such was the fear these men spread.

After paddling ashore their night vision improved sufficiently to where they could make out the topography of the coastline and see their final destination. Tonight they had to remove part of a German radar installation inside a concrete bunker on a small hillock a mile inland, and capture prisoners if possible. They initially always had the element of surprise, which was paramount to the operation and keeping more of them alive. There was a high price to pay for these missions but Churchill was adamant that it needed to be paid. And thankfully there were always volunteers willing to risk paying that price, for King, country, family, friends, or just because the rest of the services were boring. Over the years Brits have always answered the call, and done it with remarkable fortitude and vigor. Stinger and his mates were no different to any before, or any who would follow. Though their cause was probably more righteous than anything before or since.

Reaching the beach they hauled their light boats over the sand and into the grass, covering them with camouflage netting. Two men remained behind to guard the boats and prevent ambush while the rest immediately headed off inland, carrying their heavy loads of weapons, ammunition and explosives, the officer in charge leading the way, half by memory and half by map. They had all studied the sand model and each knew his role; how to get there, how to do the job, and how to get back out. So the idea of the plan went anyway.

After a hard slog for ten minutes they reached a point two hundred yards from the concrete structure, above which stood the tall steel girders holding the electronic device that transmitted the beams. Beams that guided German bombers onto targets over London and all the ports of England.[*] The boffins at home needed to know the workings of the device, so they could come up with a counter-measure or, instead, turn it into something useful. The part they needed was inside the building itself, surrounded by barracks of regular troops. From the information local human intelligence had gathered the troops were not supposed to be combat quality, since most of the combat battalions were either in the deserts of

---

[*] Lorenz beams were an early German radio navigation system that led to the 'Battle of the Beams', whence British boffins were forced to develop counter-measures such as radio frequency jamming and distortion of the radio waves.

North Africa or slogging through the mud in Russia. However, that was by and by, Stinger and his mates would kill everyone, no matter how qualified, in order to complete the task at hand.

Fire teams were set up with the Brens to provide covering fire during the escape while the remaining six crept forward in total silence in the pouring rain. Music was coming from inside the building, scratchy radio tunes from Paris. Everyone was relaxed inside the building, warm and cozy out of the weather, unaware of the drama about to unfold. A lone sentry walked to and fro outside the building, shielding himself from the rain and hardly paying enough attention to save his own life, let alone the lives of his friends inside. His life ended quickly and mutely at the point of a sharp Sykes Fairburn. His body unceremoniously rolled into a culvert out of view while one of the commandos put on his cape and continued the relentless guard duty, without anyone any the wiser. The new guard motioned the rest forward and they sprinted over the newly laid concrete road in their rubber-soled boots, making hardly a sound. Reaching the building, two took up position outside the door and another two at each of the windows. The two at the door burst in and immediately shot three Germans dead with silenced pistols. Four more quiet shots came through the windows, which took care of the remaining inhabitants. In three seconds the building had been taken, in almost total silence. The guard outside walked up and down as though nothing was going on. Two commandos removed tools from their packs and started to dismantle the fragile electronics component they needed. It would fit easily inside a large backpack when completely taken apart, and that would only take a few minutes, though it would seem much longer to those waiting outside.

The guard rapped on the door, signaling company. Two of the commandos immediately left the building and hid in the shadows behind a storage shed, waiting for the imminent arrival of what was probably only the replacement guard. As soon as he was close, one jumped out and held his hand over the man's mouth while the other embedded the knife deep into the side of his chest. There was no sound, just sheer horror on the unsuspecting man's face. Stinger had never seen that look of horror before and tugged hard to remove his blooded blade as the body collapsed to the ground, the cold dead eyes starring back at him. Stinger's mate dragged the man into the culvert with the other.

The rest of the team, finished with disassembling the device, had already placed explosives set to go off in ten minutes, or by tripwire, whichever was first, by which time they should all be away from the beach. They picked up the fire team on their way out and made their way along the original path. Once on the wind swept beach the explosion lit up the night sky for a few seconds, the rain muffling the rest of the sounds. Lights appeared behind them and sirens wailed. A few seconds later they were hauling the boats back into the swell of the North Sea and paddling for all they were worth to get away from the shore, while lights on the shore frantically searched the surroundings for any signs of movement.

Ahead, a quick red flash from the submarine let them know of its position and they clambered up the slick salty sides, packed their equipment down the hatches and passed the sensitive electronics to the waiting boffin. The rubber rafts were released of air and sunk with weights. Altogether it had been a very successful mission, though a simple one. The only thing Stinger could remember, however, was the look on the face of the man he had killed just a few minutes earlier. A look that would haunt him for a lifetime.

Later missions wouldn't bother him as much, not outwardly anyway. It wasn't as though they got easier each time, just that the need to remain removed from the human cost was paramount to the safety of the men around him and the success of the missions.

Stinger killed many men after that, but for some reason that one affected him in a way he never spoke of, and never wanted to. His shattered leg had somehow seemed the inevitable reward for what he was doing. Payback almost. At the time, delirious with pain, and with a soldier's conscience gnawing at him, that by getting injured he had let his mates down, he had resigned himself to losing his leg and ending the agony, but his wife had thankfully saved him from a life of one-legged despair.

For her dogged persuasion, not only to Stinger, but towards the doctors all too eager to remove a man's leg, he knew that the only way he could thank her was to be good man, live a good life and "treat her proper like," with respect and honesty, although her method at the time had been a somewhat curt: "Dammit Sprite, you're my fucking husband, behave like it!"

Chapter Five

Sabine O'Connor, Admiralty, London, England / May 1982

A woman's perfume tells more about her than her handwriting.
– Christian Dior

"STINGER! YOU ALRIGHT MATE?" the barkeep said.
"What? Oh, yes. Thanks. Just thinking too much. Must be time for me to head on home now though," he said.
"Can I walk with you? I have to get to London this evening anyway," James explained, hoping to get some more information on the way.
"Sure lad. Sorry to be such a downer and that I can't help you much," Stinger said.
James and Stinger left the bar together and walked toward the Hoe, leaving those in the bar wondering what was up with the old fella. Few had seen him like that before, he was usually the glue that held them together and the humor that kept the conversation going. There was something on old Stinger's mind alright, but he couldn't make up his mind if he wanted to tell. For a long time now he thought that everything he'd done before was irrelevant in today's world, and when he saw the kids growing up and causing trouble, showing no respect, he sometimes doubted it had all been worth it. All his mates who had been left behind on the beaches of France or fields of Holland had died because of what?

"You know Stinger, I've got the greatest respect for you and your comrades, almost envious of the things you've done. Having the opportunity to make a difference in extreme circumstances, having the guts to do it and then living with the horror, it deserves a lot more than simple respect and gratitude. Though you may not see it these days, life is different, and hopefully better thank God. But it's men like you who made it possible. There's little we can do to repay you or those who are lost forever for what went on. But you have to know that there are still men just like you were, over there," James said, pointing to the huge stone walled barracks of the Royal Marine Commandos towering above them. "You'd be surprised how much like you they really are. And your little group of volunteers started it. You should be as proud as hell. I'm damn proud to live in a country that still produces men like you."

Stinger listened. He knew every word because he'd thought it himself, but until now had never heard it from any one individual, face to face, apart from the vicar at the Remembrance Service held on the Hoe each November.

Stinger stopped in his tracks and looked out over the Hoe. The moon glinting off the surface of the cold uninviting water. "We sank that ship you know. The *Albatross*. We took on her crew and sank her in sight of land. We thought it was another of Churchill's attempts to get America involved in the war."

"The *Sturgeon* sank her?" James asked.

"Obliterated her. The skipper used a two-thirds compliment of torpedoes after we placed explosives in the hold to make certain it sank and wasn't a hazard to other shipping."

"Then you came home?"

"No. We went straight on to another jaunt in Holland and lost four chaps in a badly planned operation that went horribly wrong. We thought the Gestapo must have caught the resistance man who was providing the intelligence, and broke him, because they were waiting for us, it was a disaster from beginning to end. We were supposed to be gathering intelligence for the Dieppe Raid a year later. The planners should have taken notice, it was an omen to the bigger disaster to come."

"Thanks Stinger, you're the only one who knows."

"I know. That's what makes it worse. It's as though the others have kept all the secrets and I should do the same. Nine of those submarines we used never came home, you know? It was a bit of a crapshoot to get on the right one. Some smartass came up with a ditty about them, but I can't remember it anymore." *

"Times are different Stinger. There's nothing that'll make much difference these days, it's been too long for that. Anyway, it's more for historical sake than anything."

"Hope you're right lad," Stinger said, reaching his doorstep.

James watched the old hero walk up to his house, not quite having the same hop in his step as he'd seen earlier and leaving James to wonder if he'd done the right thing. But that was nothing new. Stinger had been living that life since burying his knife to the hilt in that young German soldier's chest forty years before. For most, the personal war doesn't end when the real war does, it lives on and only relinquishes itself in the finality of life. Such is the price many pay when they are fortunate to survive.

Seeing Stinger safely home and making sure the door opened for him, James was both exhilarated and sad. Exhilarated at having found something he'd known to have been there, and sad for what he'd made an old marine remember in order to get it.

But Stinger would get over it. He went through these bouts of self doubt every once in a while and always bounced back. The following night he would be back in the local, having a pint before heading home to meet the blunderbuss. Then every Friday she would meet him at the bar and they would enjoy their weekly

---

* *Twelve Little S-Boats*, based on *Ten Little Injuns* by Septimus Winner (p. 280).

evening out over fish and chips. They were regulars, had been for years, and nothing was about to change that, not for a long time. The memories would hauntingly remain just below the surface of everyday life, but each day would go on as usual and Stinger would keep doing what was expected, continuing despite the doubts, just like a marine was supposed to.

James strolled toward the station. He needed to get back to London and ponder what he had learnt. It was all starting to make sense. The map was a mixture of bullion and secrets, red and green together. Though the reasons were still a mystery. Why would the navy go to all the trouble of crewing a merchant ship, pick up a cargo of gold bullion and then sink the lot in a great explosion off the American coast? Then not say another word, not even write a report? It was too much to take in right now, he needed some rest.

The train journey was bleak; darkness seeped into the carriage like a leach looking for blood. Torrential rain beat fiercely against the windows hiding everything from view, rivulets of water racing each other almost vertically across the thick panes of glass. The restaurant produced buckets of weak coffee and stale biscuits and spewed out the putrid aroma of overcooked vegetables. Automatic doors at the end of each carriage opened and closed by themselves at every sway of the coach, even with no one near them. Each time they opened a blast of cold air entered, bringing with it the awful stale cooking smell again. Couldn't the navy have afforded first class tickets at least? Then he wouldn't have had to put up with the kids playing their new little cassette players at ear spitting levels and thumping the tabletops like drums.

When the kids left the train James was finally able to sleep. Rolling into London at midnight he found a taxi which took him home to relief at one 'o clock in the morning.

Rising five hours later he readied himself for work, still tired from the train journey but anxious to get back to his project.

"Where the hell have you been Devlin?" the CO asked.

"Went down to Plymouth to meet an old marine who knows something about this hole in the map, sir," James replied, rather startled that the CO was there already.

"Does he now, and what did this genius tell you that was so bloody fascinating that you had to use hard earned taxpayer money for a train ticket?"

"Well sir, he said that a ship was sunk by a British submarine in that exact spot on the map."

"Rubbish!" The CO bellowed. "Absolute rot. Why would they do that?"

"I don't know sir," James answered sheepishly. "But I intend to find out."

"Like I said Devlin. Don't go looking too hard and wasting our money. There's nowt to find. Otherwise someone a lot brighter than you would have found it already. And presently we've got a lot more important things to worry about. The Argie air-force is creating drama and it won't be long before they get lucky."

"Yes sir."

James hadn't heard the news yet. He'd been in too much of a hurry to switch on the radio whilst getting ready for work. Unlucky for James, the first person he'd run into had been up the whole night re-arranging some logistics nightmare. Something had gone awry in the loading of the ships that were carrying vital stores for the South Atlantic task force. But now that encounter was over James could go down back into the dungeon, and sift through the endless reams of papers that he'd left scattered about.

Reaching his door he found it wide open. Inside was a rather attractive backside showing itself to the world, while the attached head was looking through the papers on the floor in front of her.

"Can I help you at all," James asked.

"Oh. Sorry sir. Didn't mean to disturb you. Just thought someone had left this lot here by mistake," the pretty girl said, getting to her feet and straightening her ruffled uniform, in which she looked remarkably un-naval.

"It's all in order, by date and vessel. I know it might not look like it, but I know where everything is," James said, waiting for something more.

"Sabine. Sabine O'Connor. Nice to meet you," Sabine said, visibly aware of the long undressing stare she was receiving.

"James Devlin. Same here. Look, I'm sorry. It's just that you're an unusual sight around here. I mean, it's not that common to see a good looking girl down here," James stumbled. "I'm sorry, I shouldn't say that."

"No you shouldn't, but thank you. I'd better leave you alone. Looks like too much fun to me," Sabine said sarcastically, walking away.

James couldn't take his eyes of her as she strolled away down the hall on the polished tiled floor. Her heels clacking away in true military fashion while her skirt swayed a little too illicitly for any navy he was part of. She turned around before heading up the stairs and saw him following her with his eyes. She smiled. He turned away, embarrassed.

Sabine's aroma remained in the air, providing a respite to the mustiness of old papers and mold from years of decay in the subterranean world of old London. James looked around at the various stacks of papers and had to think for a minute what he was about. Gathering his thoughts he looked over the 1941 pile again, trying to find anything on the mission Stinger had mentioned. He thought it rather farfetched and would have discounted it if he had heard about it from anyone else. But Stinger had no reason to be telling tales. There had to be something in it.

The salvage currently being organized off the American coast was supposed to be looking for a German U-boat, at least that's what the media were saying. But why look for an old U-boat, of which there were many scattered around the oceans, when there was a chance of finding bullion?

James contacted Lloyds registry and found all he could on the salvage company. It looked like they were a legitimate historical group and they'd even had a National Geographic Explorer team contracted to document the event. They had a splendid reputation to uphold, and wouldn't likely jeopardize it for anything dubious. He also got the name of a British member of the salvage crew and learned that they had stopped searching for the time being because National Geographic had pulled their team off the project.

The information rather surprised James, he'd always thought highly of the organization and thought that they would have stuck it out. They knew well enough the problems associated to salvage operations and, indeed, any enterprise involving a search for lost items whether on land or sea.

Leaving the basement to return to his small desk in an upstairs office James called the hotel where his contact was staying. It was nine o'clock on the east coast.

"Yes. This is Sean."

"Hello. Sean O'Connor? This is James Devlin from the Admiralty in London. I'm sorry to disturb you at this early hour."

Sean looked at the clock on the sideboard. The caller had said "early hour," yet it was nine. Still, it seemed like the middle of the night. The late night hadn't yet worn off and he was still groggy.

"Yes. Hi. What can I do for you?" Sean asked.

"Sean. You're involved in a salvage operation. I'd like to ask some questions if I may. When would be a good time? If you're agreeable that is." James said.

"Can you give me an hour? Had a late night last night, you know. I'll get sorted out and be waiting for your call in an hour," Sean said, hoping James wouldn't call, he just wanted to sleep.

"Certainly Sean. Thanks very much for your time. I'll get back to you at ten, your time," James said, replacing the receiver.

"What's going on Devlin? You finished with that map yet?" The CO bellowed through the open door.

"What? Sir? No Sir. I'm just following a lead and checking with someone in the field. I'm calling back in an hour to find out what's going on over there," James said rather nervously.

"Who is this contact Devlin? And where did you find out about him?" The CO asked.

"Lloyds, sir. Told me there was a British diver on the salvage crew, a Mr. O'Connor. So I contacted him this morning."

"Well? What did he tell you? Anything worthwhile for all the time you've been wasting?" The CO asked.

"Nothing yet sir. Calling back in an hour, it's early there."

"Early! It's nine o'clock in the damn morning! What's wrong with this gentleman? Can't he get out of bed in the morning!"

The CO was enjoying himself, having fun at a subaltern's expense. "Okay Devlin. Carry on. I'll give you a couple more days. But then it's over. We'll lay it to rest for another ten years," the CO said, walking away with a large satisfied smile on his face.

In an office down the hall Sabine couldn't help but listen. A name had sparked an interest; Sean O'Connor, her brother's name. She ducked quickly into the safety of her office as the CO strode past, oblivious to her presence. Or so she thought. Sabine wore the wrong scent to be oblivious to anyone.

Chapter Six

'Short' Larry, Eastern Seaboard, United States / May 1982

Old age has its pleasures, which, though different, are not less than the pleasures of youth.
– W. Somerset Maugham

"LARRY! WAIT UP," Sean shouted.

"Hey lad, what's up?" Larry turned and said, surprised to see someone following him out of the bar.

Sean jogged and caught up to the stumbling man and rested a hand on his thick shoulder. He thought there was no way he would let the opportunity pass to have a few more words with the only person he'd met so far who was the least interested in their salvage operation. Someone who seemed to have information to share and actually wanted to share it.

"Larry. How about we find somewhere quiet to talk. I think you've got something in that stubborn head of yours that might be worth listening to, and I'll make it worth your while," Sean said.

"Stubborn is it! Aye, well you may be right. But it's comes from years of seeing things others choose not to. If that makes me stubborn, so be it. So, what's on my mind that you want to know?" Larry said, walking on.

"You know what we're doing here, and you've got a good idea of what might be out there, and what isn't. So why not tell me exactly what you think and maybe we can get you a trip out on the *Ulysses*. You'd have some fun," Sean said, in hope.

"Aye, it'd be fun for me, but what about them others? I doubt they'd want an old fart like me hanging around their fancy-dudy instruments. I know I'm a bit o'a drinker and tend to piss folks off pretty easy," Larry said.

"You let me worry about them, and you worry about telling me what happened out there all those years ago," Sean said.

"It's a deal. Why don't we go o'er here and have a brew?" Larry said, pointing toward an old shack on the edge of the beach, hidden from view by the tall spindly sand grass.

Entering the shack through a dilapidated and well-weathered wooden door, that looked as though it would fall apart at the slightest draft, Sean looked around. The place, though dark, was amazingly clean and tidy. A cloth was even on a small round table and plates were laid ready for breakfast, two chairs waiting for customers. At the other end of the room stood a large, comfortable, high-backed chair, and alongside a side-table that held a neat stack of hardcover books. The air was fresh from the ocean breeze which wafted in gently through the net curtains, creating a shimmering of light across the floor. Sean expected a woman to come in from the kitchen at any moment.

"Beer lad?" Larry asked.

"Yes. Please Larry," Sean said, still a little surprised.

"You thought it would be a shambles didn't you?"

"No, no. Well, to be honest, I wasn't expecting this. This is immaculate Larry. Well for a chap anyway," Sean said.

"Aye well, not many gets to see it. But those that do are always a little surprised," Larry said.

"I'll bet. It doesn't seem like you. But I hardly know you."

"No matter, Sean. My wife kept this place in tip-top shape her whole life. It was her home away from home. She loved to come here at weekends and anytime she could spare, just so we could spend time together, alone. It let us get away from world for a few days so we could regain some sanity." Larry explained.

"Sounds nice Larry. You must have had a good relationship," Sean said, picking up on the past tense.

"We still do. She might not be around anymore, passed away twenty years since, while I was away at sea, but I still think of her here, and that's why I keep the place as it is, out of respect. It keeps her memory alive. So long as the place is clean I know she's here somewhere," Larry said, looking around the room for signs of a friendly spirit.

"That's nice Larry."

"Grab a beer lad and sit down."

Sean sat on one of the chairs by the kitchen table and looked at the plates, which seemed to be waiting patiently for morning.

"Always lay the table before I go out. We always did that. She liked to drink too, and it made it easier in the mornings. Old habits. She taught me all my old habits. Least that's what she used to tell everyone anyway. And you know, she was probably right."

Sean sipped his beer and looked carefully at the old man in the chair across from him. He looked sad from years of hard work and drinking. Yet there was something calming about his manner. He had a confidence that seems lost to most people, especially those in their later years. It was as though he knew something no one else did, and didn't care whether anyone wanted to know or not. He was totally happy with his lot, in this tiny shack that from the outside world looked as though it would evaporate any second. Sean asked why the inside was so tidy and the outside so rundown.

"Simple," Larry said. "When we weren't here we didn't have to worry about it. It always looked so bad that no one would ever think to bother it. Wife said that it's what's inside that matters.

Guess that's why she married me, because I never was much of a looker. She must have seen something inside of me she liked."

They both sat for a while, sipping their beers in silence. Sean taking in the sounds of the ocean and enjoying the cool breeze coming in through the small windows. Larry listening to his wife in his thoughts, softly reminding him to use a coaster.

"Suppose you want to hear about that ship, the *Albatross*?" Larry asked.

"The one you mentioned in the bar, yes. But are you sure there's no U-boat from '41 out there?"

"Sure as anyone can be. Grandfather was convinced there were never any U-boats here until December 1941, after Pearl. Though rumor has it there was a submarine in the area somewhere around the time that ship was sunk, but it was likely British or American. Some fisherman found a few bodies floating in the sea after the ship went down. Although they looked as though they'd been dead for a while, and not just recently from the ship sinking. The strange thing was they were all wearing German underwear," Larry said.

"But surely that would mean a U-boat?" Sean asked.

"That's what someone maybe wanted us to think. The bodies don't make sense though, unless they were previously fished out of the water somewhere else, and aboard the ship awaiting a proper burial," Larry explained.

"Could be. So what about that ship?"

"Well, my old man said his father had heard three separate explosions from the ship. To him they sounded like torpedoes, and he'd heard them before, on a convoy over the Atlantic in the First War, so he knew the sound. Then there was the major explosion. The one that devastated the ship, and the only one that most people remember hearing. That's when local folks went out looking for survivors, but found nothing. It was completely obliterated and everyone thought it was due to un-vented tanks. But there would have been a lot more wreckage had it exploded on the surface. It was obviously already submerged when the big explosion tore it apart."

"From what, a submarine?" Sean asked.

"Who knows? That's the mystery. But it was a sub that sank her first. But not a German one."

"How could you possibly know that for sure?" Sean asked.

"Well, nothing's for certain. But there's evidence that points otherwise," Larry answered.

"What evidence?" Sean said suspiciously.

Larry walked over to a well polished chest of drawers resting against the wall and removed an old yellowing piece of paper. He handed it to Sean.

"Looks like a brass rubbing of some kind," Sean exclaimed.

"It is, kind of. Except it's from the casing of a torpedo that was dredged up by my father's fishing boat 20 years ago. Scared the crap out of the whole crew when they saw it hanging in the net. My father, though, got close enough to do this before they cut it loose again. He rubbed the markings which show it wasn't made in Germany, as clear as day it is. Case closed I'd say," Larry said, rather pleased with himself.

"Well if this is real… is it?"

"My old man did it, and he wasn't prone to practical jokes, though you'd have to have known him to realize that," Larry said.

"Can I make a copy of this?" Sean asked.

"Sure lad, if you think it'll help. Just bring it back. It's a memento, like everything else around here, including me."

"Thanks. Larry you're quite the character. Seem to know a lot, but don't care if people listen or not," Sean said.

"Used to care. But as old as I am, and probably a little too much drink, everyone started to think I was the village idiot and stopped listening. So I figured it wasn't my job to educate the ignorant. There's others who get paid to do that, but even they aren't heeded anymore either," Larry said.

Changing subjects as frequently as the arrival of more beer, they soon got onto present day politics and, inevitably, the Falklands. Larry, like many Americans, couldn't understand why Britain would exert so much effort, at such a risk, for nothing more than a sheep farm in the South Atlantic.

Sometimes Sean wondered the same, but could easier understand the principles that constantly drove the British to do such things. He tried to explain the rationale that originated from the Norwegian hordes who had been among the first to invade the British Isles. Not just the warrior spirit, but the deeply held conviction that looking after each other was paramount to survival, protecting what was theirs, their kin and their country, indeed everything that their livelihood was based upon. And from the moral standpoint, that people just cannot be allowed to show up and take everything away – even though that's exactly what the Vikings had done.

It did nothing to quell Larry's doubts, though, brought about from a few years more experience, during which he'd learned that it really didn't matter that much. Especially when blood is spilt and friends and family come home maimed, or not at all.

"Larry. It's been a pleasure. I haven't enjoyed an evening of conversation such as this in quite sometime. I've missed it. We should do it again, soon. But in the meantime I've got to get going. I have to do some research in the morning. I'll let you know when we head out, and you can be sure of an invitation," Sean said.

"Thanks son. But you've really got to get yourself a life if you think this was fun at your age," Larry responded.

Shaking hands they parted. Larry settled back into his comfortable armchair and picked up a book, half reading, half reminiscing over evenings with his wife. Sean returned to the hotel with the casing rubbing, eager for morning so that he could learn more about what Larry had provided. As soon as he could he would call his sister. She had a job at the Admiralty in London. But right now she would be getting ready for work on the other side of the Atlantic, so he'd have to wait until morning.

Chapter Seven

Sabine and James, London, England / May 1982

Friendship is unnecessary, like philosophy, like art... It has no survival value; rather it is one of those things that give value to survival.
– C. S. Lewis

SEAN PICKED UP THE PHONE on the first ring. This time he was wide awake, refreshed after a shower and caffeined enough to jump start a Chevy.

"Sean? Thanks very much for giving me your time. I'll try to keep it brief," James said.

"No problem. What can I do for you?" Sean asked.

Sean knew it would have something to do with the salvage. Why else would the admiralty be interested? He hoped to get more information for his own interests, since the person asking would provide that just by the nature of the questions. The fact that the Admiralty was interested, in itself, proved he was onto something. He just needed a little more substance, something tangible to persuade the Geo crew to remain.

James asked a series of questions and Sean provided honest answers. Though neither really got what they were after. Each thought the other the holder of the greater knowledge. Sean deliberately didn't mention the rubbing from the torpedo that Larry had given him because he wanted to find out more about it first.

After half an hour James thanked him and ended the call. A little disappointed in the lack of information, but not put off to the possibility of trying again.

Just then Sabine entered the office and closed the door behind her. This was rather a strange action from a female officer in the Admiralty, where open doors were a form of protection.

"Sir. Can I speak with you?" Sabine asked directly.

"Yes, certainly. Of course, what is it?" James said.

"I heard my brother's name mentioned earlier, when the CO was grilling you."

"Your brother?"

"Yes. Sean. Sean O'Connor."

"Of course!" I'm sorry, I'm not good at last names." James said honestly, and thought, "especially when distracted."

"No. That's fine sir. I was just wondering… well, why?"

"Oh yes. Well… I just finished calling your brother actually. I was inquiring as to what he thought he might find on the salvage operation. Since it might link with my research," James explained.

"He's not in any trouble then?" Sabine asked.

"Good Lord no. Why would he be?" James said.

"Oh, he has a bit of a reputation. But thank you sir. Sorry to trouble you."

"It's not a problem. Anything I can do to help, just let me know," James said, hoping that she would indeed require his help again, for anything.

Sabine opened the door and walked away with what seemed like a strut, leaving James more than a little intrigued.

There were too many coincidences playing a role. But for now he was enjoying the pleasant aroma of perfume and the vision of breasts silhouetted ever so subtly against the lamplight. Then he realized he'd already spent too much time in the basement.

Sabine thought James was so unlike most of the boring men she'd met in the offices around the stuffy Admiralty building. He was also somewhat different to the active officers she'd met during the parties she attended. She thought James was upset at having lost the opportunity to excel in the active side of the service, but then he appeared happy with his lot in life, and was just trying to do his best with whatever came his way. It was probably the youthfulness in him that kept the optimism alive. Whereas most of the older officers in the building had since found that hard work, effort and loyalty, generally went unrewarded, and had settled into a more lax attitude. Sabine also thought James rather handsome, which was why she was starting to make him notice her.

James was still thinking of Sabine walking away when an idea crossed his mind. He didn't think the CO would go for it, but there was no harm in trying. The phone call with Sabine's brother had instilled a further interest in the investigation and if he could just get to America he might be able to sort the mystery out for good. Then no one else would have to bother with it ever again, even though it was just a job assigned to short-timer junior officers on their way out. Something to keep them out of trouble and away from sensitive procedures prior to termination from service.

He sat behind the ancient typewriter and began writing a justification letter. He had been quite good at these sorts of presentations ever since school, when he'd always won the prize for collecting the most donations for African famines, and any other worthwhile cause that came down the pike.

Two hours later his hopeful letter was sitting on the CO's desk, awaiting his arrival in the office the following morning, when James would either receive a rocket of negative abuse, or a rocket of affirmative abuse citing the enormous cost during a time of national emergency. But James was hoping that the CO would see it as a way to get him out of everyone's hair for the duration.

He had also offered to use up some holiday time to keep the costs down, and with military flights regularly going to the Americas it shouldn't be too hard.

James was sweating a little as he left the note on top of all the paperwork, each piece of which was no doubt far more important. He left the office and walked toward the exit, expecting to hear a tirade following him, but none came. He could look forward to that in the morning.

Leaving the building the sun was still trying to shine through the cloud layer, but as is usual for the city at this time of year, not having much luck. He walked the long route to his favorite pub, which was filling up steadily with office workers. And as much as he hated most of the pretense, he knew eventually he would have to become one of them, unless he managed to find a job that took him out of the city, which he thought highly unlikely.

Arriving in time to secure his righteous seat at the end of the bar, he ordered his favorite pint; London Pride. From this seat on a sunny day he could see all the pretty girls walk through the sunlit doorway in their light summery dresses, not leaving much to the imagination. Today wasn't so good, though. Not only was the sun unobliging but neither were the summer dresses. Instead, London's hideously boring black business suit was the uniform of the day.

Leafing through the broadsheet left on the bar by a previous customer he noticed his local team lost again. He raised his eyes in disbelief as to how they could possibly lose to such an opponent. In doing so he caught the attention of someone familiar watching him in the mirror behind the bar; Sabine. She was sitting at a small side table, by herself, obviously amused at James's exaggerated expression of disgust.

James picked up his beer and made his way to her table.

"Mind if I join you?" James said.

"Please. Help yourself."

"What's so funny?" James asked.

"The look on your face while you were reading the paper. You were so animated," Sabine responded.

"Oh, that. Sunderland lost again. I need another team," James explained.

"That would be an understatement. When are you going to get up to the Premiership? You're in London now you know."

"As if I could forget it."

"You don't like it here?"

"Not so much. I need to be outside. In the country, or on the sea," James said.

"But what's not to like here?"

James caught the double meaning, and was having a difficult time not letting his eyes wander down to the delightfully low opening of her blouse. He could only imagine what was hiding in there. It was probably wonderful. She leant forward to tempt him.

But she wasn't there just to flirt. Whether James knew it or not she didn't really care, because she also enjoyed the attention for attention's sake and was simply used to getting it. This age-old ploy has been used ever since humans stepped into clothing. Some just know how to better use it. Sabine was a consummate expert.

"Nothing here I don't like," James said, being completely honest for the moment.

She already knew that. She could see that he was paying too much attention to her eyes, concentrating too hard on not letting them stray. And yet his thoughts were so obviously involved with his lower peripheral vision, causing his eyes to involuntarily dilate. She knew the signs and was both flattered and satisfied with her efforts. But with oh so little effort.

"Have you eaten," Sabine asked.

"No. I usually just grab something at home after a couple of beers here," James answered.

"Well tonight why not be dangerous and join me? I'm going to that Italian place over the road. That's if you can handle it."

This Sabine was totally different to the one he had noticed at the Admiralty. She was direct, forceful and very confident, almost too confident.

"I might be up for it, if you promise to be gentle," James said.

"Can't do that. But I promise it'll be fun."

With that, James couldn't finish his beer fast enough.

"No. No hurry. We'll have a couple here, like you normally do, and then head over. Give the other wankers a chance to clear out so we won't have to leave for the second sitting," Sabine said.

"Okay. What are you having?" James asked.

"Scotch and water, double. Thanks," Sabine said, already expecting the question.

"Back in a minute."

James walked over to the bar and ordered a double Scotch and a beer for himself. The barman gave James a nod, and looked over at Sabine with a look, which said: "Lucky bastard."

"You seen her in here before Pete?" James asked.

"Nope. Never 'ave. Awful shame that as well." Pete replied.

"Cheers," said James, smirking as he walked away.

James was aware that he'd been searched out. This was his local, and she had never been here before. It was unlikely, though not uncommon, that a girl would go out alone without intending to meet up with someone.

Going back to the table James placed her drink down, bending sufficiently to get a better look at what was on offer. Sabine sensed it, looked up and smiled. "Thanks," she said.

"Cheers," James said, in the middle of sitting down. "You don't come in here much do you? I mean, it's my local, at least my after work local, and I've never seen you in here before."

"No. First time. But then I don't usually come into bars by myself, unless I want to meet someone," she said.

"Who are you meeting?" James said.

"You of course, silly."

Sabine knew James was probably aware of her motive, but not all the reasons behind it. She had decided to come clean when James was at the bar. He was clearly a decent guy, and besides, it looked like he'd asked the barman something about her. She couldn't, or didn't want to, get into deeper lies and decided to forestall any interrogation as to her motives.

"I just thought you could tell me what's going on with my brother a little more. I never hear too much from him and my parents are always asking," she explained.

"Well, you could have just asked me at work. You didn't have to go to all this bother," James said.

"Bother? What bother? I also wanted to find out more about you. Isn't it obvious?"

She was honest. She was interested in James. Her interest had been sparked the first time she'd seen him in the basement. And in that they both had something in common.

After more small talk to get to know each other, and getting to better trust one another, Sabine reached into her rather large handbag and passed a piece of paper over the table. It was a flimsy piece of facsimile paper, much like the old waxed toilet paper in the toilets of the recruits' dormitories.

James looked at it carefully. It was difficult to see exactly what was on it, but it looked like some kind of tracing.

"It's a rubbing, from a torpedo," Sabine said.

"What?"

"Torpedo. World War Two torpedo. British I think," Sabine said, somewhat pleased with herself.

"Well, it is in English, but that doesn't mean that it's British. It could be American," James explained.

"Yes. But it was fired before America was in the war."

"It could be a training torpedo," James said.

"Maybe. It was dredged up off the eastern seaboard, near where Sean's working."

James came alive immediately. "Where did you get this?"

"Sean. He faxed it to me today," Sabine said.

"He never mentioned it to me."

"He doesn't know you, so why would he trust you?" Sabine said. "What does it mean?"

"Could be a lot of things. If I'm looking at this date correctly, it fits perfectly with what I've been finding."

"Which is?" Sabine asked, watching James intently as he studied the poorly transmitted document.

"You've got to keep this under wraps and not tell anyone, especially anyone at the Admiralty. You agree?" James said.

"Yes, of course. What is it?"

James described his theory of what happened to the *Albatross*. He didn't know why any of it happened, but by piecing together Stinger's story he knew there had to be a good explanation. He just hoped he could find it, and that his CO would let him find it. He didn't have long to go at the Admiralty and he needed access to all the files, so he would have to hurry.

Through dinner they talked over everything that Sean had left out in his earlier conversation with James. Time flew by. But now they had to leave. James called a taxi and they shared it, first dropping Sabine off at home, alone, and then returning home himself. She thought he was being a real gentleman, albeit a silly one after all her efforts. But something was on his mind that would only get sorted after meeting his CO the following day, or rather later that morning. Despite the desire, the instinctual animalistic urge, the long legs, her delirious musky scent, and her obvious willingness, he knew that he needed as much rest as he could get. And he knew he would never get any rest staying with Sabine, and neither would he want any, on any other night but this.

Chapter Eight

Ulysses, Eastern Seaboard, United States / May 1982

Neither should a ship rely on one small anchor, nor should life rest on a single hope.
– Epictetus

SEAN WAS HOPING THAT HIS SISTER, Sabine, had unearthed new information that would justify National Geographic remaining with the salvage operation. In all likelihood the search could lead to something far more interesting than anyone had originally thought. All he had to do was persuade the moneymen to allow National Geographic to stay a little longer. He was also willing to utilize more help from Larry.

"Hey guys, this is Larry. I told him he could come on the next trip. He knows the area better then anyone and knows the history," Sean explained to the gathered group.

The crew looked around at each other with mild trepidation after briefly studying the older man in front of them. He didn't look much like a seaman, although he was clearly rough around the edges, leading them to believe he'd had quite the life. So, one by one the group gave their silent but reserved approval. Besides, none of them had any better ideas than the one Sean had told them over breakfast. At least they would still be working the job they enjoyed rather than sitting around looking bored.

Ulysses was readied for another week, which was all they could afford. Sean was confident they would find something in that time with Larry's help, and because they were now looking for something entirely different. Indeed, a few of them had already seen some of the wreckage they were looking for, although at the time they hadn't been interested in the remains of merchant ships since they bore no relationship to the submarine they were after.

Larry remembered the location of where his father had fished out the torpedo all those years ago, and had consciously stayed away from the area ever since. From the underwater maps they had made during previous searches Sean figured they could accurately guess the direction the torpedo had been fired. And armed with that, they could determine the line on which the *Albatross* would have been sailing prior to her destruction.

On the open sea Larry was once again in his element. He loved the shudder of the ship as it tore through the waves, sending plumes of salty water over the decks. He still had his old sea legs, with better balance than the others, and more than a few of the crew were envious at Larry's confident disposition while on the deck. There he was, right out in the thick of it, drinking coffee as though he was in his backyard watching waves wash on the beach, and never spilling a drop. It was hard to believe this was the same old man they'd seen getting teased in the bar a few nights earlier. Sean could see the crew slowly realize their dreams again, and with the help of this old sailor it might just all come to fruition.

They reached the spot where they had previously abandoned the search and retraced their steps a couple of miles. From triangulating prominent features on the distant coastline, Larry decided that this was as good a place as any to start. Sean designed the search grid according to the weather and they hoisted the sea rover over the side again. The cameras were functioning correctly and pictures were soon coming through on a selection of monitors in the cabin below. Larry was in his element on deck watching the hands complete their tasks while Sean made sure the tapes were recording everything. This was all brand new high-priced equipment, much of it having been used only a couple of times before and it had a tendency to be fickle.

After a couple of hours they were back in their normal routine of drudgery and boredom as they studied the murky images on the screens in the front of them. Larry, still on deck, had no time for technical innovations, he was too old to learn something new, especially something he himself would never use. He therefore kept himself to the more practical aspects of the voyage, like keeping all the coffee inside his cup. Larry noticed that this small talent seemed to impress the others and had long understood that credibility was gained in small donations.

Stuck well into the routine of their search grid each crew member was either assigned a position or was resting and awaiting a position. They only had a week in which to find the ship and they needed to work every one of the twenty-four hours every day, and, moreover, not miss anything. They all knew that this simple task required uninterrupted concentration.

The days went by without so much as a glimpse of anything and the crew was, once again, becoming despondent. Larry started to receive some disparaging glances, though no one was willing to follow up with words. However, he privately wondered how long that would last. The hardest thing about credibility is not so much the earning of it, as the keeping of it.

Entering the cabin, Peter interrupted a conversation between Sean and Larry. "Sean. Remember those boxes we saw just before we finished the last search grid?" He asked.

"Yes." Sean said. "What of it?"

"Well, I've been going over the tapes and I think what we are looking for might be there," Peter said.

"Where was that?"

"If we stay on this current search pattern we'll run into it again on the last run. But that'll be on the last day. Not leaving us much time to explore further," Peter said.

"So what do you suggest?" Sean asked.

"We're not running into a debris field on this search, whereas we were before. I think we should split the difference and start nearer to our previous ending position."

"Larry, what do you think?" Sean asked.

"Makes sense. We'll still be online for the torpedo run, and seeing as you found something there we should take a look. We're not doing much good right now and your time and the crew's patience is running out," Larry said.

"OK. If Pete's sure, and you think it's okay, we'll do it." Sean said. "Pete, why don't you knock out a new search pattern for that area, seeing as you seem to know the location? And while you're at it we'll pull in the toys and let the crew know what's going on."

It took a few hours to retrieve the equipment and stow it for the move. In the meantime Peter had plotted a new search grid using the tapes as a guide. A few hours later they were in position and searching. They had lost half a day's work, but if they were nearer the goal they knew it will have been worth it. It was a big 'if' however, and apprehension was running high; some thought it better to have been patient and stay on the course they originally agreed. Notwithstanding that, they were all professionals and even with frustrations creeping in they kept it to themselves, except for a few intense arguments over dinner one night. Larry managed to keep himself out of it with Sean protecting him by suggesting a smoke on the deck.

The following day, the fifth, they started running into a little debris. Nothing that could be immediately recognized but it was, nevertheless, hopeful. At least now there was something to keep them interested on the monitors, because without anything to look at it had become exceedingly difficult to maintain concentration.

"Sean. You're needed below," one of the crew shouted.

Sean's heart raced a few beats as he went down to the cabin. There already were Larry and Peter, eagerly watching the monitor.

"Look, there, see it?" Peter said.

"I see mounds of sand," Sean said, confused as to what he was actually supposed to be looking at.

"I'll pull back the zoom. Now you see it?" Peter asked.

"Railings... buried in the sand. Can you pull out further?"

"I can, but then you'd see nothing. It's too dark. But we need to hold it here to make a smaller grid with the rover," Peter said.

"Alright. Do it," Sean said.

Orders were shouted to the wheelhouse and the ship made motionless except for the roll in the swell. Crew members not assigned to anything were piling into the cabin in anticipation of finally seeing something. There was nothing spectacular, but hopes had been raised with the slowly growing debris field. Everyone strained their eyes to be first to spot something in the murky waters in front of them.

"What we need in here are three people to study the screens. Everyone else out. We'll all get a chance to monitor the progress, but for now we need to keep our eyes fresh and interest piqued. So everyone not immediately involved find something else to do until we call you for your shift." Sean explained.

There were a few groans, but overall everyone knew that the request was sensible and left.

"Good job lad," Larry said, looking at Peter once the room had cleared.

"Thanks. Everyone played a part," Peter said.

"Aye, but you played the major part in this, so don't be so modest. Take the credit when it's due, because it never seems to last long," Larry said.

Peter just looked up and nodded. He knew exactly what Larry meant. He'd always taken the brunt of most things going badly because he was the techie, and the easiest to blame. But now he was brimming with quiet pride and enjoying it.

On the screen was clear evidence of what they had spent so much time looking. A massive debris field. Though much was still unidentifiable there was still a lot to be explored and documented. Not least the large steel boxes which seemed to be in a reasonable condition compared to the rest of the ship.

Sean organized the first two divers and briefed them as to what they were looking for, what was expected of them, and what was to be brought back to the surface. It wasn't an easy task. The depths were deep, the conditions not good and the visibility was poor. Yet the divers were experienced professionals and eager to get on with the job.

Also eager to the task were Sean and Larry in the cabin. They could make out the movements of the divers and gave instructions on positions. The first object of major interest was the largest piece they'd seen so far, the large chest.

After digging away at the seabed, cables were strapped around the casing and soon the large box was being raised toward the surface, something it hadn't seen for over 40 years. There is an air of intense fascination in finding and retrieving a lost object, especially from the depths of the ocean. *Ulysses* and her crew were, once again, fortunate to be a part of that history.

Chapter Nine

Spooks, Eastern Seaboard, United States / May 1982

Government is not reason; it is not eloquent; it is force. Like fire, it is a dangerous servant and a fearful master.
– George Washington

TWO MEN APPEARED AT THE *Albatross* bar while the crew of the *Ulysses* were engaged in the sensitive task of retrieving the items from the seabed. These men were not the usual contingent of tourists or sport fishermen. They were easily distinguishable as government men, G-men, taxmen or spooks, generally disliked and always made to feel unwelcome in these parts. These two in particular looked too much like the IRS, which meant unwanted intrusion into some poor local's privacy.

"Can I help you gentlemen?" The landlord asked bluntly, making the fact plain that they were not at all welcome. But glad to have the custom all the same.

"Beer would be good. Bud?" One of the men said.

"Sure. Coming up. You here on business?"

"Sort of. We're here to check on a salvage team out there. Know anything about it?" The man said.

"Not much. They came in a week ago after they ran out of money. But then they went back out so I guess they must have found some more," the landlord said.

"Are they due in anytime soon?"

"I wouldn't know. You'd have to ask them," the landlord said, realizing he'd said too much from the disapproving looks he was receiving from the other patrons.

The locals were all ears to the conversation and becoming more suspicious of the two strangers as the conversation unfolded. One of the men was writing everything down as the other subtly interviewed the landlord between sips of beer. But, the landlord had reversed course and was remaining quiet, quickly removing himself from the conversation on the excuse of serving customers. Leaving the two men pondering over their notes.

"They after Larry?" One of the locals whispered.

"Don't know. Think they're more interested in the salvage team," the landlord said.

"They're not IRS then?"

"Don't seem to be, but you never know," the landlord said.

"Go ask 'em where they're from."

"Go ask 'em yourself. I've got a business to run."

Andy took his cue, slipped off his barstool with a practiced motion and walked casually over to the two men at the other end of the bar. All eyes immediately went to Andy. Good old Andy. They could always rely on Andy to ask the questions.

"So," Andy said, nodding and searching for recognition.

The two glanced over briefly and went back to their notes.

Andy, not used to being ignored so blatantly, stood taller and stepped closer.

"So." Andy said, nodding. "Not from around here then?"

"No." The talkative one replied.

"So." More nodding. "Where do you hail from then?"

"Not from around here."

"Upstate maybe?" Andy said, motioning northwards.

"Maybe."

"So." Andy said, nodding like he knew what was going on before skulking back to his barstool.

"Nice one Andy. You showed 'em," said a familiar whisper in the shadow.

Andy raised a middle finger salute to the shadow and returned to his beer. At least he'd tried, which was more than the rest had done. Sometimes he hated this bar, but it was the only one around.

The two men finished their beers, put a couple of dollars each on the counter and left.

Everyone immediately got up from their seats, watched them step up into the big Suburban and drive off toward the pier.

"Strange two that. Up to something," the landlord said.

"Aye, up t'something," a voice said. "Maybe we should send Andy out to follow 'em, see what they're up to."

The landlord turned to look at Andy, still at the bar. All he saw was a thin finger sticking in the air out of the gloom.

The Suburban rolled heavily down the street, its reinforced tires crunching the crumbling tarmac. The oversized, perfectly polished vehicle looked completely out of place next to the rusty pickups that were commonplace near the dock. The windows were tinted, giving it an even more eerie appearance, and there was something very different about this particular vehicle that no one had noticed. It was sitting lower to the ground and had upgraded struts to take the extra weight of the steel armor plate beneath and around its sides. This was a vehicle from the fleet at Langley. One of the newer CIA additions generally used to ferry VIPs around. The back of the vehicle held an arsenal of weapons with which the occupants could even fight off a small air attack. Yet it wasn't going to find anything to fight in this sleepy little seaside town, and apart from the people in the bar no one seemed to care much about it. The projection of power, the pretense, had been a waste, and they realized that should have come in the Taurus instead.

Alongside the dock they first went to see the harbormaster. All they needed was a rough position of the *Ulysses*, then they would know if the crew was close to recovering the salvage that was reputed to be laying on the seabed, and had been for 40 years. They had been tasked with not allowing the salvage operation to succeed if, indeed, it was their intention to find this particular cargo. But before blundering into what might be a basic salvage operation they had to make sure, otherwise people would assume that there really was something to hide, which would lead to all sorts of amateurs showing up looking for treasure.

In all honesty they were not too keen on their task. It seemed like a bit of a waste of time, one associated with nothing more than removing their presence from the office. They were older agents, but without seniority, and disgruntled over the recent promotion of a junior university educated agent above them, simply because she was a she. The 'she' in this case had tasked them with this mundane job while she further greased her nose, or whatever else she liked to grease, in the vast inefficient bureaucracy that was known as the Agency. When they had started twenty five years ago it was relatively streamlined, and a person could prove himself and advance on abilities and a job well done. Not simply by looking cute in a short skirt.

The harbormaster, a good local, provided them with what he thought a likely position for the *Ulysses*. However, unbeknownst to the two men, it wasn't the correct location. Prior to setting off he always asked the locals to provide him with a course, in case a storm came up or someone was late returning. Since it wasn't an official request, and didn't require paperwork, everyone obliged. So he knew pretty well where the salvage crew were but provided the suits a location twenty miles distant. The harbormaster didn't know these two from Adam, and it was already proven that Adam couldn't be trusted.

The two weren't the least suspicious. The answer had come easily and voluntarily, and besides, why would the harbormaster protect outsiders on a ship not associated with the area. What the men didn't know was that one of their oldest locals, Larry, was onboard. And although he was considered by some to be the local drunk, he was, nevertheless, a local, and, in this case, also had seniority. They all expected the same from each other no matter the apparent elusive and often abusive nature towards each other.

The Suburban made its way back the way it had come. Its next stop was a bar on the outskirts of Langley, Virginia, where they mingled with a few other older agents to complain about the current state of the Agency, and count the days to retirement.

The harbormaster, in the meantime, called the bar and told the landlord about the two strangers who had been asking questions. He was happy to hear they had received the same intransigence at the bar, apart from Andy of course, and used the radio to inform the *Ulysses* about the town's inquisitive guests. That was all he could be expected to do since he didn't know what was going on and really didn't want to.

Several hours later there was a hubbub of excitement onboard ship. The first box was nearing the surface after been hauled up slowly on the end of the long, non-spinning, German steel cable. All eyes were looking over the ship's side to where the cable emerged from the ocean. The whirring and clatter of the winch the only sound penetrating the lapping of the waves as, foot by foot, the steel rope wound its way neatly onto the spool.

The surface of the water was oily dark, with the only contrast coming from the spray being whipped up by the waves slapping gently against the ship's side as it swayed back and forth, back and forth. Peering into the depths in front of them no one could yet see the box nearing the light, but the high tensile straps had already broken the surface, meaning only a few feet remained beneath the surface before the cargo would show itself to the world once again.

A cheer erupted as the steel chest cleared the ocean for the first time in 40 years. The last of the salt water poured off its surface, sliding down its sides, as if an unwilling hand was losing grasp of a valued possession. The steel containers were caked with rust after so long in the depths, but still sturdy enough to hold the contents rigid and secure in their confines. They were now free of the ocean and swaying heavily under the gantry. Hooks were produced and two members of the crew gently guided the heavy cargo onto the deck of the *Ulysses*.

The apprehension was both massive and oppressive. Sean felt as if he could cut the air with a knife. Larry was the only member calm with anticipation, even though he should have been more excited than anyone to see what had been laying a few miles outside his front door. Sean removed the straps from the cable, letting them fall to the deck and then lashing the end of the cable down. Already hands were touching the boxes, feeling the decades of rust, feeling for the history as if it were tangible. They looked at each other without saying a word, silently deciding who should have the honor of opening the first box. Without hesitation all eyes went to Larry.

"No lads. It's your show," Larry said, breaking the silence.

"But it's your neighborhood Larry. Your story. You do it," Sean said, handing over a large mallet.

Larry took a small swing at the large rusted padlock, but the box stayed closed.

"Come on Larry. Hit the bugger with those big meaty hands o'yours," someone said excitedly.

Larry grabbed the mallet tighter and took a larger swing, pounding apart the latch in one great effort. The lid hopped a little as the seam separated, letting out a stream of oily water. In that split second one or two of the men saw a slight yellowish glow as the available light caught something shiny. Multiple hands grabbed for the lid to pry the old hinges open. Larry smacked the hinges with the mallet and the lid squeaked open, revealing the contents. An audible gasp filled the air and then, except for the sound of waves lapping at the ship's hull, complete silence.

Chapter Ten

James, Eastern Seaboard, United States / June 1982

Men go abroad to wonder at the heights of mountains, at the huge waves of the sea, at the long courses of the rivers, at the vast compass of the ocean, at the circular motions of the stars, and they pass by themselves without wondering.

– Saint Augustine

JAMES SAT BACK IN THE CRAMPED seat onboard the Boeing 747 as it climbed to its cruising altitude. Thirty thousand feet below Ireland was in full view. The tiny hedge-lined fields creating a disorderly mosaic of greens and browns amidst the larger grey blue expanse of ocean beyond. James rested, watched the slowly changing scene and sipped on his gin and tonic. He was visibly relieved to be airborne. Not from any fear of flying, but to be finally away from the office and on his way to America after days of persuasion to his cause.

The CO had initially balked at the idea of James traveling to the U.S.A for nothing more than what he thought was a waste of time, waste of effort and a waste of taxpayers' money.

"Remember what I said lad," the CO had thundered. "Don't go looking too hard. There's nowt to find, or someone a lot brighter than you would have found it already!"

James had almost given up but Sabine had pressed him. In a surprisingly short time she had become an inspiration, although exactly why he didn't know. Maybe she was just too damn cute to ignore. James's next attempt caught the CO in a bad mood after he'd received further tragic news from the Falklands; the South Atlantic Fleet was having a hard time of it, being little more than a collection of sitting ducks under scant air cover from marauding French jets being flown by some very brave, and very capable, Argentinean pilots. This time, though, James showed the CO the case rubbing, albeit against Sabine's wishes, and it seemed to spark his interest. Then, in a moment of controlled anger, he agreed to let James go to the salvage site to investigate. Although it might simply have been James's repeated requests that wore him down, a desire to get this insufferable individual out of the way so that he could concentrate on more important far flung issues. Either way, James was ecstatic as he turned to leave the office.

"You had better come back with something more valuable than an old rusty torpedo," the CO barked, through a slight smoky haze created by a previous visitor's pipe tobacco.

"Yes sir." James said, trying hard to hide his excitement. "Thank you sir."

"Now bugger off and leave me alone," the CO bellowed.

With that, James was on his way. It would be his last task before being released from the service and he wanted to do well by it. He also wanted to impress Sabine. But most of all he wanted to reinstill his faith in himself. Sitting back, he tried to relax as the Atlantic Ocean rolled on beneath him, but the anticipation was too much, his brain too active.

Arriving at Charleston, the beautiful old historic city in South Carolina, James rented a car and started driving north. After three hours he pulled up outside the *Albatross* bar, just as a large black Suburban was leaving. From what he could see, the bar was the only one in town.

"Jesus! Another one!" Andy said, looking towards the door.

The whole bar looked up and watched as James entered. He wasn't used to being the center of attention and had only ever seen this happen in Westerns. He walked to the bar self-consciously, trying not to look too long at anyone, and asked for a beer.

"Bud?" The landlord said, holding up a bottle.

"Thank you. Please." James said, thankful that the landlord had made it easy, because he had no idea what 'Bud' meant.

"Something strange going on. We haven't had this many visitors in years," Andy said.

"Why don't you go on up and ask where he's from Andy?"

"Get lost."

James leaned against the bar and looked around. All the eyes in the room were still on him, some subtly, some not so, and he began to feel uneasy. He made an attempt to smile at a group in the corner but got no response, just cold hard stares in return so he sat down and faced the bar.

"Nice weather you have over here," James said.

"Where you from then?" The landlord asked.

"London."

"London? As in England London?" The landlord said, as if there were two.

"Yes, that's right. I'm here to see Sean O'Connor. He's on a salvage operation somewhere out there." James said, pointing out the window. "Know him?"

"Good lad that," Andy chimed in.

"Yes, well, I don't really know him but his sister arranged for me to meet him," James said.

"So you know Sean then?" The landlord said.

"Well, no. As I said, not personally. But we talked on the phone. I'm a friend of Sabine, his sister."

James slowly gained acceptance and relinquished the slightly worrying notion of being in *Deliverance*. Being more open and honest than the previous two suits this new stranger in town didn't seem to be hiding anything, so the defensive walls were lowered a bit. And once they heard him speak, with an accent that properly accentuated every single word, the locals rather enjoyed listening to him, even mocking his pronunciation in friendly sort of way.

"Hungry?" The landlord asked.

"Yes, starving! What's on offer… fish and chips perhaps?"

"Nope. But fish and fries is," Andy said, smiling, as much as to say that everything in America was the same but different and always better.

"Guess I'll have fish and fries then, please!"

During his meal James learned a little more about the salvage operation and was told that one of the locals had also gone along, someone who said they knew more about what they were hoping to find. But James would have to wait until morning before he could get a boat out to see them, if there was one to be had. This was still a suspicious group and James rather suspected they might not be helpful on that front, even though they had become infinitely more friendly towards him than when he first arrived.

James also heard about the two government men who had left just before he arrived, which explained the cold reception he'd received when asking the same questions not an hour later. He wondered what interest the American authorities might have in the proceedings, or whether it was merely the same as he.

There was definitely something afoot and he was glad that he'd made the effort to persuade his CO to let him come. All he needed to do now was come up with something tangible to justify his trip, and satisfy his boss back home. The Falklands wouldn't go on forever and he'd have some explaining to do if he went home empty handed after "wasting taxpayers' money."

After dinner James took his leave and explored the small town and its harbor, quickly realizing that anything happening offshore would immediately be noticed by everyone onshore. It was the only view the inhabitants had and the twinkling lights of distant tankers could be seen quite easily from the town. If something had been destroyed during the war everyone would have surely seen it, if not heard it.

As James walked along the beach to go back to town, to arrange for somewhere to stay, a King Air 200 flew low overhead, going directly out to sea. An event that would have been unusual to most people since there was nothing out there except the Atlantic Ocean. But James didn't think much of it.

The agile little King Air had originated from Norfolk, Virginia. Onboard were more government men; field operatives from Langley, experts in solving problems one way or another and ordered to the case after the previous agents had been debriefed. These two, knowing that they wouldn't get anywhere with the townspeople, arranged for a Company aircraft to do a fly past of the *Ulysses*. The position of which they knew exactly thanks to Coast Guard radar.

Sean and Larry were still staring at the contents of the steel box when the plane flew over. They hadn't heard it coming because of the noise from the winch directly behind them but they saw the dark flash of its shadow and looked up to see the aircraft do a tight turn once it passed over them. Someone immediately threw a tarp over the box.

"Do you think they saw?" Sean asked.

"Not sure. It'd be hard to see something on one pass like that," Larry said. "But who knows?"

The plane made four more low passes and the crew gave them a polite wave each time.

"Who the fuck are they?" Larry said.

"Your guess is as good as mine," Sean said. "But we'd better decide what to do before we go down again."

Once the plane had disappeared over the horizon one of the divers lifted the tarp for another look at the contents of the box. He grabbed one of the bars and scraped it with his knife.

"Don't get too exited," the diver said.

"What?" Sean said.

"This ain't what you think it is."

"Let me see that," Larry said, grabbing at the bar.

Larry took the bar and looked at the recent scrape. He saw the dull grey lead showing through the thin outer gold plating. Picking up another he scraped it against the box with the same result.

"Well, why do you suppose someone would go to all this trouble?" Larry asked.

The group of men looked despondently at each other. One moment they'd been richer than they all thought possible and then back to poverty in a heartbeat. They were confused and began to get very pissed off.

"Well that sucks," Larry said.

"Yes. Yes it does rather," Sean said. "But you're right. Why would anyone go to this much bother?"

Sean was already trying to make sense of it. There had to be a reason, and wherever the reason was the story. It was moments like this that gave his life purpose; a mystery to be solved, the story he'd always wanted.

National Geographic were less than impressed, however. "Time for us to go. There's nothing for us here."

"There's a story here somewhere," Sean said. "There has to be." Trying desperately to get them to reconsider.

"When you find it give us a call. In the meantime we've got other fish to catch. Let's wrap it up, take us back to shore. Sorry, it's orders," the team leader said.

Sean couldn't do anything but what they asked. They'd been putting up all the money and from this moment there wasn't any. It had been a miserable operation from the start, fraught by one disappointment after another. Maybe it was time to call it quits.

Sean gave the order to ready the ship and head for shore and the men slowly parted to go about their tasks. Larry, meanwhile, was tinkering with one of the lead bars and trying to put the pieces of the puzzle together.

"What are we going to do with this?" Larry said, pointing to the box.

"Souvenir," Sean replied, sarcastically. "To remind us of the success of the operation."

Chapter Eleven

James, Sean and Larry, Eastern Seaboard, USA / June 1982

The job of the artist is always to deepen the mystery.
– Francis Bacon

JAMES WOKE THE FOLLOWING MORNING and looked out of his tiny bedroom window directly into the rising sun. Below the glare he noticed a new ship in the harbor. *Ulysses* had returned quietly during the night and discarded her crew. The National Geographic Team left as soon as they'd packed their gear while Sean had stayed with Larry at his cottage, drowning their sorrows as the ship's permanent crew remained onboard, readying everything for shipping out in the afternoon. A new destination beckoned. Salvage ships are expensive sought after commodities and don't remain idle for long.

James dressed and walked straight down to the harbor. The crew told him where Sean was and pointed him in the direction of Larry's cottage. Entering Larry's driveway James didn't notice the tarp covered crate sitting in the back of the beaten up pickup. It just looked as though the springs had gone and was sitting low. James rapped on the door.

Opening the door Sean recognized him immediately. Despite never having met James he still knew the rigid uptight stance of a Royal Navy officer.

"James Devlin I presume?" Sean said.

"Yes. Sean O'Connor? Nice to finally meet you."

"Who's that lad?" A voice in the back said.

"That's Larry. It's his place. Come on in, I'll introduce you. You'll like him," Sean said. "Larry, this is James. I told you about him last night, remember? Friend of my sister. By the way, how is she James?"

"She's very well. She would have loved to come but the navy is rather busy just now."

"So I've been seeing. They've got their work cut out for them down there. Quite the party," said Sean.

"Hello son," Larry said, coming from the kitchen with two cups of coffee. "Here, have this one, I'll get me another."

"Thank you sir," said James.

"Navy man then!" Larry said, on hearing the 'sir.'

James thanked Larry for giving Sean the rubbing, saying that it had been instrumental in getting permission for him to travel. Then Sean explained why they'd had to stop the salvage operation and return early after finding nothing but boxes of lead. James was enthralled at the find of the ship, but confused about its cargo.

"That makes no sense at all," said James.

"Larry has a theory," Sean said, looking at Larry to continue the conversation.

Larry explained that during the war all countries were sending bullion back and forth, in payment for war matériel or after being plundered. Great Britain was doing most of the sending. So was Russia later. Even Germany and Japan were doing it. Anyone with any connection to the sea at that time knew someone who had either been on a bullion ship, or convoyed with one. People didn't always agree with it. There was a certain amount of callousness in demanding money for matériel when a country's soldiers were dying while using the equipment gold had bought, and for what was in all the allies best interests.

When the *Albatross* was sunk off the coast everyone had naturally thought it had been the target of a U-boat. It wasn't until the torpedo was discovered much later, with British markings, that people started to think otherwise. But no one was particularly concerned by then, there was too much going on. Everyone was either busy digging out of a depression, finding work in the armaments factories springing up around the country, or signing up and getting ready to fight in one theater or another.

Larry went on to explain that as soon as he saw the lead in the boxes he realized why the torpedo had been British. They were simply hiding the fact that the gold was not gold, that much was obvious. The bodies found floating at the time had always been suspicious because their injuries weren't consistent with that of an exploding ship, and the German underwear just gave the game away. But again, no one made issue of it at the time.

Larry also suggested where the fake gold might have originated; a member of the *Phoenix's* crew had lived close by and once mentioned being involved with transferring a suspicious cargo to a freighter at sea before they went to the Pacific. The local bar was even named after the ship as a sort of memorial.

"That's quite a story Larry," James said. "Still makes no sense though."

"Does if you don't have the money you say you have," Larry responded. "As I remember Britain was close to being bankrupt before we even started, largely by American policy and neutrality forcing them to pay cash for every gun and bullet they needed. So to what lengths would you go to protect your country?"

"Good point," said Sean.

"Yes, but... ." James was interrupted by a commotion outside. Two large Chevy Suburbans appeared at the front of the cottage and six men appeared and spread out. In the road there was a flatbed truck with a forklift being unloaded.

"What the fuck?" Larry said, going toward the door.

"Be careful Larry," Sean said.

"Who are those guys?" James asked.

Before Larry reached the door there was a loud repetitive knocking. He opened it to two men, the other four were spread out behind them. They flashed a couple of badges too quickly.

"I'm afraid we're going to have to confiscate the crate on the back of the truck over there. It's the property of the United States Government," the stockier of the two men said.

"And you are?" Sean asked.

"Agent Kowalski, sir. This is Agent Smith."

"Smith? Really? Do you have a warrant or something?"

"The police use warrants sir. We are here as a direct order from the United States Government, for national security, and you are not from here, are you sir," Kowalski said, not making a question.

"National fucking security, for a few bars of lead. What are you talking about?" Larry said.

"Sir! We're here to remove the bullion you recently salvaged without proper documentation and without permission from a known war grave," Kowalski said.

The forklift was already off the truck and heading toward the back of Larry's old pick-up in the yard. One of the other men was removing the tarp covering the crate.

"Do you really think we'd leave a few million dollars of gold bullion laying around in the back of a pick-up? Like I said: It's nothing but lead," Sean said.

"We'll see," Kowalski said, and motioned to the man on the pick-up to check the contents of the crate.

The crate was opened once again and there for all to see was the glint of gold. The man picked up one of the bars, feeling its heft before scratching it with a penknife. He looked up and shook his head.

"So if that isn't the gold, where is it?" Kowalski said.

"Enough of this crap. Take these men away. We'll get answers to that later," Smith said.

"Like we told you: There is and never was any damn gold. What's in the truck is what we brought up from the bottom and we haven't touched it since. Do you think we weren't disappointed? If you think we'd stick around here with that much gold in the backyard then someone's got their head so far up their ass their brain's devoid of oxygen," Larry said. "And where the fuck do you think we'd get a bunch of gold plated lead, overnight?"

On hearing Larry's tirade the other three men moved toward the door, ready to counter any aggression or attempted escape. They shouldn't have worried, James, Sean, and Larry were too incredulous to think about escape. James was even looking around for the cameras, convinced he was on some stupid TV show. None of it made any sense.

"You guys were in the plane yesterday?" Sean asked.

"Yes, that's right. We've got pictures of you opening the crate, with a bar of gold in your hand," Kowalski said. "Here's a photograph to remind you."

"Lead," Sean said.

"So why did you cover it up so quick when you saw us."

"One, we didn't know who the fuck you were, not that that would have really mattered. Two, we didn't know then it was only lead. Three, do you think we would have left the rest down there if it had been gold, knowing that you'd seen the location? What the hell would you have done? Sean said, before calming himself: "Enough, the best way to sort this out, and to get you to believe us, is to view the tape from the Geo crew. Because they filmed it all!"

"It's all lead, every bit of it." A man on the pick-up shouted.

"We'll take it anyway. Load it up." Smith ordered.

The forklift driver placed the tines under the edge of the pallet and pulled the crate back until he could get a better bite, going forward again to lift the crate from the pick-up's bed. The springs creaked in relief as they were released from the weight and the pick-up instantly became a few inches taller. The crate was placed on the front of the flatbed truck and the forklift loaded behind it, all covered by a large canvas tarpaulin. Three men loaded into a Suburban and followed the truck as it headed down the road.

Kowalski handed Larry some paperwork and said someone would be in touch. In the meantime, no one should say anything and they were not to undertake any more salvage operations in that area until notified. Agents Smith and Kowalski then left.

"Well! So nice to be in the land of the free!" James said.

"And they wonder why people move to Idaho and don't pay taxes," Larry said.

"So what do we do now?" Sean asked.

"Not much we can do? There's no money. There's no gold. No U-boat. And now no cargo at all. All that's left is the brilliant memory of one big cluster." Sean said. "I need a drink. How 'bout we go to the bar and tell everyone the good news?"

"Walk or drive," Larry asked. "Pick-up's empty."

An hour later there were a few very angry locals in the bar. They'd listened intently to Sean and Larry's story and found it hard to comprehend. They'd seen stories like this on television but never believed them. Now it had happened on their own doorstep.

"Call Hugh Downs, 20/20, he likes a good yarn." A pissed-off voice said.

They would have been even more upset had they known a United States Navy salvage vessel was heading toward the wreck, with orders to retrieve what they could and destroy the rest. Teams of trainee divers spent a week practicing underwater demolitions until nothing was recognizable. It wasn't until the following week when environmentalists discovered rotting fish washed up on the local beaches that people became suspicious. The Coast Guard was then drafted to release a statement saying a foreign freighter had been fined for flushing its tanks too close to shore. But there was no oil on the beaches, just a strange filmy scum from the residue of underwater explosives.

With the evidence now gone all that was left was the story.

Chapter Twelve

MI5, London, England / June 1982

Contrary to popular belief, Britain never had an official Intelligence Service until 1909. Prior to that, the myth that British spies were everywhere was both a fiction of novelists and the legacy of Queen Elizabeth I's ardent protector, Sir Francis Walsingham.

– Author

WITH NOTHING TO SHOW FOR THEIR efforts the salvage team was permanently disbanded. The other Brits managed to find work on the west coast while Sean decided to head home. Saying his goodbyes to the crew, and Larry, he was despondent and his thoughts revolved around the necessity of finding another line of work. Inane government rules and paperwork were making this one too hard to deal with. But he couldn't have known how little he had scraped the surface of government meddling.

Sean and James traveled together. Sean taking the chance to quiz James on his relationship with his sister, while quietly appreciative in the knowledge that James was probably better than any other man she'd found thus far, and for that he was grateful. It was the start of a long friendship and they both seemed to sense it.

They arrived at London's Heathrow early in the morning, cold and wet, not particularly welcoming after coming from the warmer climes of the east coast, and not conducive to raising their spirits.

Going through the immigration hall was normally a breeze for a Brit; one just had to show the photograph in the hardback passport and keep walking. However, as James and Sean neared the kiosk this time they sensed otherwise. Two men appeared and watched as they approached.

"What's this now?" Sean said, motioning ahead.

"Spooks," said James.

James had had previous dealings with Britain's Secret Service while serving overseas in the navy. The navy was a good cover for agents and enabled them to get into countries more easily than modern tightly controlled airports. He'd originally liked the idea, and once even thought about transitioning, but after seeing some of their methods he had changed his mind.

"MI6?" Sean asked.

"Maybe. More likely MI5," James said.

"What's the difference?"

"MI5's home based. MI6 is overseas intelligence."

"Passports please, gentlemen," the immigration officer said.

They handed over their passports and the officer nodded to the two behind him.

"Could you both come with us please," one of the men said.

"Is there a problem?" James asked. "I'm a Royal Navy officer on assignment."

"We know who you are sir. There's no problem. Come with us please."

They were led into one of the interview rooms and asked to wait. One of the spooks remained in the room while the other left to use the phone. James and Sean looked at one another with mild dread, unsure of what was about to happen but convinced that they hadn't done anything untoward to warrant their detainment. Sean walked to the water fountain and the door opened.

"Gentlemen. Sorry to make you wait. I'm George Kerrigan. Yesterday we received information from our American cousins stating that you discovered something of interest in the States?"

"Not really. Not unless you think a few lumps of lead are interesting?" Sean said, still bitter about the enterprise.

"Lead. Yes, that's true. However, this is not so much about the lead, the tangible qualities of it, as it where, but more about its existence. Does that make any sense?" Kerrigan said, questioning himself rather than anyone else. "Well never mind," he went on. "What we'd like you to do is agree not to say anything about it, and we'd like that in writing, just for the record. So you need to sign the Official Secrets Act as your guarantee that you won't… won't say anything about it, that is."

"Why? And who exactly do you represent?" Sean asked.

"We are from a section of government of what you'd call MI5. Our job is to protect Great Britain from outside influences and what you've discovered could be a problem. I'm sorry I can't divulge more, but we don't know it all either. We are just servants to the government, as you also are Mr. Devlin." Kerrigan said.

"I'm a little confused as to why this lead is such a threat to the British Government," said James.

"Not for me to know, or wonder why," Kerrigan said.

"Theirs not to reason why, theirs but to do and die." James said, reciting Tennyson. "We've hopefully surpassed that notion by now so I don't believe that for a moment. I need to know more, certainly before I sign anything."

Kerrigan stood up a little taller. "Being a Royal Navy officer you should really know better, Lieutenant Devlin, because you've already signed the act and well-know that just because you don't understand something doesn't mean that it's not insignificant and not a threat. In the bigger picture, as it were." He said.

"The bigger picture! Tell me about this bigger bloody picture and maybe I'll change my mind," James said, getting heated.

"The decision is not yours to make I'm afraid. Since being a terminating serviceman I'm sure you'll be requiring references for your future. Signing, therefore, would be best for everyone," Kerrigan said, bluntly, tired of the direction of the conversation.

"I see. And what do you have to threaten Mr. O'Connor with?" James asked.

"Come now gentlemen. There's no need for this. If I knew something I'd tell you. I don't, so let's get on with it and we can all go home," Kerrigan said, honestly. For he didn't know, in this he was just a messenger, and getting shot for it.

"No. Com'on, I am interested. What are you going to threaten me with?" Sean asked.

"I was hoping not to get into that, but if you insist," Kerrigan said, not really caring not to offend any longer and removing a large manila envelope from his suitcase.

Sean peered in to look at the contents. The photographs were all of Sabine, naked, and seemingly enjoying herself in a variety of intimate poses with another woman. Sean was visibly shocked and immediately became angry. Not because of Sabine or what she was doing, he'd always known that side of her, he was her brother after all. But because someone had deliberately, and obviously, taken these photographs with the intention of blackmail.

"When were these taken?" Sean demanded.

"Three days ago," Kerrigan said.

"Three days! We hadn't found anything three days ago!"

Kerrigan just looked at him. He was good at his job and had used the same tactics repeatedly in getting what he wanted. He always kept a card to play and when necessity required it he played it perfectly. He was a professional in a world of subterfuge. Few got the better of him.

Sean and James looked at each other, resigned to the fact that they didn't have a choice. James hadn't seen the photographs but guessed the envelope must have contained something damaging, either to Sean or someone close to him. Sean knew he couldn't do anything. His little sister's career would be ruined if he refused. They signed.

"Thank you gentlemen. Please remember the penalty for reneging on this agreement," Kerrigan said, sliding the envelope back into his suitcase. "I'm returning to London. Could I give anyone a ride?"

"You've got to be fucking kidding me," Sean said, striding out the door to retrieve his luggage from the conveyor.

Sabine was waiting for them in the arrivals hall. She looked wonderful and was exited to see her two favorite men together. Driving to London they told her of their dealings with the security agencies of two countries and of Sean's frustration at not finding what he'd wanted. Sabine had found some information of her own, though, by doing some simple library research, and had come up with the same theory as Larry. They talked it over during the busy rush hour drive into the city, on their way to breakfast.

"But there's nothing we can do about it now," Sean said.

"There's always a way. You've just got to make choices,"

"Yes, but I can't make some of those choices anymore."

Sabine caught James's eyes in the rear view mirror and they seemed to warn her off continuing the conversation. James figured the pictures must have involved her somehow; Sean wouldn't have caved so easily if they had been of him.

Chapter Thirteen

Sabine and James, London, England / June 1982

The man whose life is devoted to paperwork has lost the initiative. He is dealing with things that are brought to his notice, having ceased to notice anything for himself.
– C. Northcote Parkinson

SABINE WAS THE BEST THING James could have seen at the Admiralty on his first day back at work. But the brief glimpse of her while being escorted to the CO's office told him things were not good. She had a sympathetic look in her eyes as though she knew what was about to happen.

"Good morning, sir." James said.

"My bloody mornings might start being good once you're no longer here," the CO bellowed.

"Yes sir," James said.

"Have you any idea of the scale of shit you've unearthed Devlin?" The CO said, staring at James and awaiting an answer.

"No sir. I didn't think there was a problem sir. Well, not until we ran into the spooks at the airport." James said.

"Spooks! They weren't just any bloody spooks Devlin. Those men were ordered to welcome you back into the country by the bloody Cabinet, sent personally by the bloody Home Secretary! I have been asked, repeatedly, in no uncertain terms, by I don't know how many bloody people, why the hell I had let you travel to

America. Good God man! If I'd known the trouble it would cause I would have laid you up in the brig for the duration. What the hell is going on?"

"Nothing sir. Well... no. Really... nothing sir. It's just that the CIA, we think the CIA, maybe the FBI, turned up to confiscate the salvage sir. That's all. I have no idea what all this is about either, I'd only just arrived when all this happened." James said.

"Well somebody very important wants to clip this and keep it very quiet. And I expect you to oblige. I have more important bloody things to worry about than you and a bunch of misplaced lead. Everything we have in the South Atlantic is either wearing out or getting itself sunk, and we don't have any replacements. The politicians are just now realizing the abject bloody foolhardiness of their cutbacks and now they're doing what they always do best; smothering everything in bullshit. And mark my words, two months from now the same fucking assholes will be doing the same fucking thing."

Just then Sabine poked her head in and delivered a package to the CO. "Here's that package you wanted right away sir," she said, sneaking James an empathic look on her way back out.

"Sorry sir," James said, continuing with the conversation.

"You bloody well should be. When are you finished Devlin?"

"End of the week sir,"

"Anything lined up?"

"Not really sir. Thought I'd take some time off and think about it," James said.

"Don't think too bloody hard Devlin."

"No sir."

"From now until then I don't want hear or see you, not until the end of the week. Understand? In the meantime stay out of trouble. I don't want any more calls from mother."

"Yes sir."

James left the office and went straight down to the basement, slightly in shock from the bollocking. He hoped Sabine would be there waiting.

"How'd it go?" Sabine asked.

"Phew! Not too bad, I suppose, under the circumstances. He's got a lot on his plate and too busy to worry about a short-timer," James said, trying to put a brave face on it.

"That's good, and just as well." Sabine said. "It'll give you a few days to figure out what's going on."

"You've got to be kidding me! Three different groups have now warned me off." James said. "Two of which can be especially nasty. And besides, I'm done with this dog and pony show. I've looked through all this stuff for hours and there's nothing to find."

"Maybe you should look to see what isn't there," Sabine said.

"What do you mean?" James said, tired of it all and wishing it would all go away.

"I'm an administrator. I file everything according to date, topic, people and a bunch of other criteria depending on the subject. All this stuff was filed by date, as are most of these war documents, but there are pages missing, it's obvious, and parts of the index are also missing."

"Which means?" James said, accepting that he would have to listen to more.

"Which means, dummy, that every group, every collection of documents is supposed to have an index page. So that people know what's included in the lot. There isn't one for this lot and there are obviously pages missing." Sabine explained.

"So who has those?"

"I don't know. I don't even know if they still exist or not. But you've got some days to find out." Sabine said, smiling that smile women do so well while convincing their men to do something that they'd rather not.

"Great. But how would I do that?" James asked.

"The ledgers. Everyone has to sign the ledger before getting a key to remove anything from the inventory."

"And I thought my last week would be easy." James said.

Sabine just smiled and walked away, pleased with herself. In appreciation, her hips exhibited an exaggerated sway as she almost skipped up the tiled stairs, enticing, though more forcing James to watch until she was out of sight. She knew he was watching. She didn't strut for nothing. But neither was she going to turn around to give the game away. James was hooked and she was reeling him in, methodically, with all the guile of a practiced seductress.

Receiving his orders – for although it seemed like a simple request, it had, in fact, been an order of the female variety – James went through all the papers again and documented likely gaps in the dates. Once he'd got a general idea he returned all the material to the inventory and requested another collection. The clerk took the returned boxes and disappeared along the long shelves, giving James a chance to peak through the ledger. But there were too many pages to search and the clerk's footsteps were soon back.

"Here you are sir," the clerk said, passing a couple of files over. "Could you sign the book please sir."

"Thanks," James said. "Maybe you could help me some more. I'm trying to find out when those files were last removed. Any idea of how I might do that?"

"Well sir, the files themselves should have a list of who and when each file was removed, like a library book, that's the system. But if they don't, if the list goes missing, records like that are also logged in the ledger, but not in this ledger; it's too recent. Offhand, though, with the ones you have there, for instance, it's obvious that no one has removed them for quite some time; too much dust on the box, you see?" The clerk said, wiping his finger on the top of it. "But if you need exact dates we've got a stack of ledgers that go back to 1810, maybe even before that. You could look through that lot if you like."

"How big a stack?"

The clerk raised his hand above his head, to about eight feet.

James shook his head and said: "No other way?"

"Not if the individual index page is missing sir. That would have everyone's name on it, again, like a library card," the clerk explained. "But these old files have rarely been looked at, and I would remember if they'd been taken out in the last two years."

"OK. Well never mind, thanks anyway."

"Sorry I can't help you more sir," the clerk said.

James walked out and tried to think what to do. Thinking being difficult since he really didn't care anymore and just wanted to finish his last week and get out. He was tired of beating himself up against the establishment and oceans of paperwork with no end in sight. But he also didn't want to disappoint Sabine, didn't want to look like a quitter in her eyes, so in the end he knew he'd have to find a way.

Once James was gone, the clerk picked up the phone and said: "He's just left sir. He asked about the missing pages, but didn't push it. I think he's giving up."

James had sensed the clerk wasn't being totally honest. He'd appeared too helpful. People in those positions generally act put out when someone shows up to make them work. James was already thinking of a way to utilize Sabine's charm so that he could better access the records without the clerk's presence. He had the impression he was now being watched wherever he went, and tried to act normally, or as normally as one does when one is on a short string. He returned to his office and leafed through his termination papers through want of nothing else to do. There were still documents he needed to get signed; not least the CO's final release and recommendation, which he didn't want to screw up but wasn't much looking forward to.

After work he met Sabine for a drink in what had become their local. He asked her if she would be up for a little role-playing, if it wouldn't get her into trouble. She jumped at the chance and even suggested the method. Listening to her explain her intentions, James was quietly wishing he could have been the recipient. The clerk didn't know how lucky he was going to be the next day.

The following day was exceptionally slow. James brought a large suitcase giving the impression that he was removing all his personal effects from his office. However, his bag contained a thermos of coffee, small bottle of whiskey, sandwiches for a night's work, a razor and a change of clothes.

The clerk was usually glad to leave around five but today Sabine appeared at his door fifteen minutes beforehand. Like every other man in the building the clerk had seen her around, although not being an officer knew he never stood a chance. But that didn't stop him from fantasizing about the possibility and when she appeared at his doorway looking like she owned the place he was instantly overawed and smitten. Beneath her issued but tightly tailored blouse she wore a beguiling non-regulation bra that was even more uplifting than normal, causing the uppermost buttons on her crisp white shirt to visibly stress, allowing the clerk the merest glimpse of the flesh beneath.

"Afternoon ma'am," the clerk said, trying to keep his eyes up where they belonged.

"Hello. Captain Lawton needs all the 1957 files associated to batch number K5209/23-6-57." Sabine said.

"Right you are ma'am," said the clerk, scurrying away.

Sabine popped a button and sprayed a little perfume into her cleavage. She'd long known men were drawn to her scent ever since being a schoolgirl. She didn't really know why but she made the most of it every time it suited her. Although on more than one occasion in the past it had gotten her into trouble before she had learned how to better to use it. The clerk didn't stand a chance.

He returned from between the shelves carrying a large dusty box. Sabine knew it was one of the largest boxes because she'd specifically asked James the night before. And he only knew by chance because he had seen it on the shelf and subconsciously wondered what on earth has been happening in 1957.

"Oh, it's rather big and dirty isn't it?" Sabine said.

"Sorry ma'am. I'll clean it off for you," the clerk said eagerly.

"Would you?" Sabine said, placing a subtle hand on his arm.

That clinched it. What with Sabine's intoxicating aroma, her wonderfully hoisted breasts, the sultry voice, and now the subtle touch, no man could have resisted.

"You know. Would you carry that upstairs for me? I really don't want to get my shirt dirty," Sabine said, pulling her shirt down tight until another button almost popped.

"Well I'm not supposed to leave the room ma'am."

"I think it'll be alright, just for a few seconds. Everyone has left anyway. But if you'd really rather not...."

"That's fine ma'am. I've got it. Lead the way," the clerk said, wanting to be around this woman for a few moments more.

Sabine walked out and the clerk followed, savoring the aromatic wake behind her. Watching Sabine climb the steep stairs ahead of him almost made walking difficult and he lowered the box in an attempt to hide any embarrassment. Once in the office Sabine went straight over to the sunny window and turned.

"Just leave it behind the door please," she said.

"Right ma'am."

The clerk placed the box down and looked up to see the light streaming through Sabine's thin white shirt, revealing the beautiful dark lines of her bra. When she bent to pick up her jacket the straps of her suspenders were just visible through the taut material of her skirt. The clerk was soon in dire need of a cold shower.

"Well ma'am, if that's all, I had better get going," he said hurriedly.

"Thank you so much. Goodnight," Sabine said, and closed the door behind him.

The clerk walked uncomfortably back down the stairs with Sabine's aroma still in the air. He grabbed his jacket, locked up the office and immediately left to tell his mates in the pub about the stunningly hot female officer who had just come on to him.

James was also aware of Sabine's presence as he made his way down the steps before walking casually into the records room with his suitcase. He quickly found a shadow in the far end and wasn't noticed when the clerk returned to lock up. The clerk should have done a cursory glance around the room if only to make sure no one was getting locked in, but he had other things on his mind. The day had ended remarkably well for him.

James had about fourteen hours to find what he was looking for. But he didn't really know where to start, or indeed what he was looking for. He went for the ledgers first. The clerk had mentioned a stack eight feet high, which meant an awful lot of people had required documents over the years. But when he found them there were actually only five large volumes. Pouring himself a cup of coffee from the thermos he started at the date the *Sturgeon* sunk the *Albatross* and worked forward.

The light faded quickly as the evening wore on. James couldn't very well turn on the lights in case a roaming security guard noticed them through the glass in the door so he removed a small reading lamp from his suitcase, clamped it onto a shelf above him and continued going through page after page of the ledger. Occasionally stopping to give his eyes a rest and to have more coffee. At midnight he pondered if it was all worth it. Then he thought about Sabine and what she was doing, and longed to be with her instead. The faintest remnants of her scent still lingered and it comforted him. He inhaled it, and imagined holding her as she slept, feeling her smooth skin and the warmth of her body next to his. She was an intoxicating woman. Every sense he had had opened up to her. He was caught.

His eyes were getting weary, it was hard to concentrate, each page looking like the one before. Not really knowing what to look for didn't help either, but he hoped something would seem out of place or he would recognize a name. Then the handwriting would change as clerks were routinely rotated through, usually just when he'd become accustomed to a certain style.

He was in the files of 1956 when he noticed a consistent name appearing in the sign out column. Lieutenant Harrison seemed to have been especially interested in the same files James had found. Maybe he was just another short timer given the task to keep him busy. But James seemed to remember seeing the name somewhere else, when he'd been a Captain. There was no way he'd still be in the navy, but he might still be alive. James copied down the name.

The date was also interesting; it was in the midst of the Suez Crisis and Britain and France had just caved to United States pressure and were leaving Egypt, after invading it to protect their interests in the canal. The argument for Britain vetoing a United Nations resolution – the first time it had ever done so – and going to war, would be repeated early in the next century, in another area of the Middle East, this time by the United States. Powerful nations in decline apparently pursue the same mistakes as their colonial predecessors.

Lieutenant Harrison was the only name James had come up with after eight hours of searching. So after finishing with the ledgers he roamed the shelves with a torch and briefly looked into what he thought might be intriguing boxes, only to find more mundane papers. Many of the secrets from the Second World War had already been released, so he doubted he would find anything interesting by chance, and certainly not among so many records. The missing papers would probably never be found. He resigned himself to the fact and had a sandwich and some whiskey.

With another five hours to go before he could leave, James then went on a search for maps. He found an old cabinet with a series of large flat drawers, all containing naval maps from between 1940 and 1945. They were all in bad shape with many of them actually falling apart. They had obviously been aboard ships during their early life and been roughly handled ever since.

James opened the drawer for maps of 1941 and a name jumped out at him; *Sturgeon*. It showed the submarine's exact location off the eastern seaboard, with the later part of its route originating in Newfoundland. Then there was a zigzag route to England with rendezvous markings for fuel and victuals. A definitive turn in its course clearly meant something had occurred at that location, which seemed to substantiate Stinger's story. James rolled up the map and put it in his suitcase.

He was tired. He'd been up since five the previous day. Finding no more coffee in the thermos he decided to have a nap and leant back to rest against the shelves. After a little more whiskey he soon fell into an uncomfortable sleep. Subconscious thoughts warned him consistently of the danger of sleeping too long and his backside bore the problem of sleeping on a cold floor.

James woke up when he slipped to the floor four hours later. It was just before seven in the morning. He was cold, stiff and thirsty, but he couldn't leave yet. He had to wait for the clerk to return and open the door. And he hoped Sabine would remember to be there, otherwise he'd have more than explaining to do.

Sabine was indeed waiting right outside the door when the clerk finally showed up at eight, later than usual. He couldn't believe his eyes, he'd thought of nothing but Sabine all night and here she was again. Her scent wasn't as intoxicating this early in the morning but she was still a very welcoming sight.

"Good morning," Sabine said. "I'm sorry. I forgot to sign out last night. But Captain Lawton doesn't need the files now anyway. Could you fetch them down for me, please, while I fill out the paperwork?"

"Um. Yes ma'am, okay. Could you watch the shop for me? I'm really not supposed to leave," the clerk said.

"Certainly. No one will get through me. I guarantee it."

"But I'll bet there's a lot who'd like to try," the clerk thought.

As soon as the clerk left James appeared around the corner and gave Sabine a big kiss on the cheek.

"Thanks gorgeous," James said.

"Anytime," she said.

"Dinner tonight?"

"If you're paying I'm there. See you later," Sabine said.

James left the doorway and hid in a store cupboard until the clerk was back inside the records room. As soon as the door closed he ran up the stairs to his office, hoping to run into no one in his rather disheveled appearance. He closed his door, removed his shirt and started to replace it with a clean one.

The door flung wide open. "Devlin! What's going on?" The CO bellowed.

"What? Sir? Oh, the shirt, sir. I helped a lady change a tire on the way to work. Thought I'd better change the shirt too."

"Good turns. Good lad. Come and see me this afternoon. I'm away the rest of the week and need to get your paperwork finished. And I don't want to see you back here next week asking for it. You hear?" A more congenial CO said.

"Yes sir. I'll be there. Two o'clock sir?"

"Fine," the CO said, and waited for a moment, thinking that he should say something else to a leaving subaltern, but then left.

James was visibly relieved. For a second he thought he'd been caught and used an old schoolboy excuse in haste. Though he wouldn't have been able to come up with an equally quick reason as to why he had a fresh shirt in a suitcase; nobody picked up dry cleaning on the way *to* work.

By this time James was hungry so he left the building and walked to Parliament Square for breakfast. A touristy coffee shop had some small but very expensive muffins that would have to suffice until lunchtime. He relaxed, read the paper and watched as hordes of commuters went off work. Looking over his coffee at the long dejected faces under a cloudy sky he doubted that he would ever miss it.

Chapter Fourteen

Sabine and James, Oxfordshire, England / July 1982

Sadness is but the precursor to happiness. Such is the hope that drives us forever forward.

– Author

JAMES'S LAST DAY WAS A DISSAPOINTMENT to say the least. It was the typical end to a short and unhappy career. Not one old friend was there to see him off. They were all on ships, having big and small adventures, many of them still in the South Atlantic, and he hadn't made any new friends at the Admiralty because everyone had been so busy with the fleet down south. Plus, he was a short timer, there was little point in forming friendships with a short timer. So James simply collected his belongings, walked through the doorway for the last time and out into the unwelcoming street.

It was pouring. A heavy July rain was cleaning the grime from the streets in torrents, and spray thrown up by London's double-decker buses was being hurled across the pavement in waves onto unsuspecting tourists. James didn't have an umbrella, or his cap, but in his present mood he didn't much care. He looked up into the ominous looking clouds and strode away, indifferent to the drenching, indifferent to the world around him.

After barely fifty yards he was soaked to the skin. Then, from an alcove, a figure stepped out and placed an umbrella over his head, and instead of rain pounding his skull he felt the warmth and breath of a woman. She was also wet but looked wonderful for it, even with a tear in her eye.

"I'm sorry I wasn't there to see you off James," she said. "It must be horrible. I can't imagine."

"It's okay, really, much as I expected. You make up for it," James said, and thoroughly meant it.

He pulled her close and hugged her tightly. He had so many emotions swirling around that he just held onto her, enjoying the moment, the relief, while around them London bustled, oblivious to the two new lovers in the middle of the pavement. They kissed. It was the inevitable kiss and they both understood where it would lead. James hailed a taxi.

The following morning was bright and clear, the London outside cleansed and refreshed by the rain. Inside, the sun streamed through the large window next to the bed. James woke and looked over to make sure it wasn't a dream and watched as she slept. The sunlight reflecting off the smooth bare leg draped seductively over the sheet, her hair sensually messy. She was incredibly beautiful, awake, asleep, and all the other times. Life, he realized, was good, as he leant over to kiss her.

"Coffee?"

"Humm, please," she whispered contentedly, pulling the sheet up around her.

James returned with coffee and a paper to see Sabine sitting up in bed writing her journal. A chore she usually did the night before, but she'd had other things on her mind. Purring happily against her covered leg was the large orange cat that had earlier been unceremoniously banished because it had been competing for attention. But was now back in its rightful place.

"He's letting me know whose boss," James said.

"That's right. He has seniority," said Sabine.

"I never took you for an Independent reader," James said, unwrapping the newspaper.

"Really. What should I be reading?"

"Oh, I don't know. Thought you more of the Telegraph type," said James. "Although you'd do nicely in the Sun."

"Why thank you, kind sir," Sabine said, throwing her shoulders back and tossing her hair.

Sabine knew she was good looking, from an early age men had always offered her stuff, gifts, even promotions, just to get to know her, or get inside of her. She'd once thought about putting on weight just to stop the harassment, but then someone good would come along to make her world right again. She looked at James and knew he was special. She hadn't had a night like that ever. The passion between them had been exhilarating and the room still embraced the heady intoxication of their lovemaking.

"How's the coffee?" James asked.

"Good! You figured the espresso." Sabine said.

"I had one onboard ship, couldn't wake up without it."

"I'm sorry," Sabine said.

"For what?"

"For reminding you. It must be miserable. You loved it so."

"Time for something new. Don't worry about me, I'll sort it out. Anyway, what gives you the right to worry about me, do you really think I'm coming back?"

Sabine starred at him for one horrified moment, then threw a pillow.

"Bastard!" She said.

"Through and through," he said, smiling back.

James put the pillow aside, carefully moved Arthur to the chair and slid onto the bed. He straddled her legs and held her arms above her head so she couldn't move. Looking down at her he couldn't believe his luck. He should've been unhappy about leaving the navy, but right now he was happier than he'd ever been, content and happy. He bent to kiss her. She was eager again and raised her mouth to his. It was better than the first time, more practiced, each now knowing what the other enjoyed most. The only member of the household not impressed was curled up and already asleep on the floor.

Two hours later they showered and made love again. Sabine was insatiable and James found he was more than able to satisfy that desire after being so long away from it. By the time noon came around they were both exhausted, relaxed, but energized, and toweled off before finally getting dressed for the day.

"We're going to have to eat sometime," Sabine said.

"Saturday morning breakfast on the High Street," said James. "Eggs, bacon, sausage, mushrooms, tomatoes and fried bread. A cholesterol-ridden dream."

"Sounds absolutely wonderful."

It was afternoon by the time they arrived, but the café served English breakfast all day to order. They devoured it as they had earlier devoured each other. Afterwards, they walked along the banks of the Thames, found the least crowded pub, grabbed drinks and sat outside watching rowers fight against the tide. It was warm and it felt like summer had finally arrived. At Wimbledon it was Ladies' Finals day. Everything was as it should be. And at some point in their life everyone should be that happy.

They talked about anything and everything, but always returning to what James intended to do. Although he didn't yet know he knew that he'd find something. But first he had to find Harrison. Sabine had obviously not yet given up on that idea and James was picking up on the subtle messages sprinkled in the conversation.

His last hope of finding a solution to the strange salvage operation, and appeasing Sabine, was with Harrison. He had found

Harrison's last address in the Admiralty records, having retired at the lofty rank of Rear Admiral, and doubted the man would have moved, unless into a nursing home at this point. James knew few people moved away from Devon once they retired there, it was an easy place for people to love, and a retired rear admiral was probably no different. James planned his trip for Monday, after enjoying the best weekend of his life.

James and Sabine's friendship had evolved into a relationship that would see them through the rest of their lives. They realized, given modern life, that they might not always be together, but they already knew they couldn't live without each other.

At this moment, fully embraced in the enthralling heady excitement of new love, they were not to know that there would be years when they would never see each other, but then one would call, or just turn up, and they would instantly revert to the easy familiarity and luxury of that perfect relationship. Although often living apart they each knew the other was there, somewhere, it gave each of them comfort, grounded them, even solidified their relationship in some way, and both were confident they would be together in the end.

Chapter Fifteen

Walter Harrison, Devon, England / July 1982

If you reveal your secrets to the wind, you should not blame the wind for revealing them to the trees.

– Khalil Gibran

BOVEY TRACEY IS A QUIET, mostly untouched, typical English village in the west country bordering Dartmoor – visiting Americans call it quaint – and its secluded surroundings next to the moor have made it a popular host to a plethora of retired ex-forces personnel from all the services. It also has more than its fair share of public houses, which might be why so many ex-military types migrate there in retirement. A variety of pewter mugs hang behind many of the bars and represent just about every rank in the Army, Navy or Air Force. Captain Harrison was not outdone, his mug was hanging in the *Cromwell*, a pub with prominence right in the middle of town. Harrison was 68 years old and still fit as a fiddle from walking the four miles into town and back every single day to enjoy a pint or two of Best Bitter.

Harrison was currently talking with a young lad who had just quit the navy and had bought him a pint, and who apparently had a lot of questions. Harrison's wife had been only too happy to drop James at the pub, knowing it would give the other regulars some respite from her husband's endless stories of the sea. James had made a last minute appointment but the captain had forgotten and walked down to the pub for his afternoon pint as usual.

"Aye lad. Navy's a good life. If I had it again I'd do it again. Cheers," said Harrison raising his glass.

"Don't use the tankard then sir?" James asked, looking behind the bar.

"No 'sir' lad. It's Walter. And no, tankard's alright for impressing the tourists, but it makes the beer taste like shite."

James laughed. He already liked this man. His age portrayed an untruth because the years of doing what he loved had kept him young. They ate and discussed events in the Falklands. Walter was quite vocal about the tactics being used and the navy's heavy reliance on modern technology, but clearly proud of all the men involved and more than envious of their amazing successes.

After getting a couple more pints of bitter James slowly steered the conversation around to the War. Harrison was like an encyclopedia on the topic but when James mentioned the *Sturgeon* he was visibly shocked and stopped the conversation in its tracks, immediately querying James as to how he had come by the name.

"They had me research a wreck during my last month at the Admiralty; one of those maps with a pin missing, you no doubt know the drill. I think it was just a job to keep short timers out of trouble," James said.

"Aye lad, I do remember. They did the same to everyone who came through I think, the injured ones anyway. No one ever found anything though. Waste of time if you ask me."

"But you did, didn't you Walter?" James said. "You found something."

Walter went completely quiet and thought for a moment. He hadn't realized how much James already knew.

"You did find something, though, didn't you?" James said again. "And you made sure that no one else would."

"That was twenty five years ago. It doesn't matter now. And it's best kept quiet anyway," Walter said, feeling a little like he'd been ambushed.

"That your decision Walter, or the navy's?" James asked.

Walter placed his beer on the table, turned and stared intently at James without really realizing what he was doing, his mind elsewhere, pondering whether it was time to release his conscience and pass the secret to someone else. He had carried it for so long and was getting tired, maybe a younger opinion would invalidate the necessity for the continued secrecy. But it was akin to giving up a valued possession, even though it was a torment, a burden of responsibility for which no one living even knew.

Walter wasn't at all sure whether he should explain anything, not even to this honest young subaltern who looked as if he was not only seriously interested but resolutely trustworthy. Beating about the bush for a while, allowing him to gather his thoughts, he then made the decision as he spoke, going on to describe what he had found and the reasons for removing the documents:

In the fifties the country was still rebuilding itself after the crushing devastation of the war. Even so, it was again fighting in Korea and Malaysia, but steadfastly refusing to be drawn into the chaos in Indochina, first by the French and later the Americans. Africa was a cauldron of violence and the Middle East was bound to erupt sooner or later, especially as Britain was having political difficulties about how to resolve the problem of Egypt and the Canal. But the greatest threat by far came from beyond the Iron Curtain. The threat from the Soviet Union was very real in the minds of politicians. Conflicts were exploding all over the world and promising to engulf people in the greatest catastrophe of all; nuclear obliteration. The only thing that stopped it was having two equally powerful opposing sides, both willing to fight small wars in obscure places instead of one all-for-nothing, head-to-head, deciding catastrophe. Which was fine unless you lived in one of those many small obscure places that endured decades of conflict for the benefit of the two great superpowers.

With the arms race in full swing, billions being spent, new and more deadly technology was emerging almost daily. Nations spied on enemies and friends alike, and people of all creeds died under the unfurled banner of patriotism. With commonwealth countries recoiling after their selfless bloody contribution during both world wars, and independence finally rewarded after decades of wanting and waiting to the Jewel in the Crown of the Empire, Britain's greatest friend and ally was now the United States. And yet even these two great friends spied on each other.

"Ever think why some secrets are released after thirty years, some after fifty and others never?" Walter asked.

"Waiting for people to die, situations to change, or still a threat to national security," said James.

"Sometimes. But it's one thing to protect secrets about an enemy, it's another to protect secrets about a friend. Those should never be released. Would you tell a stranger that your best friend was sleeping with his wife?" Walter said.

"I see your point. But what's it got to do with the *Sturgeon*?" James asked. And as he said it Larry's theory came charging out from the subconscious again. Everything pointed back to the bullion, or the lack of it.

"The war created tough choices and those decisions, more often than not, were based on solid intelligence, meaning that friendships were often flouted when intelligence included information detrimental to one friend or another, it was stored for safekeeping, as it were, just in case. You know, of course, what we did to the French Fleet at Mers-el-Kébir? Christ, even our own men were thrown into suicidal missions. Commandos up and down the coast were shot as spies, air force pilots shot, and then there were those poor sods we sacrificed at Dieppe, to name just a few. It was win or lose, life or death. Total war. Those of us who survived did so simply because of luck and because others didn't. Friendships were used and abused, pure and simple. It may well have been all for the greater good, and the rhetoric will always portray honor and glory, but everyone used everyone. It was basic, fundamental, dirty survival," Walter explained.

"I agree, and I know what you're getting at. The Americans bled us dry before entering the war, and they only did so after the Japanese attacked them at Pearl. But what does this all have to do with a few pieces of lead in the Atlantic?"

Harrison made up his mind, being active in the navy during the war he'd initially heard about it on the wind, that great travelling windmill of rumor aboard every ship of the line, but then later from an official source, making it verified, classified, 'For Eyes Only' stuff.

"To some it's known as 'Churchill's Gold.' Apparently the gold never existed, or rather it existed but it was not available, while it was still being held as loan collateral, but the pretense that it did exist, and available, was invaluable to Churchill. It bought us time by allowing Britain to continue the Atlantic runs. The money might have only purchased decrepit old destroyers but they were still quicker than German U-boats and the skippers more than earned their pay hunting and killing those bastards. Without those destroyers' protection Britain wouldn't necessarily have starved but it would have been damned close, and we would have been completely defenseless. Everything we had was being sunk, destroyed or wearing out faster than it could be replaced. That probably sounds familiar to you. Pretty soon we would have had nothing but rocks and iron gates to throw back."

"But surely, America must have found out about the bullion long before?" James asked.

"Oh yes. Eventually, I'm sure. But by then the secret had being going on for so long that it became sacrosanct. They certainly knew before the Korean War and pressured for British help, which was provided. That's not to say we wouldn't have given it anyway, Korea being an early test for the United Nations, fighting the domino effect of communism and all that. Then they put pressure on us to leave Suez so that they could step in to fill the vacuum and get closer to Middle East oil. Vietnam, Indonesia and Cuba are other examples." Walter explained.

"But that's crazy. Why not just come clean?" James asked.

"You'd have to ask the politicians that, though I'm sure most of this latest lot don't know one way or another, or care. The longer a secret is kept the bigger it becomes and the more difficult it is to swallow. So too does the value of money, not that that's the issue any longer. But how much do you think fifty million pounds worth of gold bullion in 1940 is worth now? "

"But that's still not a problem. We could pay it."

"Of course we could. It would just mean juggling the books a little so no one knew where the billions were going. No one would ever ask questions," said Walter sarcastically.

"OK," James said. "But once it's in the open it would be finished. Let the chips fall where they may and to hell with it."

"You're right of course. But you have to remember there is no common sense involved in these things. Countless half-truths and outright lies are consistently used by politicians to justify ignoring common sense. Even the most brilliant among us would have to admit to having no idea of all the variables involved. Only the blindingly ignorant, or a politician, thinks that they have a handle on things. The bigger picture always holds surprises," Walter said.

"The bigger picture. That was just explained to me recently, in no uncertain terms," said James.

"It shouldn't be totally discounted. People can't always get their mind around complex issues, and to make up one's mind based on only the parts they do understand is flawed."

"But not only do we expect our leaders to understand the issues, even the complex ones, we expect them to act honorably in making decisions." James said.

"Expect what you want. But that's not what you're going to get, and I don't think you're that naïve to think so," Walter said. "Political decisions are based on what's good for the country, after, of course, what's good for the politician, since he's unlikely to make a decision beneficial to the country if it's detrimental to his own job and agenda. Rarely are decisions made anymore from a purely selfless moral standpoint, that's one of the biggest problems we face today. Although, it has to be said, Britain does have a slightly better history in that regard when compared to many other empires. America, for example, will screw you blind if it benefits America, but they also sincerely believe that what benefits them benefits everyone. It's a simplified insular viewpoint, but the proof is written in stone in their foreign policy and trade practices. Again, look at Cuba. Look at Indonesia."

"So why did America never demand payment?" James asked.

"Initially, Britain literally couldn't pay. Britain was broke for years after the war. Then it became more valuable as a hold over the British Government. As time went on they couldn't make it public because the people would see it as the conspiracy it was. What would happen to U.S. world opinion if populations around the globe knew they had held such a seemingly trivial thing over a friendly nation, especially a major ally, in time of supreme need and desperation? It's paramount to national blackmail."

"What you're saying is that the two countries are inextricably caught in the same lie. Neither can now disclose it. But if that's the case, why is it still a threat to the British?" James asked.

"Simply because the nature of the British Government makes it more honorable, and they still, even now, have more to lose." Harrison said, alluding to something else he was not willing to say. "Also, the person who initiated the lie is one of the greatest people this country has ever produced. Churchill is far more than just a national hero along the lines of a Nelson or a Wellington. This country exists in its present state largely because of the man and his legacy. Politicians the world over still compare themselves to him, albeit in fits of delusion. He is venerated by peoples across the globe, been on other nation's stamps! Who would tarnish the reputation of a man they routinely compare themselves to? These politicians are exceptionally conceited people."

"But so far nothing serious has really happened. Just a little friendly pressure here and there to win political support."

"Tell that to the dead soldiers. But aside from that, it's only because governments on both sides have been mostly honorable, so far, or as honorable as they can be expected to be given we're talking of politics... the inherent nature of the beast demands a gross of hypocrisy. Most politicians in the post-war years knew each other personally and understood and respected the hard decisions each had to make. They formed strong global bonds. Eisenhower was a strong voice of reason during the Cold War, along with Churchill. They both knew the enemy well, needing to thwart its moves and keep it at bay, but they also knew the danger of antagonizing it too much. Neither wanted World War Three on their hands. If Eisenhower hadn't been president in '52 the hawks in Washington might well have started a nuclear war in Korea. Kennedy actually used Eisenhower as an early adviser and followed a similar vein, when he was able. Imagine what would happen if that hawkish mentality ever found a president amenable to their fanatical ideology." Walter said.

"Can you really foresee that happening?"

"God forbid, not in my lifetime! But yes, I can," said Walter.

"Anyway, this is all mere speculation. Where are the original documents, do you still have them? And what in them was so damming?" James asked.

"The documents are long gone. I made sure of that. A secret can only remain if there is no trace. Then it becomes nothing more than legend, or conspiracy." Walter said.

"Then more dangerous or harmless?"

"Hopefully harmless, depending on who holds the power, of course. Let's finish this conversation over coffee. Fancy a walk?"

"Certainly sir.... Walter." James said.

Leaving the pub they turned right and walked down the hill towards the old Bovey Bridge, exactly the same as Cromwell's New Model Army crossed in 1646. Turning into the park they followed the river until the path merged with a disused railway line, and walked a further mile and a half before reaching a large secluded manor house on a steep and narrow one track road.

"I can see how you stay fit. Walking up and down this every day," James said.

"Exercise is the key to a healthy life. And since I like my beer I am equally attached to exercise, or I would very quickly end up like the fat beer bellies back in the pub," Walter said, patting his stomach with one hand and pointing backwards with the other.

The manor house was quite spectacular from the outside but James never got to see inside. Walter led him straight through the arch to the garden and a small studio where he obviously spent a great deal of his time. On a sturdy side table a pot of coffee was already percolating away. The aroma reminded James of a coffee roasting shop he used to pass on the way to school. It mixed surprisingly well with the smell of old books and pipe tobacco, occasionally obscured by the heavy sweet scent of flowers wafting through the open door from his wife's well manicured garden.

"Mary, my wife, you've obviously met her already, she sees me walking up the road and comes down to put the coffee on. She's quite wonderful." Walter said.

"You're a fortunate man."

"Yes, I know," Water said, looking up toward the house. "She'll be polishing the silver, writing, or potting some plants for the garden. Can't relax you know, whereas I can spend hours in here with my books, some good tobacco, the occasional Scotch and a decent coffee. Fortunate isn't an adequate term for my life."

James could see it was ideal. He could imagine a life such as this for himself some day. And for a moment he contemplated what Sabine might think of the arrangement. Looking around, he saw black and white photographs of ships on the walls, some of which were in their death throes. The remainder of the wall was a veritable library, mainly naval history through the ages. But lately there seemed to have been a change; a political theme squeezing its way onto the shelves.

"Have you read all these?" James said.

"Of course. What's the point in having them otherwise?"

"And the political stuff?"

"Yes, that's new, of course. Knowing what I know hasn't been easy and I've recently found that I need to justify my decision more and more as time goes by. Reading these proves I've at least tried to do the right thing. Not that it was a lot. I simply aided the subterfuge. I didn't create it." Walter said, passing a cup.

"Thanks," James said, taking a sip. "This is really good. I think you're right in what you did, if it helps."

"It does. Thanks James."

They talked all afternoon and well into the evening. Mary brought down sandwiches at seven and they ate together. James sensed Mary was relieved that Walter had finally talked about his personal demon. It was as though the responsibility had changed hands and a weight of conscience was lifted. Although she never knew what it was about. In that, he had tried to protect her as well.

An hour later James took his leave. He'd had an interesting afternoon and his perceptions on politics, foreign policy and military intervention had changed a little. In one afternoon he had become what most would consider a cynic. But as Walter tried to explain, a cynic is someone who believes that some people, those more often in power, are really driven by selfishness, which is different to what most people assume it to mean. Politicians, by their own admission, are egotistically driven and, due to the very nature of politics, complete hypocrites. They have to be, although it can make them go crazy in later life; it's not easy to live with two completely opposing and opposite views, and be forced, perhaps by policy, to agree with both.* The world is littered with tyrants who began with good, or rather moderate, intentions. To control those political characteristics the people need to regularly question politicians' decisions and actions, to be the checks and balances that are normally inherent within the system but which are often mislaid, or willfully abused. To do that effectively one needs to be endowed with a healthy dose of cynicism, even if only to play devil's advocate. The age of dogmatically believing a politician out of pure loyalty or patriotism is long gone, if it ever really existed at all.

---

* Psychologists describe this condition as 'cognitive dissonance.' Far be it for me to offer advice, but the interested reader might do little better than explore this human malady, for it explains much about politicians and leadership. In that regard, Norman E. Dixon's classic, *On the Psychology of Military Incompetence*, is an excellent starter. And for this I need to thank a good friend, an avid reader, a prodigious giver of books, and my occasional editor, for which I shall be forever indebted; Mr. Stephen Stutzbach.

Chapter Sixteen

Sabine, James, and the Police, London, England / July 1982

Some word there was, worser than Tybalt's death,
That murder'd me: I would forget it fain;
But, O, it presses to my memory,
Like damned guilty deeds to sinners' minds.
– William Shakespeare

SABINE FOUND IT HARD TO BELIEVE that a long succession of British governments would go to such lengths to protect Churchill's wartime secret. It seemed absurd after so much time. Especially since the issue really wasn't that important any longer. But James explained that too many decisions had already been made with the sole intent on keeping it secret, and many of them had been embarrassingly poor decisions. James recounted Coventry's wartime history when, once the thirty-year secrets were released, a deceased Churchill was initially accused of sacrificing the city in order to protect Ultra; the breaking of German wartime Enigma codes. However, it wasn't until *all* the facts became apparent that the majority of historians concluded that the city couldn't have been saved anyway, even if all of Britain's anti-aircraft artillery had been moved to Coventry, which, had it been, would have left other cities even more vulnerable. But as with all modern sound-bite news reporting, by the time the real truth was realized, the initial story had gained so much traction that it was unstoppable.

"After all," James said. "Most people get their news from a few snippy headlines in the tabloids, while flipping from the blow-brushed tits on page three to the sports page."

"That's a nice complimentary way to sum up the collective intelligence of the country," Sabine said.

"It's the country's biggest selling newspaper!" James said.

"Maybe, but everyone also knows it's a comic."

"Really, you think so? Either way, those newspapers are still tools of propaganda and people vote because of what they read in them." James said.

"You're a sad man."

"It's a fact of life. How many times have you seen a headline crucifying someone? Then when they're found innocent the paper issues a one-inch retraction between the gossip column and the insurance ads. Which do you think everyone remembers?"

"What does this have to do with Churchill?" Sabine asked.

"Not sure. I've forgotten," James said, smiling.

Sabine slapped James so hard even the cat felt sorry for him, instantly jumping from the chair to rub around James's legs as if to apologize for her behavior.

"Well, he seems to like you now, so at least someone does."

"Making friends all over, that's me. By the way, how's Sean doing?" James asked.

"He's okay, I think. Something upset him while he was in the states, he's laying low for a while. I know he likes you. He told me so the other day and he's never said that about anyone I've ever known." Sabine said.

"I like him too. You're just like each other, same perspective on life, same sense of humor. The only difference is… he's nice."

"Oh really!"

Sabine got up to put the kettle on. She was wearing James's white office shirt and as she bent over to retrieve the milk her shapely backside peeked out from beneath.

"Though you do have some redeeming qualities," said James, tilting his head to one side to get a better view before following her into the kitchen.

She heard him come up behind her and turned. James was already kneeling. He placed his hands underneath the shirt and pulled her to him. Her aroma was sweetly familiar, enticing and intoxicating, as his tongue reached out to taste her. She widened her stance and accepted the pleasure.

Fifteen minutes later, feeling nicely relaxed, Sabine said: "You know what's happening here don't you?"

James smiled and nodded. He'd known from the moment they were under her umbrella on that wet London pavement. He pulled her to him once again and kissed her, she could taste herself on his lips. They knew it was more than just a passionate weekend and as they talked their explorations fueled a desire for more.

When they rested they discovered they had much in common. They understood each other perfectly and seemed to sense what the other was about to say before saying it. It was uncanny. Even Sabine's cat, Arthur, liked James and that little hairy brute didn't usually like any man that would mean sharing Sabine's affections.

"So what do you intend to do about all this?" Sabine asked.

"Nothing. What can I do, and what would be the purpose of talking about it? No one has anything to gain," said James.

"You could write about it. Sell an article. Let people know the truth," Sabine said.

"Let people know the truth! You know that's bullshit. The newspapers would twist it, sensationalize it and trash everyone's reputation who has ever been associated with it... including mine. Besides, Harrison kept it to himself for years. The least I can do is the same.... the least we can do. There are three of us involved in this," James said.

"Well it's not my concern, but you should talk to Sean. He's more invested in this than us," Sabine said.

"You're right, I should have done that earlier. My mind has been elsewhere," said James.

"Not just your mind," Sabine said, all too seductively.

They had dinner at a local pub and arranged to spend the following weekend with Sean, although James planned to talk to him first during the week to explain what he'd discovered about the salvage. Also, it was Sunday, and Sabine had to work the next day. And since James needed to find work he decided to leave in the evening, knowing that if he stayed any longer neither of them would ever get anything accomplished.

It had been an exceptional weekend and his life had changed forever. On the one hand he had ended a career in which he'd always hoped to retire, and was now out of work, and on the other he felt strangely contented. Although exhausted. Keeping up with Sabine had tested his stamina as much as hill running ever had, although it had been significantly more enjoyable. But even apart from the sex, he had finally found someone who actually meant something to him. It had been so long a personal drought that he'd resigned himself to never finding anyone to share his life. On his way home James's unstoppable grin and flushed appearance revealed his happiness to anyone who took the time to notice.

Someone was noticing, and James, too late, saw the man waiting in the shadow of his doorway and stopped in his tracks.

"Mr. Devlin?"

"Yes?" James said, suspiciously.

Another man appeared as if from nowhere and behind him a car pulled up to the curb.

"Could you spare some time and come down to the station sir. I'm afraid there's been an accident," the man said, showing his Metropolitan Police credentials.

"Uh, yes. I suppose so. What's going on? I mean, who's had an accident?" James asked, fearing for a family member.

"Mr. Harrison, sir. I believe you spent the afternoon with him yesterday?" The man said.

"Yes. That's' right. We spent the afternoon at the pub and then went to his studio. Is he alright?" James said.

"Not exactly, sir. He's dead."

"Dead? But... but he was fine. We just had drinks together and he was fine," said James.

"Please sir. Could you come down to the station and answer a few questions? Just routine you understand. Apparently you were the last to see him alive," the policeman said. "It's just routine."

"But his wife, she was there also," said James.

"I'm afraid we found her too sir."

The news hit James like a punch in the stomach. How could this be? He was utterly confused and starting to worry that the police might think he'd had something to do with it. In the circumstances it was natural to assume so. James revisited the afternoon in his mind, trying to see something strange, something untoward, something that would solve the problem and get him out of this mess. But there was nothing. Poor Walter. And his wife too. What on earth could have happened? James stepped into the back of the dark saloon and was driven away to a cold tiled room at the police station. It was all a blur.

"Mr. James Devlin. I'm Inspector Killian. Sorry to bring you here so late. But we didn't know where you were. You weren't at home. Where were you sir?"

"I was with a friend all day," said James.

"Does this friend have a name? Can we contact them?"

"Yes, certainly," James said, and gave them Sabine's address and phone number.

Killian passed the information to a colleague who quickly disappeared. James assumed the other policeman was going to check on his whereabouts during the day, see if he really did have an alibi. James couldn't be certain but gathered from the direction of questioning that they didn't actually suspect him of anything. But they were clearly reaching for something without being too specific. It was as though they were hiding something. And although James knew they wouldn't let on to what they knew, since it might adversely taint his memory, he still believed that they weren't asking the right questions.

"What was the cause of death? I mean he seemed to be so fit for an older gentleman," said James.

"He was murdered sir. There's no sign on the body, but his studio was broken into, leading us to assume an intruder of some kind." Killian explained.

"I see. When was this?" James asked.

"Late yesterday evening. The gardener found them both this morning."

"But I was with him early yesterday evening," said James.

"Yes, we know. And until an hour ago you were our chief suspect. But now you have an alibi," Killian said.

"I do?"

"The Harrison's neighbor saw you leave and we have you on video filling up with petrol in London two hours before he died. And your friend, Miss O'Connor, has just verified where you were yesterday evening." Killian said.

"I see. So do you have any ideas? Who else might... "

"None sir," Killian interrupted. "That's why we needed to talk to you, to see if you saw or heard anything, or suspected anything. For instance, what did you talk about?"

"Oh, just old navy stories really. I recently left the service and Walter's... Mr. Harrison's name came up regarding something I was researching. Nothing special really, just a mutual interest," said James.

"I see. What exactly?"

"What?" James asked.

"What exactly were you talking about? What was subject of this mutual interest?" Killian asked.

"Oh, a shipwreck off the American coast. An old freighter during the Second World War, that's all," said James.

"You seem to have talked about it for quite some time if you met after lunch and stayed until evening," Killian suggested.

"Walter had been tasked with doing the same research I was doing, only twenty-five years earlier. I thought he might have found something that I didn't and went to find out," James said.

"But you're no longer working for the Admiralty."

"No. But I was still interested. For myself."

"So did he?"

"Not really, so we got onto other topics instead; navy stuff, politics, the Falklands mainly, stuff like that. We seemed to get on. I think we became friends. I liked him," James said. " He's a pleasant man. Was... "

"I'm sorry." Killian interrupted again, trying to get on with the questions. He was clearly in a hurry. "Does anyone else know of your conversation with Mr. Harrison?"

"No, no one. Except for Sabine obviously. And her brother perhaps, that's Sean. No one else though."

"I see, and what's Sean O'Connor's interest in this?"

"He was involved in the actual salvage operation, that's all. But it failed, so just a passing interest I'm sure." James explained, realizing that he might have said too much while still shocked over Harrison's death.

"And would you know where Mr. O'Connor was last night?"

"No. No idea at all." James said honestly.

Killian asked more questions, for which James apparently had all the right answers. But James still had a notion that something wasn't right. It didn't feel like a routine session and he felt the questions were somewhat ambiguous, steering him elsewhere, but he couldn't quite put his finger on it.

After a couple of hours James was driven home. It was dark and he didn't know which police station he had been taken to. Having not been in the area before he made a mental note of the turns until he saw something familiar. It was then he suspected something. There were an unusual number of right turns, leading him to think that they might have been going round in circles. But he didn't say anything, he wanted away from these people.

Back at his flat, James immediately called Sabine and told her what had happened. She was horrified to hear of Harrison's death, but knew something must have been wrong for the police to have called and enquired about James's whereabouts the previous night. She was relieved to hear that he was alright, at least, and offered to drive over for the night. He gladly accepted.

Being in her company again felt so natural and he relaxed immediately. They slept comfortably until five o'clock, when Sabine had to return home to get ready for work. They arranged to meet that evening and she left James in bed to finish sleeping.

He didn't sleep for long, he was showered and dressed by seven and driving off the A38 into Bovey by ten o'clock. When he arrived the gardener was mowing the lawn in front of the house.

"Hello there," James said.

"Aye, morning. Nice one today I'll bet," the gardener said, stopping to look up in case he messed up his perfect line.

"James! What on earth brings you back so soon?" A voice behind a bush said.

James turned to see a bush tremble before Mrs. Harrison appeared, carrying a set of secateurs and a basketful of trimmings.

"Mrs. Harrison? I... I thought... "

"Good Lord James. What's the matter? It looks like you've seen a ghost. Would you like some tea? Walter will be delighted. He's been driving me crazy ever since you left. You sparked his imagination and got his mind working overtime again. He's got books scattered everywhere," Mrs. Harrison said. "Don't worry though, it's good for him."

"Walter? He's alright? And you're alright?" James asked.

"Yes of course. Shouldn't we be?" She said. "Come on James, let's have a cup of tea. It looks like you need one. Long drive was it?"

James followed her into the house that he hadn't seen before. On the way he stared down the garden to the studio, expecting to see something. What was going on, he wondered. Had he been dreaming?

"Walter! Come down. See who's here!" She shouted.

Into the kitchen strode a very healthy Walter puffing on his old Capri pipe. There were no obvious wounds, certainly no sign of any sickness, and no suspicion was apparent.

"James lad. Good to see you. What brings you back so soon? Forget something?" Walter asked.

"Um. No. I was passing and thought I'd drop in to thank you once again for the other day," James said, coming up with excuses and hoping Walter didn't discern the untruths.

"That's fine lad. Glad you stopped by. Though it's a bit of a coincidence," Walter said.

"Why's that?" James asked.

"Well, I had a call from the Admiralty yesterday. Completely out of the blue. Someone asked if I'd been contacted by anyone unusual lately. Seems as though they found my name on a piece or paper laying around and were worried," said Walter.

"Really. Who was it, do you know?"

"No idea. Some senior officer I gathered, I forget the name, it didn't ring a bell. But then it wouldn't after so long, would it?"

"That is a coincidence," said James. "Could I have a word?"

"Certainly. What's on your mind James?" Walter asked.

James looked over at Mrs. Harrison, making sure she was out of earshot, and explained to Walter that he didn't want to worry her, to which Walter said that his wife had seen him through a lot and wasn't about to get worried. So James explained what had happened the previous night and why he'd shown up unannounced looking as though he had seen a ghost. At the time he'd become suspicious at the line of questioning. Then there was the strange drive home afterwards. James suggested the Harrisons go away somewhere. He was worried for their safety.

"It has to be someone playing a joke," Mrs. Harrison said.

"It's quite a sick joke. But no, these men were very real, very serious, and they clearly wanted something," James said.

"That phone call. It must be connected," Walter said, looking over to his wife in expectation for an answer. She usually had one, but not this time.

"It's no coincidence." James said, something is going on.

The Admiralty. James had a funny feeling about the Admiralty. Now that he thought about it he remembered having a moment that seemed odd, but it had been quickly obscured by something or someone, his thoughts had been interrupted and he had completely forgotten about it, until now. But he couldn't for the life of him remember what he was doing or to who he was speaking when it occurred.

He left the Harrisons again and asked if he could call them, just to make sure they were alright. He suggested, again, that they might go away for a few days, but they rejected the idea out of hand. They told him to be careful, since he'd obviously got himself into something. Walter assumed it must be something to do with their recent discussion and strongly advised James to leave the matter well alone and not talk about it to anyone.

James agreed, and knew if that's what was really happening these events had been a warning that he was stepping out of his depth. It had been a rather sick warning, however, but the message had been received loud and clear. He couldn't forgive himself if someone got hurt because of his interest in an outdated conspiracy. An interest urged on by Sabine, a sibling's attempt to alleviate her brother's frustration over the failure of an operation for which he'd put up most of his savings after the contract had ended. James wasn't looking forward to telling Sabine he was finished with it.

Thankfully Sabine was more relieved than disappointed, although she was mad as hell that someone could have gone to such extremes to warn James off. She was slowly discovering the reasons for Sean's inherent mistrust of governments and their propensity for hidden agendas.

Chapter Seventeen

Winds of war, London, England / April 2003

I think if you have faith about these things, you realise that judgment is made by other people ... and if you believe in God, it's made by God as well.

– Prime Minister Tony Blair

THE THOUGHT OF THE NATION GOING to war again, for the fifth time in the six years the Prime Minister had been in office, was incredulous to most people. The Brits, usually first in line for a fight, and proud of it, were however, dubious to the merits of this one and questioning not only its justness but its morality. Britain had not been attacked or threatened and neither had an ally. There was no Iraqi link to the terror organization blamed for the Twin Towers destruction in New York eighteen months earlier, despite Vice President Cheney's deliberate, and very vocal, rumor mongering to the contrary. The whole thing looked like Britain was simply playing the role of lapdog to the Unites States, and this did not sit well with most of the British people. They voiced their displeasure and concern in true style and marched by the thousands around parliament, Downing Street, Trafalgar Square and in many other cities around the country. Indeed, the whole world replicated those efforts on a massive scale, in scenes not witnessed since Vietnam.

The Prime Minister's mind was made up, however, and mass demonstrations, cabinet resignations, army chiefs' reservations and even contrary intelligence, were all unlikely to change his decision; born from a stubborn, innate, dogmatic belief, apparently brought to him by God himself. This was typical for a Prime Minister who was well known for his dictatorial approach to government, albeit entrenched within an historical democratic institution of the ages. Moreover, the reasons given to the public, and parliament, for agreeing to war, under American guidance, of course, were lacking any concrete evidence. Indeed, the cherry picked intelligence offered was extremely vague and seemed designed to validate a decision already made.

As war approached, the number of people across the world strongly against it grew steadily. A host of governments were also totally unimpressed by the spin emanating from both the White House and Britain's Parliament on a daily basis. It was seen as little more than fear-based propaganda designed to incite. The United Nations, hypocritically always blamed for being ineffective by many of the more hawkish members of the United States Government – the United Nations main stumbling block is usually the veto of the United States – refused to pass the resolution put forward for war, preferring to continue with arms inspections, which seemed to be working, albeit painfully slowly. The resolution failed, however, maybe because of a stream of insults hurled from arrogant senior officials in the White House, stating France and Germany to be the 'Old Europe' that should step aside. Such inane talk naturally resulted in lost trade for American businesses and for America, in return, to ludicrously, and somewhat vindictively, rename its fries 'Freedom Fries.' It was as if children at a summer camp had suddenly become leaders of nations.

A few probable, interspersed with a myriad improbable, reasons for justifying war quickly sprouted, and, collectively, were given credence under the questionable notion of patriotism; meaning that only if you agreed with them were you a patriot. Then, once each reason was proven false in turn, apparently by dastardly non-patriots, it was finally portrayed as a war to liberate the people of Iraq. Yet anyone with only a token understanding of recent U.S. history knew this to be preposterous. Moreover, the likelihood of success in such a strife-ridden, ethnic-torn, and religiously fractured country was a pipe dream – most people understood that the country would be hurled into a civil war as soon as the great coalition left Iraq to pick up the pieces and govern itself. Nevertheless, the coalition – the United States and Great Britain, with a few sundry nations – kept to their agenda and pressed ahead regardless, hoping to pass the point of no return when the arguments against war would eventually be nullified, by its beginning. At which point billions of dollars were expected to be 'voluntarily' handed over by uninvolved and uninterested nations to pay for the reconstruction of a devastated country. Little, however, was forthcoming to explain that the real recipients of the funds were huge American transnational corporations run by the Vice President's cronies. Hardly surprising considering the circumstances to which these same individuals were so embroiled within their own unethical behavior; to them it was just business as usual, not the gross conflict of interest that it so obviously was.

Of course, the blind hypocrisy was visible to anyone even remotely interested. The United States had, only too happily, funded the oppressive and brutal regime of Mr. Saddam Hussein over the previous decade. Even while he had been busy gassing Iranians and Kurds in the north of his country – the United States knew of this reprehensible act but kept it quiet until it needed the propaganda for its own interests later. Also, there exists a long muddy history of funding brutal dictators over democratically elected, but un-allied, leaders. The problem was that most people were not interested and many were too ignorant to even know the war never, in fact, really ended when Mr. George Bush bragged to the world that it had. It was, as Churchill stated fifty year previous, just the "end of the beginning," or the first battle in a longer more protracted campaign. A war is not over simply because one person decides that it's over. Wars generally end when either: both sides agree, one side is annihilated, or someone gets bored and goes home. The insurgents in this case certainly weren't going to agree, get annihilated, or get bored and go home. Because they were already home.

Most experienced military persons – which none of the hawkish, neo-conservative, self-proclaimed Christians in the White House were – knew that the inevitable guerrilla insurgency would be far more costly in lives and silver than the war itself. The risks were obvious to all with more than half a brain. Indeed, American military doctrine openly states that a guerrilla campaign that maintains and grows is, by definition, winning. The Americans had, after all, gained practice in this field and were remarkably successful with the insurgency they covertly ran in Afghanistan against the Soviets. This evidence didn't provide much in the way of confidence to the soldiers on the ground, however, who were being attacked and dying almost daily, and whose morale was being sapped rapidly.

When the number of Americans killed in the subsequent guerrilla insurgency surpassed those killed during the declared combatant stage, documents started to appear which proved a long suspected hidden agenda: Six years earlier, several future members of the United States Government had been openly conspiring to attack several countries considered to be hostile to America. By 'hostile' they simply meant those sovereign nations not submissive to American demands. The reason for war, then, was to institute stability within the region. By 'stability' read 'submissiveness', and agreeing to American trade practices.

The population in the United Kingdom was becoming increasingly disenchanted with New Labour's golden boy and current Prime Minister. All the issues: Suicide of a well-liked and competent civil servant; cabinet resignations; requests that the PM not turn up at a memorial service by parents of deceased servicemen, and falling polls, were all taking a toll on his health. He succumbed to a common stress related heart complaint. It wasn't serious enough for many people, however, because he returned to work almost immediately. Yet it raised concerns that he might, contrary to popular belief, actually have a conscience.

What was it that drove the Prime Minister to suck up to the United States to such a level that he was willing to risk and waste British soldier's lives in a war of choice?

Clearly it wasn't for money, liberty, moral values, or just to stand alongside a friend. It was thought to be for an egomaniacal desire for recognition on the world stage; to be remembered for a place in history, as a statesman, even a Churchillian statesman.

Well, he would certainly be remembered, but not for his original want or desire. Afterwards, he even forsook his Church of England faith for a Catholic version, his religion so strong and resolute that it was, for him, an easy stroll across the aisle.

Hidden among the throngs eager to popularize morality issues and conspiracy theories there were also a few who thought they understood the real reason. Up to now they had kept quiet, abiding by a longstanding mutual agreement. They each worried that repercussions from its publicity would create a cauldron into which the coalition's major participants would be flung, possibly leading to mass disorder and civil disobedience not seen in years.

One of these individuals had decided to make his way to Iraq.

Chapter Eighteen

Sabine and Sean, Oxfordshire, England / October 2003

I reject any religious doctrine that does not appeal to reason and is in conflict with morality.

– Mohandas Karamchand Gandhi

SABINE O'CONNOR WAS RELAXING at home over a glass of Australian Shiraz and a good book. Her latest cat, Lana, purring in her lap, content in the warmth generated by the wood fire a few feet away. The room was simple, cozy, but very comfortably furnished, everything matched perfectly the seventeenth century surroundings. The familiar salivating smells of a roast dinner were wafting from the kitchen, where the large Aga oven was slowly cooking the joint. The beef having been left on the doorstep that very morning with a note from her brother, inviting himself to dinner after watching the Rugby World Cup at the local pub.

Sean, an infrequent visitor to the cottage since their parents had died three years earlier, clearly had something he wanted to talk about. Sabine assumed the visit was something to do with yet another of his upcoming adventures, searching for something he was always unable to find. He would, no doubt, ask Sabine for the usual favor; that of looking after his fat black lab, Sheila. Sabine would, of course, just as she had done on all the other occasions, and which was the main reason for Sheila's condition; too many leftovers. Lana wouldn't be too chuffed with the idea, however.

Impeccable timing had Sean ringing the doorbell just as Sabine was removing the abundant tray of meat and vegetables from the oven. "You're just in time to carve Sean!" Sabine shouted toward the opening door.

Sean walked into a busy kitchen. Sabine was arranging the trays, plates and cutlery while Lana followed every step, rubbing against Sabine's legs and reminding her to drop a morsel. Sheila, already in the kitchen, having galloped in from the car, was expecting more than a morsel and making every effort to let everyone know, but wise enough to stay clear of Lana's well practiced claws while on her territory. A lesson she had learned long ago and still owning the scars on her nose to prove it.

"Hey gorgeous! Smells fantastic as usual," Sean said.

"As usual? You only come when you want something."

"You know me so well sis. That's why you're my favorite sister," Sean said, slicing off a dark sliver of outside meat.

"I'm your only bloody sister. By the way, how's your old girlfriend's sister?" Sabine said, knowing the fascination Sean had had with his girlfriend's sister, and rubbing in the reason as to why she was now the ex-girlfriend.

"You win. Let's eat," Sean said, smiling. "I'm famished."

Sitting down to the small table in the sitting room they caught up on recent events in their lives. Sabine sat listening but waiting for the inevitable favor to emerge, as it surely would after the first bottle of wine was gone. Going to the kitchen to find a piece of bread to mop up the gravy, Sean picked up the next bottle on his way back, one that he'd brought with him and one he knew Sabine especially liked.

"Well Sean, where is it this time?"

Sean was caught unawares. She usually gave him a chance to broach the subject slowly, or at least open the wine first.

"Middle East. Journalist gig. It's a good opportunity. I've been waiting for this sort of thing to come up, and a national has contracted me to cover the story," Sean explained.

"Where in the Middle East?"

"Iraq." Sean said gingerly.

"You've got to be fucking kidding me. You're not going to Iraq!" Sabine said, visibly shocked.

"It's not so bad. Things have quietened down a bit and I'm following one of the NGOs, an aid agency. They're not a target."

"I can't fucking believe you. With what we know about why this bloody government is there, you're going to play a part in it. You're mad," Sabine said, "and bloody hypocritical."

"It's an opportunity I can't give up. I've looked forward to this gig for a long time. I know it's a screwed up policy, but it's done, now we have to put things right."

"Put things right! You're buying into the bullshit Sean, right to the letter. I never thought I would see you do that of all people."

"For years I've been doing what I thought was right and what do I have to show for it? Now I have a chance to make my name mean something, for me. I need this one Sabine."

"Make your name mean something! How's your name going to 'mean something' being associated with this crap? Especially when someone discovers what you know? Besides, you *are* a success. You've done half a dozen different things. Most people are totally envious of your life and what you've done."

"Most people are ignorant." Sean said.

"Maybe they're the lucky ones."

"Ignorance being bliss, you mean?"

They sat in silence. Sabine inwardly fuming. Eating the meal but not savoring it. Sipping the wine but not really appreciating it.

"So when are you leaving?" Sabine finally asked.

"Two days. The airport's open now so I can catch a flight."

"Nice of you to give me some warning."

"Thought it best not to give you too much notice, you would only have worried longer. You don't mind Sheila do you?" Sean said, leaning down to pet the dog by his feet.

"You know I don't. She's a darling." Sabine said.

"Thanks Sabine. You really are the best."

"Uh-huh. Fuck you."

In agreeing to disagree they tried to enjoy the rest of the meal. Sean described the morning's game and told of running into old friends from when he'd lived in the area. Sabine mentioned she had seen James again, the first time in three years. He was busy writing and had asked her for permission to use some information she'd provided years earlier from the Admiralty, but had never used in his last book.

Sean always liked James and thought it a mistake that Sabine hadn't continued to make a go of it. They had been so good for each other and everyone who'd ever met them was instantly jealous of their easygoing relationship. But it wasn't to be. And they were now suffering the results of a separation that had no reason and seemed to have no ending.

Sean was a frequent visitor to James's London flat. It was handy for when he was traveling since he could stay in London overnight and recoup before heading home to the country. When together, and after a few customary beers, they would pretend to be twenty again and chase girls around the neighborhood bars. James was never as lucky as Sean, but having Sean around increased his odds exponentially, Sean was a girl magnet and little about him had changed in twenty years.

Sabine and Sean shared the washing up and spent the remainder of the afternoon reminiscing over their long disappeared family life. Before it got too dark they tried to walk some of the excess weight off the dog. Afterwards, Sean agreed to stay the night, but explained that he would have to leave for London first thing in the morning.

While they were both in the living room talking, Lana was curled up on the floor at the base of the Aga. She was comfortable near the heat and the flickering bluish screen on the kitchen counter was hypnotizing her. Unknown to its furry audience the television was describing another day's bloody events in Iraq.

The BBC newsreader explained that the violence in Iraq was spiking, showing a specific increase in the targeting of relief organizations, including even the Red Cross and those associated with the United Nations, and mentioned that personnel within those organizations could no longer be guaranteed safety around their places of work. Although this was a standard risk for people venturing into war zones the tone of the warning was dire. Several smaller NGOs had already postponed their arrival as a result and were waiting events out in neighboring Jordan. To put the indiscriminate viciousness into perspective, after being specifically targeted twice by al-Qaeda insurgents in the last two months, the United Nations had been forced to remove all of its staff members. It was a signal that the already appalling situation was only going to get worse. Even though, according to the U.S. President, the war was over, 'Mission Accomplished.'

Had Sabine or Sean watched the BBC news that evening things might have been very different for all of them.

Chapter Nineteen

James, England / October 2003

Great is the guilt of an unnecessary war.
— John Adams

SINCE LEAVING THE NAVY TWENTY years earlier James had moved around in a variety of jobs. He'd even had a spell trying to sell cars before realizing he was useless at it. Then he found a position on a large cruise ship which was easy but incredibly boring and he didn't last long at that either. Back on land, he found himself meandering around the country until he found a niche; tracking down European ancestors for wealthy Americans. He had always enjoyed the English countryside and mixing that pleasure with visiting historic old churches suited him perfectly. He was exact in his work and his very proper English accent endeared him to the myriad of rich American women hoping to discover that they were related to royalty. It also paid rather well and his success grew by word of mouth alone. He became especially sought after when one very satisfied client actually did discover that she was related to royalty, Scottish royalty, and later wrote a well-received women's magazine article bragging the fact.

His job demanded frequent travel to the States, delivering both the good and the bad news. Most of his female clients were, even despite bad news, happy with the results and more than eager to invite this perfect English gentleman into their immaculate east coast homes. And if he was in the area he enjoyed staying at the *Albatross*, just for old times sake, although no one he knew was there anymore. All the old timers had disappeared into retirement homes or had died. The previous landlord's daughter now owned the bar. She was a cheerful chubby woman who thrived on arguing baseball stats with her regulars, but knew absolutely nothing of the sea barely a hundred yards from her doorstep.

The part of the job James really enjoyed was visiting old, often forgotten, churches all over the country. He would stay in the locality and get to know the villagers in the evenings while at the pub. He found a lot of his information this way and met many wonderfully strange people hidden in the backwoods of the English countryside. Some of whom had never left the village in which they were born. One such person, living in a small Devon village, Gidleigh, described why: "Well, my mother told me I should go to Exeter and buy a suit for my dad's funeral. So I walked along to the train station in Moreton. I waited a while, but the train never came, so I came home."

"Why didn't you look at the schedule?" James asked.

"Well, when I looked down from the platform, I could see someone had stolen the rails."

"When was this?" James asked.

"Nineteen-eighty-six."

James knew that the Moreton to Exeter line had been removed in the seventies and was now a public bridle path. It seemed as though some people just needed any little excuse not to make the effort to leave town, even briefly. But each to his own, James could see that they were happy in their lives.

When Sean was on his way to Iraq James had offered his London flat, as was usual. However, he couldn't be there to enjoy another evening with Sean because of a work commitment in the

States. A week earlier Sean had called explaining his intention and James had congratulated him on finally getting the opportunity that he'd been waiting for. But James had been busy at the time, and hadn't really thought through the implications, not that they were any of his business anyway.

Later, when Sabine called in tears after Sean left, James realized his error. For as good a friend as Sean had been over the years he should've made an effort to see him before he left. Guilt emerged as he was talking with Sabine and he felt bad, not just for Sean but for Sabine also, being the one left at home to worry. James knew she'd seen Sean go through the wringer during the last twenty years, ever since the salvage episode with *Ulysses*. The information he had been entrusted to keep steadily ate away at the core of his ideals. Sean's previous naïveté, that the government existed solely for everyone's best interests, had been irretrievably shattered. And although many people know it to be so, they tend not to dwell on the fact. But Sean was different; he had been witness to, and had seen proof of, one of the greatest longstanding deceptions and he could never forget it.

During the run up to war Sean had written countless letters to the press demanding accountability and honesty. Sabine had kept some of them and sent copies to James while he was traveling. Sean wasn't anti-war in the true sense, he just wanted to make sure that the war, any war, was justified before sending men to do violence and accept death as a result, which he assumed was no different to how most people thought. Sean had agreed somewhat with the country going into Afghanistan, in the way that it initially did, using special forces and local manpower to quell competing warlords and the fanatics and terrorists that were hiding amongst them. Iraq, however, was not a hotbed of terrorist activity, and never had been. And just like everyone else he could see that removing forces from Afghanistan would only further enable the

Taliban, which, of course, it did. In effect, wasting all the previous effort and, moreover, wasting lives.

Sean's dislike for George Bush and his crèche of pseudo-Christian fools was total and he could never comprehend the Prime Minister's fascination at being Bush's personal lapdog. It was demeaning. Watching Tony Blair parade himself around alongside George Bush, pretending to the world they were statesmen, made Sean want to puke. Blair's ballooning ego would not allow him to remotely comprehend that he might be being taken for a ride by forces way beyond his control, designed by manipulative people a lot cleverer that he. So it went on, despite serious reservations from a variety of high profile political figures and high echelon militarists. Then, slowly, the fragile intelligence was torn asunder piece by deceptive piece, leaving nothing but a series of outright lies visible to the public. But this was alright according to Mr. Blair, because according to him the war was being waged in "good faith." A term that instantly put a big dent in the endless rhetoric that none of it had anything to do with 'crusading'. An irony that apparently went completely over the Prime Minister's head.

It was around this point that Sean decided he could no longer keep quiet about Churchill's legacy. He began writing letters to the newspapers, even turning up to his local MP's surgery. But everyone ignored him, thinking him a bit of a paranoid crackpot. The papers even placed him on their blacklist – their bosses, or more importantly their advertisers, and their leaking politicians, didn't want to hear another word from Sean O'Connor.

It was during his third meeting with a local MP that Sean realized someone else might be listening in. This time the MP had a series of questions for him, almost appearing interested, which was unusual because he'd always felt he was just being politely placated. Then, to prove his suspicion, when he left the office he was followed.

Sean was a lot more mature than when first confronted by the Secret Service twenty years earlier and decided to make things more difficult for them this time. After a lot of amateur subterfuge and chasing around – in the front door, out the back, kind of stuff – he was eventually openly arrested, although released by his lawyer thirty minutes later. But that had given a couple of MI5 agents time to remind him that he had, indeed, signed the Official Secrets Act. An agreement that lasts forever; guaranteed for life, as it were. And that any transgression would immediately land him in Wormwood Scrubs, an unpleasant 19th century prison built by convict labor on an old London dueling ground.

In his present mood, though, Sean didn't care and wasn't very helpful, exposing the agents to a selection of expletives he hadn't used in years. But it made him think that he might actually be onto something, that maybe past forces were pressuring the Prime Minister, and that he was pushing the right buttons. It would explain a lot. The constant re-evaluation of lies was not only hiding an agenda over Iraq, but also protecting a secret that had got so out of control that people were now dying because of it. Maybe this was the final payoff. Either the guilt or the bullion's monetary value had finally become a soldier's worth, a nation's worth.

It was this that inevitably drove Sean to Iraq. Before leaving he hurriedly mailed a package to his sister, via her favorite pub. She would understand. She was family. The Lamb Inn in Burford, Oxfordshire, would be the recipient of documents that could either tear apart the foundations of government or, he hoped, make it see sense and return the country to its long-held and long-respected values of morality and justice. The very things that his grandfather, and many other grandfathers, had fought and died for 60 years earlier. It was a tall order born from wishful thinking, for those days are long gone, even if they really existed at all.

Chapter Twenty

Sean, Baghdad, Iraq / November 2003

How many times over the centuries have peoples tried to conquer Baghdad, Fallujah, Kut; each time doing the same thing, each time expecting something different? Is that not the definition of insanity?
– Author

SEAN HAD BEEN IN IRAQ for two weeks, temporarily attached to one of the smaller, but well respected, non-government organizations, Education for Life. The group had been involved to some extent in hotspots all over the world and was now firmly entrenched in Iraq, helping some of the more educated local women start up schools in impoverished areas of the country. They strongly believed education was the cure for many of the world's ills and had designed their mission accordingly. Sean was collecting information for an article on the organization, its members and the many children for whom they were all working. He believed strongly in their mission and wanted to give them notoriety from which they might gain more funding. He was also sending in daily reports to a national newspaper and trying to be insightful to the few optimistic events unfolding in and around Baghdad. The pessimistic view already being exceedingly well documented by reporters from all over the world who had gathered in the city at the end of the invasion. The BBC, however, had recently been reporting that insurgents were starting to go after more soft targets, in an attempt to further hamper reconstruction efforts by stemming the flow of charities and relief organizations coming into the country. With the coalition unable to provide security, due to insufficient manpower, the tactic was working.

Sean could hear and occasionally see the results of the pessimistic view. There were explosions daily and automatic gunfire was rife across the city, and yet average people got on with their normal day despite the risks. The main targets for bullets and bombs were American soldiers, so people prudently, and very subtly, gave them a wide berth and didn't mingle too much, except for the children, who stood around hoping for handouts despite their parent's misgivings.

The American soldiers passed out candies and footballs in an attempt to seize 'hearts and minds' – a phrase coined to describe the British counter-insurgency strategy in Malaysia. But the Americans couldn't quite grasp the concept and free candy was not helping. Sean wondered what on earth made them think the parents of these kids would be happy for them to be receiving candy, not only from strangers but from Christian strangers? After all, how many American parents allow their kids to accept candy from anyone? It was abject naïveté. The whole misplaced adventure was steadily developing into a colossal failure, based largely on an inherent arrogance in not trying to understand the culture and willfully ignoring the fundamentals and responsibility of being an occupying power. It wasn't simply that American politicians didn't know, it was becoming more apparent that they didn't know they didn't know. After all, most of them had had so much experience themselves of war, having managed to duck at every opportunity.

Sean, however, although heavily entwined between the good and the bad, was trying his best to remain optimistic. The people with whom he was dealing, Iraqi and various foreign volunteers, were the nicest, hardest working, most forthright individuals he had ever met and nothing, but nothing, seemed to keep them down for long He found their courage and optimism not only surprising, but profoundly contagious.

One incident that would have brought most western schools to a complete standstill and grief-ridden for weeks happened late one afternoon, just before the kids left for home: Their teacher, an ambitious young Iraqi girl, with no obvious affiliation to one sect or another, was arranging papers for her class's simple homework. She walked to the open window – most windows hadn't had glass for months – and looked out to make sure the American soldiers were guarding the exit so the kids could leave safely. The small classroom of children, ranging from eight to fourteen, watched as she shuddered slightly, stepped backwards, and then turned to look across the room toward the startled kids with an expression of shock and disbelief, before falling to the floor dead.

By chance, a stray bullet had caught her in the middle of her chest and she had died within seconds. At first there was little visible blood on her loose clothing yet all the children knew instinctively what had happened. They ducked under their tables immediately, fearing an attack, just as she had taught them on their first day of school. She would have been proud.

The next day, all the kids were at school as usual, playing football in the dusty playground and waiting for a new teacher to appear. One did, and after briefly introducing herself they returned to their routine; teacher teaching, children learning. The incentive that drove everyone to work so hard for these kids was the endless hope that their future would, one day, be better. Better despite the insurmountable odds against it.

These types of events went on every day all over the country and everyone just continued on, much like it must have been in London during the Blitz. Sean realized, however, that in the world of running water, individual cars, electricity and all kinds of unnecessary luxury, the west had largely forgotten that the greater human family is incredibly resilient and adaptable when the simple things in life, like basic survival, become paramount.

For the past two weeks since the teacher had died Sean had been working with a new purpose. Though still writing his articles for the newspaper he was becoming more embroiled with the day-to-day work of the NGO. Not for the first time in his life was he helping other people and rekindling a feeling of innate satisfaction. Although in his position he was infinitely more fortunate than those around him because he was being well paid. Whereas the others were making do on a pittance, if anything at all. All the Iraqi women were volunteers.

The fourth week of his contract was ending and he was due to go to Kuwait to do an article on the huge American base situated in the desert. It was reputed to be larger than many cities by some of the other journalists who had been there. It was also where a western journalist could mix with the opposite sex, and do so without worrying about cultural sensibilities. Sean would have preferred staying put, but moving the contracted journalists around was a common practice designed to get the most out of them by keeping them interested and busy.

With just three days to go Sean was walking along the street with his interpreter-come-security-guard, Ali, a middle-aged Iraqi who looked like he'd fought in every war in the region for thirty years. In the streets they passed by rows of stacked household electrical appliances; fridges, stoves, microwaves, music centers and many other types of household items. All displayed by hopeful vendors vying for trade. They stopped at a corner teahouse in the midst of TVs and microwaves to talk to the owner, who Sean already knew as a parent of one of the children at the school. A couple of weeks ago the boy had approached Sean saying he had found a camera in the street after an explosion, but that it didn't have film, so Sean promised to find him a roll. Sean was always concerned about the parent's perception of rich westerners giving gifts directly to the kids, instead of asking the parents first, so this gave him an opportunity to get the father's perspective on his child's education while he gave them the film to then give to their son. Sitting down among a group of elderly men all sipping hot tea, Ali asked the questions for Sean and in overly exaggerated mannerisms explained the responses.

The shopkeeper was obviously thankful that his children had the opportunity to go to school. Maybe they wouldn't have to be shopkeepers. But he was not optimistic for the future. Experience had temporarily removed optimism from his vocabulary.

"After all. What happens when the Americans leave?" The shopkeeper asked.

"You like the Americans being here then?" Sean asked.

"No. I don't like Americans. Very rich, very arrogant. They should leave soon," the shopkeeper said.

"But what will happen when the Americans leave?"

"What will always happen. Things will go on," he said.

Few westerners would understand this contrary conversation. Yet it was how the local people felt and how they expressed their pragmatic attitude. Here was a clash of cultures and another few more years of forced western liberation was still old fashioned imperialism in their eyes. Nothing was likely to change that. Sean's problem was how to interpret the statements for a British audience at home without bias. Or rather interpret the statements so that they wouldn't upset the advertisers who were funding the newspapers. The usual analogy being: "My enemy is my friend until my greater enemy no longer threatens me."

The shopkeeper's son was excited that he now had some film, and running in and out of the shop taking pictures of everything, even the convoy making it's way up the street in the distance. The father said something that Sean assumed to be "don't waste it," but it looked like he was going to be ignored. After fidgeting with the camera some more the boy politely asked Sean if he could take a picture of him with his father. Sean was flattered and they both agreed, sitting side by side while the boy carefully framed his first portrait. For that brief moment everyone in the shop seemed to forget the war and watched as a young boy got great pleasure from a new toy. Maybe it would be the start of a career. Something new and interesting to look forward to. A new beginning.

The war came back with a thunder as the convoy raced past outside – their usual speed to avoid ambush. On top of the vehicles soldiers brandished mounted Browning machine guns, the soldiers outwardly brazen yet wary, and very very alert. Hidden nervous eyes scoured surroundings through goggles and sporty sunglasses, with drivers constantly looking for exits from potential attack. It wasn't a matter of if they were going to get hit, but when. The recent bloody days had provided greater incentive to be even more vigilant, and a recent visiting politician's misplaced rhetoric hadn't helped their efforts for hearts and minds, or done anything to enhance their own ability to stay alive.

As the boy framed his picture Sean heard the first vehicle rumble along the narrow road, followed by a swirl of dust that engulfed the shop and obscured a small group of men mingling in the alley on the opposite side of the street. One of them held a long tube with a large bulbous end. The soldier atop the third vehicle let out a warning to those behind as he swiveled the machine gun on its circular track and the vehicle behind lurched forward. But not quick enough. A burst of fire from an AK 47 tore into the gunner's arm at the shoulder and he collapsed into the Humvee. A rocket propelled grenade then raced toward the next vehicle, but missed. Instead, it devastated another target. The teahouse was obliterated in an ear-shattering explosion. Searing shrapnel, splintered glass, concrete and chunks of flesh, were all hurled outwards in a great blinding flash.

Sean died instantly. Being only feet from the nucleus of the blast, he was killed along with Ali, the shopkeeper, his son and everyone else inside the once sedate teahouse. All that remained was a mass of choking dust and debris, and an ugly coagulating mixture of blood and dirt. The soldiers had raced ahead taking their wounded with them, unable to return any effective fire in the confined space. The attackers fled as fast as they had appeared. Amongst the wailing and shouts of anger no one would know, or say, who they were. Politicians would say they were foreign jihadist terrorists, but to the dead and surviving families it didn't matter. They simply blamed "the other side." And so it went on.

Life also went on. To remain sane local people immersed themselves in a collective resilience and tried to forget such events quickly. Iraqis had long ago been forced to inherit this British-styled 'stiff upper lip' after the country had been arbitrarily carved from the shank of the Ottoman Empire by the League of Nations, with little thought to religious, ethnic or cultural heritage. For as long as people could remember it had been that way, French or no French, Turks or no Turks, British or no British, Americans or no Americans, for a hundred years.

After the teahouse had been picked through by the security forces it was left as rubble. As testament, and another grim location, to the increasing violence predicated by endless sectarian squabbles onto Baghdad's bloody landscape.

Chapter Twenty One

Sabine and James, Oxfordshire, England / November 2003

When a man and a woman have an overwhelming passion for each other, it seems to me... that they belong to each other in the name of Nature, and are lovers by Divine right.

– Nicolas Chamfort

THE GUILT JAMES FELT FROM NOT seeing Sean before he left for Iraq was minuscule to the sorrow he now endured. Sabine had not come out and specifically blamed James for Sean's journey, nevertheless, he knew she was looking for a convenient scapegoat. For now, James was willing to fill that role. He loved her and was desperately trying to console her in any way that he could, and in any way she needed. If that meant taking some small part of the blame, so be it.

They sat either side of the fire not saying a word. Both staring into the flickering flames, remembering the past and stifling tears. Each flame seemed to spur a new memory and their thoughts were torn asunder trying to make sense of fleeting neurons bouncing off the synapses. Then, a memory would instill a brief comforting calm and flames would dance in the shadows of unconsciousness; a happy thought momentarily dulling a tormented brain before a new flittering brightness sparked another thought, rekindling a notion of responsibility and guilt once again. All culminating in the great unanswered 'what if.'

Sabine's thoughts were eventually diverted by Sheila and the warmth of a friendly muzzle nudging her, demanding attention. Sabine looked down into the dark, sad, wanting eyes, put her hand on Sheila's head and let the tears flow. They released her, allowed the inevitability of sadness to envelop her and in some natural way free her. She looked over at James. Although unable to see him through her misty eyes they beckoned him.

It was a forgiving look. A sad, desperate, forgiving look. A look that lifted the heavy veil of guilt from his heart. James felt a rush of release as blood and air were once again able to surge unfettered through his body. His face was red from sitting too close to the fire and when he rose he felt decidedly chilled. He knelt on the floor, Sabine on one side, Sheila on the other, his hands full, comforting both. Standing up, he lifted Sabine from the chair, wrapped his arms around her little body and hugged her for all his worth, neither of them wanting him to ever let go.

They had both enjoyed this level of affection in the past. What had happened to it? Had the need for a worthwhile life destroyed it? Sabine moved the hair from her teary face and stared at him, feeling the curves of his face with her fingers as if for the first time, and opened herself for a kiss of desperation. A kiss that would liberate her from the cruelties of an uncaring world and liberate him from the anguish of the preceding weeks.

Nervous at first, James finally, and fully, obliged her desire, knowing full well the commitment and inevitable responsibilities for agreeing to such an act. In those few moments they rekindled their lost years of intimacy, explored each other as if strangers, but instinctually aware of each other's cravings. After years apart they were now together again. As they always should have been.

"Sean would be happy. To see us together like this would make him happy." Sabine said.

James knew it to be true but there was nothing he could say. Anything he did would just restate the obvious, initiate more tears, ruin the moment. He just held her tighter, enjoying the closeness, the warmth, the aroma, the comfort within the subtle sensual tension, the feeling of being home without being home. What a pity such realization comes so frequently only after a loss.

"Tea?" He said.

"Yes. Good idea, let me put the kettle on. I need to give Sheila her dinner anyway."

The dog heard the two operative words in the same sentence, launched herself into the kitchen and waited, tail wagging in anticipation as her paws tapped a tune feverishly against the slate floor. For the first time in ages they both laughed.

While Sheila devoured her dinner they stood together by the warmth of the Aga oven, hugging each other and appreciating the comforting closeness of unfettered love. Sabine nuzzled her head to James's chest and inhaled, enjoying the musky familiarity of his masculinity. She could feel the sensual urge build up inside of her. The smell was a trigger, the initiator to pleasure.

James became aware of the rush of hormones overcoming her, as if her scent had jolted a long distant but forgotten primeval instinct from within. He wondered if she had noticed his growing bulge, an involuntary response to the tension between them. James relished the moment, relished the feeling, but he wasn't sure. Was it was still too soon?

It wasn't. She placed his hand firmly on her breast, lifted her head and offered her lips to his. It was an experimental kiss, born of desperation but this time more gentle, more sensual, and more resigned to its inevitable outcome. More time to explore each other's taste, inhale each other's aroma, sense each other's desire as their tongues met and delved to rediscover what they had missed. Their previous practiced proficiency had disappeared as with the years, so this was like a first kiss again; awkward, sloppy, and yet exhilarating in its anticipation.

James moved his hand slowly to Sabine's crotch and felt her tense up in delight, letting out a short shallow groan of pleasure before pushing her hips forward to meet his hand, inviting from him a stronger response to match her increasing urge. His hand ran down her skirt, feeling the firmness of her thigh through the thin material. Reaching lower he felt the bareness of a leg, trembling a little as the touch of flesh heightened his pleasure, and returned his hand up her bare leg, back to warmth. He could feel her wetness and rubbed her gently, savoring the moment before pulling aside her underwear and inserting a finger. She sighed in instant pleasure and hung on to his neck, pulling him closer and forcing herself onto his hand while she kissed him. He retrieved it, smelled the scent on his fingers that drove him wild and offered it to her.

"I want more than this," she said, before sucking on a finger.

James lifted her onto the front rail of the Aga and knelt down before her. Remembering what he enjoyed most she raised and spread her long legs, openly enticing him, no longer teasing him. Wanting his mouth all over her and his tongue inside of her. He kissed the soft skin of her inner thighs, ran his tongue delicately around the edge of that delicate fold before placing his mouth over her, his tongue exploring her moist inner warmth. She grabbed his head and forced herself against him, wanting him to do she knew not what but wanting it anyway. He responded. He worked at her, delving deep into her one moment and teasing her the next. She grabbed the overhead rail, leant backwards and thrust her crotch up and forward, grinding herself forcefully against his face. Her pace quickened. Her thighs tightened around his head. He searched for air when he could, his mouth full and his face sodden. He looked up to take a breath.

"No! Don't stop! Don't stop!" She demanded.

He stood, undid his belt, dropped his trousers and entered her. She leant forward and kissed him, enjoying herself on him and him in her. He thrust into her. Faster. Slower. Deeper. Faster. She became wanton, in desperate desire for ultimate satisfaction. In an instant she wanted it all and pushed him backwards, out of her, off her. She forced him back onto the oak table and climbed on top, straddling him and steering him inside of her once again.

She was in her element, in control, and leant backwards to remove her blouse. He leant forward to unsnap her bra and she shoved her bare breasts into his face. He knew what to do; he held a breast firmly in each hand and rolled his tongue first around one and then the other as she rocked and gyrated back and forth on top of him. He could feel the warmth oozing from her and dripping between his legs. He couldn't hold much longer. Who could? She was an animal, full of desire and wanting nothing than to be satiated. He continued to tease the nipple of choice, tasting the sweat from between her breasts while reaching behind to feel the crack of her tight little ass. She winced in pleasure and rode harder, faster, backwards and forwards, grinding further down onto him. He could feel the peak of pleasure welling up inside her. Her groaning more steady, her movement more determined and precise. She had found the spot and she was intent on keeping it, keeping it right there.

"Don't move? Don't you goddamn move!" She almost spat, as she got closer.

Her groans became longer, deeper, as she bore her full weight down upon him. He could feel the tip of him touch her deep inside on each downward thrust. She sat upright, her breasts magnificent as they lifted upwards, taut and perky, the sweat on them glistening as they bounced gloriously up and down in evening light. She was a picture, a classic erotic picture of pure unbridled sexual pleasure.

"Ohhhh Jesus! Jeeesuus! Yes! Yes! Yes!"

She tucked her head as the stimulation created an intense rush of sexual energy before arching backwards as the continued feeling of pleasure surged through her, engulfing her. It seemed to go on for a minute as it flowed through her veins, warming every vessel, touching each nerve of pleasure until she slowly wound down to a sedate and relaxed rocking motion. Her body shook uncontrollably as she looked down upon him, sweat dripping from between her breasts, over her belly, between her legs and onto him. She leant forward and kissed him, hugged him, not wanting to let go while the internal explosion subsided, leaving her completely exhausted, and finally satisfied.

"Thank you! Thank you!" She said.

He looked up to her beautiful and very satisfied face, enjoying the pleasure of seeing her pleasure.

"I damn well needed that," Sabine said.

"I gathered as much," he said.

"I'm sorry. I took control again, ordered you about."

"I love it. It's brilliant." James said. "Always have. You're lovely, wonderful in the sack and absolutely fucking gorgeous. I love you. Never apologize for taking control. I've always loved that you enjoy sex so much, and the bossiness... well that's the icing, a complete turn on! Damn woman, you're sexy!"

"Your turn." Sabine said, as she lifted herself off him.

She pulled him from the table and knelt down before him, taking him in her hands before running her tongue gently along the underside of his rigid shaft, still wet with her. He looked down and watched as her mouth engulfed him, feeling the intense pleasure of warmth as her breath and saliva surrounded him. She placed her hand beneath him and toyed with the loose sensitive skin as her head bobbed up and down with a practiced rhythm. Her tongue doing something he'd never before experienced as he became taut and shuddered as a torrent of unconstrained pleasure erupted into her. She held him there, perfectly still, neither moving, with him inside her, she allowing the last of the tingling tantalizing orgasm to wash through him. Her tongue ran up the underneath of him as she slowly removed her head from his crotch and looked up to him with satisfied whorish eyes from beneath her sex-crazed hair.

He lifted her up and kissed her. Both standing naked in the kitchen, enjoying the afterglow and comforting reassurance that all was fine between them. Their fit naked bodies glistening in the last of the afternoon sunlight as it streaked through the old windows. It was as good as it had ever been and they eagerly wanted to do the same again, right now. He was still hard and she still eager.

A black dog appeared sheepishly at the door, seeing if it was safe to enter before paddling across the slate floor, a nervous tail unsure of whether to wag or hang.

"Someone needs a walk." James said. "I'll take her."

"No. We'll both go. I'm not letting you go now I've got you back. And we can stop by the pub for something to eat. Just let me clean my teeth and I'll be right there."

"Come here," James said, holding out his hand.

She grabbed him and they kissed again. Holding each other as if they would never let go. Sabine was beautiful, he couldn't get enough of touching her, feeling her, watching her. Unconsciously, every single move she made was a teasing pleasure to him. Like enjoying the same pretty girl in a magazine but in another pose, only real. But with Sabine there was no posing, it was just a natural sensuality emanating from a purely seductive personality, full of desire and completely confident in the innate beauty of her body and her being.

James knew he would have his hands full from this moment. While Sheila made a subtle little whine as if to say: "Not again."

Chapter Twenty Two

Sabine and James, Oxfordshire, England / November 2003

FENNYMAN: So what do we do ?
HENSLOWE: Nothing. Strangely enough, it all turns out well.
FENNYMAN: How ?
HENSLOWE: I don't know. It's a mystery.

– William Shakespeare

IN THE DISTANCE SHEILA WAS chasing some elusive critter through the long dead grass. Every now and then she would stop, become perfectly still, pounce off all fours and end up a few feet forward, forgetting she no longer had the agility of a puppy and always landing a foot short of her prey. Then her nose would hit the trail again and the only thing visible above the grass would be her tail, like the periscope of a partially submerged submarine performing evasive maneuvers.

The chill from the stream created a mist over the low-lying fields and Sabine hung onto James's arm for warmth, still feeling the tingling inner glow of the afternoon's lovemaking. She had always been predictable; the more sex she got the more she needed. And she wanted to just dive into the long grass, get naked and have him take her once again. She knew she was insatiable at times and knew that it, and the inevitable infidelity that it had provoked in the past, had been the cause of her relationship failures. But she didn't want that to happen again. She had been given another chance with James and she didn't want to ruin it. And with the way he'd been in the kitchen she thought he might be one of the few who could possibly keep up with her.

They reached the end of the trail and stepped over the wooden stile into the lane. Sheila was still combing the banks of the stream in search of some unseen critter so they waited, watching the last of the sun sink behind green hills along the valley in the distance. The early evening air was damp and chilly but the temperature instantly dropped a few more degrees. The few ponies in the field sauntered off to wait by the gate for their evening oats.

It was a typical quiet country evening. The traffic light by the old single-lane stone bridge shone through the mist and when the air around it changed to green an unseen lone car could be heard accelerating towards town, its sound muffled within the moisture.

Sheila appeared, covered in a colorful variety of local fauna, and crawled under the muddy space beneath the stile, panting heavily but always eager for more adventures. James attached her leash and they set off for the pub down the narrow lane that wound its way along the outskirts of the village. An occasional car would come around one of the blind bends and they would hug the stone wall to give it room to pass. The pub was just around the corner.

Entering the slate floored pub the room went immediately quiet, just to give the patrons time to see who the gorgeous Sabine would bring this time. They weren't surprised. To them James was just another of her type. A type they had come to know quite well over the past few years because there had been a steady stream of handsome men vying for her attention. They had also been brief, very brief, and there was no reason for them to expect this one would last any longer, so they ignored him.

"Friendly lot," said James.

"Oh, don't mind them, they're friendly enough," Sabine said.

"Really?" James said, looking around at the cold stares.

"Yes, and when they accept you they're too friendly. And then you can't get away from them." Sabine said.

They strode toward the bar and it appeared as if the bartender had been waiting for them.

"This here is a pub Sabine, not a post office. The post office is down the street," the bartender said.

"Yes Frank, I know," she said, rather confused.

"Well then, maybe you can tell your friends that we don't accept mail for our customers, especially irregular customers. This has been waiting here for weeks now." Frank said, handing over a padded envelope.

"What is it?"

"It's an envelope Sabine. Envelopes usually contain letters." Frank said, sarcastically.

"Why'd it come here?" Sabine said.

"That's the bloody mystery. Maybe when you find the answer you can enlighten me."

"Well, thanks Frank. Sorry for the trouble. But why not just call me and let me know?"

"Because, if you read it, it says 'for pick up only' and 'do not notify' for some reason. It's all rather hush-hush and secretive isn't it? What've you been up to this time Sabine?"

"Nothing I know of, but I'll let you know." Sabine said. "In the meantime, can I have a pint of bitter and a double Scotch and water, please."

"Coming right up. Anything for the new gentleman?" Frank said, looking at James as though he was a consolation prize.

"Oh, you're so funny today Frank."

"I try." Frank said, and smiled as he tugged on the tap to pour the bitter to the very top of the glass, looking James over as he did so. "Don't say we shortchange you here sir."

"Thanks! A perfect pint." James said, attempting to placate a situation he knew nothing about while trying to get the glass to his lips without spilling any.

"Aye lad. Wish that the lass here was as appreciative."

"Frank! Stop kidding now. James, this is my uncle."

"Well, pseudo uncle anyway." Frank said. "I've been looking after this wee lass since she was 14. She used to sneak in here on her way home from school, you know, try to steal a handful of peanuts she would. Those were the easy days, though, once she started drinking it became another kettle of fish entirely, a whole lot more trouble!"

"Why's that?" James asked.

"Boys! They followed her everywhere. Hordes of them. I had to kick most of them out because they were underage and only good for being a nuisance." Frank said.

"I see. I mean… knowing her I can see that being a problem." James said, receiving a kick in the shin from Sabine for his efforts.

"You've known each other long then?"

"Well yes. We used to work together years ago. Over 20 years ago now. So yes, long time." James explained.

"Well good for you two!" Frank said, visibly pleased James wasn't just another fly-by-night lover desperate to get lucky with one of his favorite, albeit irregular, customers. "Let me top off that pint for you before you two sit down."

"Thanks very much."

Sabine grabbed James by the arm and stole him away to a corner table. Squeezing in past the fire they faced inwards with their backs against the wall, appreciating the cozy atmosphere as they sipped their drinks and rubbed their legs together under the table like teenagers. The only one paying any attention to them was Sheila, who was enjoying both the heat of the fire and the coolness of the slate floor.

"So what's this then?" James asked, looking at the envelope.

"No idea. But that's Sean's handwriting. He would always leave me things here when we were kids and playing at spies, away from the prying eyes of our parents." Sabine said. "Using the pub to send cigarettes and dirty magazines to each other, pretending they were state secrets or something."

The thought of being younger with her brother brought tears to her eyes again. She wiped away the mistiness and tried to regain control, but her mind involuntarily raced back to summer days playing in the grassy fields next to the river, before life took hold, hurling them in different directions. What would they have done differently had they understood the outcome, she wondered? What would she have done differently had she known she would lose her brother so young? The questions came in a torrent. But no answers.

"Sabine? You okay?" James asked, placing his hand on hers.

"Yes James. Just thinking too much." It was then she knew how lucky she was to have James back in her life. "I don't want to lose you this time. I'm not going to do anything to lose you."

"I love you Sabine. Always have and always will. I knew it from the first moment I saw you. Whether we were together or not, you have always been a part of my life. You've been on my mind constantly, every single day. When I thought you no longer wanted me I tried concentrating on work, traveling, but it did no good. The farther away from you I was the more I missed you."

"There was never a moment when I didn't want you either James. I just didn't… didn't know where it was all going and got scared. Stupid. Now I do know and I'm not scared. I want you. I want you in my life, to share my life, and I want to share yours too. I've missed you. I just wished Sean…" She stopped herself.

No more words were necessary. The closeness and intimate warmth of their bodies were all the communication they needed. Their hands tightened around each other and they leant inwards, sensing, smelling the other's need for comfort, for love, the desire to be loved.

Bringing them both back down to earth, they both knew, that at some point, Sabine would have to open the envelope. Did they really want to return to the real world? Couldn't they simply live in this moment?

But the spell was broken. Sabine tore open the package and emptied the contents on the table. Most of them were writings, Sean's writings. But others were copies of official government documents. And from the seals they were documents from both sides of the Atlantic. How could Sean have gotten them?

"We need to look at these at home." Sabine said, looking around the room to see if anyone else was watching.

"I can't read in this light anyway." James said. "Want another drink first? We don't want to look like we're hurrying out."

"You've got a wonderful way with the ladies, James. I've never been asked to have a drink so nicely before. So yes, let's have another. I'm enjoying the evening and I don't want to rush it away. Maybe it's the new me, appreciating what I have instead of wanting something that isn't there. What have you done to me?"

"God, you're gorgeous!" James said, leaning in for a kiss as he left to go to the bar.

"Another round James?" Frank asked.

"Yes, please, but make it two doubles this time please Frank."

"Yes, she'll do that to you." Frank said, with a wink.

James just smiled and looked back at Sabine. She was looking straight back at him from the shadows with a look that made perfect sense, but a look that he couldn't justly describe. It was a comforting look, satisfied, with the hint of a knowing smile, but only visible when the flames flickered just right. But underneath the facade there was a world-weary sense of foreboding. What was going to happen when they examined Sean's documents? They couldn't ignore them now. And to make things worse, Sabine was in love.

"I haven't seen her look at anyone like that in the 30 years I've known her." Frank whispered. "Be good to her lad."

"I intend to be." James said in all sincerity.

"By the way, you two are behaving like there's something else going on. We're not stupid in here, we pick up on things. That package changed the pair of you in an instant. So if she's in need of help in any way, let me know. She's got friends in this place. And I am her uncle. Ain't that right Harry?"

Harry had been sitting quietly at the bar since they arrived, paying no attention to anyone.

"That's right Frank. Quite the little den of thieves in here." Harry said, giving James a quick, but thorough, friendly glance.

On the way back to their table, James realized that Harry's casual glance had actually been a lot more than that. He had the feeling that he'd just been intimately frisked. That Harry now knew everything there was to know about him, had summed him up completely in the space of half a second. James was a little taken aback by the episode, or the apparent skill in which it was delivered, although not overly worried since Sabine had said they were all friends.

"Who's the guy at the bar." James asked.

"Who? Harry? He hangs about here a lot. Keeps to himself mostly but everyone knows him. He did something heroic years ago, some army-type stuff I think, but he'll never talk about it, and doesn't much like conversations lest he gets asked about it. Why?" Sabine asked.

"Well, he looked at me for a moment and I got the strangest feeling that life stopped for an instant, that he summed me up, and not necessarily in a casual way."

"Yes, that's Harry. Nothing to worry about. If he didn't like you, you'd already know. I've known these fellas for years. They were all soldiers or something once. Some longer ago than others, obviously." Sabine said, glancing over at a couple of older tweed-clad chess players by the window. "The local civilians generally migrate elsewhere. Not that they're unwelcome here, they just don't recognize, or don't understand, the hidden camaraderie in places like this. And just because these fellas aren't talking to each other doesn't mean they're not communicating."

"I see."

"I like coming here because there's no one to bother me. No one trying to flirt with me. And I genuinely like these guys. Salt of the earth and all that." Sabine said.

"I get it. Bit of a *Feathermen* touch going on then?"

"What?" Sabine asked.

"Nothing, just being silly. I like this place. Cheers! To us!"

"Cheers James!"

Frank walked over to the table to collect a couple of empties and laid a large hand on Sabine's shoulder. "Sorry to hear about your brother lass. He was a good lad. If you need anything you just let us know, okay? I mean it. Anything." Frank said.

"Thanks Frank." Sabine said and placed her hand on his. "You're good people."

Chapter Twenty Three

Walter Harrison's CBE, Oxfordshire, England / January 2004

I could hardly accept His Majesty's offer of the Garter when his people have given me the Order of the Boot.
– Winston Churchill

IT WAS SOLELY BY CHANCE James was reading the New Year's Honours List in the *Telegraph*. He surely must have been bored. Sitting by the fire at Sabine's, with Sheila at his feet, he was suffering a little from the previous night's festivities. Now, in the light of day, halfway through his third cup of coffee, he was getting accustomed to the dreadful pounding in his head. It had been a while since he had tied one on like that. Sabine's friends were a bad influence. She, on the other hand, was fine, and relishing the thought of cooking a big greasy breakfast.

It was also by chance that James noticed a familiar name. From the list of 1,350 his eyes somehow caught the 'H's. Maybe because the were in the middle of the page, or maybe because of some subconscious talent, but his eyes picked out Rear Admiral Walter Harrison (retd.) as though an arrow had pointed him there.

"Why the hell would Harrison get an CBE?"[*] James said.

"What? Can't hear you!" Sabine shouted over the sizzling of sausages.

---

[*] Commander of the Most Excellent Order of the British Empire.

James got up too quickly, instantly remembered his hangover as if hit by a hammer and slowly walked to the kitchen, folding the newspaper as he went.

"Here! Look at this." He said. "What d'you think?"

"Who knows. All sorts of people get those things, I never pay any attention. But they just don't give them away do they?"

"Well actually they do sometimes. They gave one to Anthony Blunt, the Russian spy! But Harrison's been out of the service for years, must be as old as dirt by now and hasn't done anything since he retired. It's a bit late to be dishing out a gong for something he might have done 50 years ago. Don't you think?" James said. "It says 'services to the nation,' which is a pretty broad category."

"Yes, I suppose. But I wouldn't know either way. Who'd you suppose would?"

"Don't know. One of your old soldier friends down the pub maybe." James said.

"Any excuse. Literally any damn excuse for a pint. Do I have to start worrying about you? You got more than enough last night by the look of it."

"Worrying, no. Caring, yes." James said, looking at breakfast taking shape in the cast iron skillet. "That looks delicious. And this looks delicious too!" He said, with a hand on Sabine's bottom.

"What have I told you about doing that while I'm cooking?" Sabine scolded.

"Okay. Bad boy. I'll go away again."

"No. Sit over there. This is ready." Sabine said as she slipped the eggs from the skillet onto a plate already filled with sausages, bacon, mushrooms and grilled tomatoes. "The fried bread will be up shortly!"

"This is good! I think you're a keeper." James said, eating a rasher of bacon with his fingers.

"Too right. And you're in too far to back out now." Sabine reminded him.

"I really am a lucky bastard." James said. " I really am," and got tucked into his heart attack on a plate.

"Coffee?" Sabine asked.

"Christ no! I've been drinking coffee all morning, I'm wired enough as it is."

"Okay then. While you're eating that I'm going to get a breath of fresh air and take Sheila for a quick walk. See you when I get back."

Hearing the word 'walk' Sheila came charging into the kitchen, tail spooling up like a helicopter. When Sabine opened the back door Sheila bolted, completely forgetting her age.

"Someone's eager." James said. "Hey. If you go down by the river I'll see you at the pub in an hour or so if you like."

"Sounds like a plan fit for a drunkard. Like I said, didn't you have enough last night?" Sabine asked.

"Oh, I'm over it now, and I've got a bee up my ass to see why Harrison got this medal or whatever you call it." James said.

"OK. See you in a bit. Bring the car down though. You know how stiff poor old Sheila gets after running around the meadow and laying on that slate floor."

Sabine struggled into her green wellies and shouted after Sheila before closing the door, leaving James to enjoy his breakfast in peace. As he lifted the fork to his mouth he could just see Sabine's head disappear behind the stone wall at the edge of the garden. She really was a doll. How could he ever be so lucky?

An hour later James stopped the car outside the pub. Through the little leaded light windows he could just see Sabine sitting at the bar with Harry.

"Hello James." Frank said. "How come you let this gorgeous creature out by herself? Someone might snap her up and steal her away."

"There'd be a fight, Frank. It wouldn't be pretty, but there'd be a fight."

"Spoken like a true gentleman," said Harry.

"Oh, I wouldn't have to do the fighting Harry. She would," James said, and earned a thump for it. "See what I mean."

"Aye, she's a tough one." Harry said. He was smiling but it was hard to notice.

"Did Sabine ask either of you two about the Honours List?" James said. "Specifically about a Rear Admiral Harrison?"

"Aye, she did lad, but no one has ever heard of him. Old fella is he?" Frank asked.

"Yes. Good Lord! He must be 88 by now. I met him back in '82 and he was in his late sixties then I think, because he'd been retired for several years." James said.

"Getting a gong before he snuffs it would be my guess, after doing someone a favor along the way, otherwise he'd already have one for any military service." Harry jutted in. "Typical bullshit if you ask me; just people blowing smoke up each other's asses."

"A fan of the New Year's List then Harry?" Frank asked.

"Not a lot, no. Does it show?"

"Well James, if old Herbert was here he'd probably be able to tell you, but I haven't seen him around in a while. Is he still even alive Harry?" Frank said.

"As far as I know. I haven't seen him in the obits yet." Harry said. "Probably got his head stuck in a book. That, or looking for his glasses."

"Is he local?" James asked.

"Aye. He's up on the Shipton Road, in Fulbrook. Just this side of the Mason's Arms somewhere. I dropped him off around there once." Frank said.

"Aye, that's right, one of the first cottages on Beech Grove." Harry chimed in.

"Thanks. Maybe I'll see if I can search him out tomorrow."

"Why not go up there this afternoon?" Sabine suggested.

"Are you sure? You don't mind?"

"Of course not, it's only a couple of miles outside town. Let's get this over with otherwise it'll be eating at you for days."

They finished their drinks, rousted Sheila from her sleep and ten minutes later were knocking on someone's front door. A tiny little cottage with a thatched roof that had long ago turned black with age and a doorway any normal person would have to duck to go through.

Footsteps approached the other side of the door. "Yes? Who's there?" A concerned female voice said.

"Hello. Sorry to trouble you, but we're looking for Herbert. Frank at the Lamb sent us up." Sabine said.

The door opened immediately. "I know you lass. You're one of the O'Connor kids." An elderly, very rotund lady said.

"Yes, that's right... I'm sorry...I..."

"No, no, it's been a long time lass. I used to run the bakery. You used to come in with your brother and collect the shopping for your mum."

"Oh really. Yes, now I remember, of course. Nice to see you again Mrs... Shipworth?"

"Molly lass. Just Molly. My how you've turned out!"

"I'm 40 years old Mrs Shipworth!... Molly! But thank you, you're too kind!"

"My, how the years have passed." Molly said.

"Who's there Molly? Who're you talking to?" A voice from another room said.

"It's Sabine O' Connor come to see you Herbert."

"Who? Little Sabine? What for? What on earth does she want after all these years?" Herbert shouted.

"Come on in lass. Herbert's only reading in the back room. Can I get you some tea or something?"

"That would be lovely Mrs... I'm sorry... Molly. Thank you." Sabine said.

"In there lass. Herbert's by the window." Molly pointed. "I'll get the kettle on."

Herbert was sitting in an old leather chair with his back to the window so that the natural sunlight drenched the pages of the book in his lap. He looked liked a retired professor; dressed in tweed trousers, checked shirt and what was obviously his favorite and very well-worn cardigan, complete with elbow patches. Perched on the end of his nose were a pair of old round spectacles that he peered over when everyone entered the room.

"Herbert? Hello. I'm Sabine O'Connor from down the road. This is James, a friend of mine."

"Of course! Now I remember little Sabine. Sabine O'Connor. And little Sean. How is Sean these days?" Herbert asked, while removing his glasses.

"I'm afraid Sean passed away in October." Sabine said, not wanting to get into details.

"Oh, I'm sorry lass. He could only have been..."

"Yes, I know, forty-four." Sabine said. "It was a surprise to all of us. A shock really."

"Sorry to have brought it up lass. So? What can I do for you after all this time?" Herbert asked, desperate to change the subject. "Please, sit down. There, please, on the sofa."

"Thanks Herbert." Sabine said. "James?"

James took his cue: "Well, Mr. Shipworth... Frank... down at the Lamb... mentioned that you might have some insight into the New Year's Honours List. I'm specifically trying to find out about a Rear Admiral Harrison. Walter Harrison, retired. He received a CBE." James said.

"Are you a reporter or something lad?"

"Oh no sir. I met Mr. Harrison several years ago and was just interested. That's all." James explained.

"So why not just ask him yourself if you know him?" Herbert said bluntly.

"Well, it's complicated. I suppose it can't hurt now, though. But the last time I spoke to Mr. Harrison it didn't go down too well with the authorities."

"Really? What on earth? Why ever not?" Herbert asked.

"Old war stories they didn't want telling I think. Hush, hush and all that. I was in the navy at the time as well."

"I see, that makes sense maybe. But after all this time you'd think all the secrets would be out?"

"You would think, wouldn't you? Nevertheless, it was made quite clear, to me anyway, that we had both signed the Official Secrets Act."

"I see. Well, off the top of my head I don't know anything, but I can find out if you like. Give me a few days, these things often take some time. Was he some type of hero? Do something spectacular to earn it? A philanthropist or businessman maybe?"

"Not that I'm aware of. And he certainly never alluded to doing anything. He retired as a rear admiral well before the Falklands so I wouldn't think so," James explained. "And he seemed to be living an ordinary life away from everything. What I mean is... he was living on the edge of Dartmoor and didn't seem to be associated with the service any longer, or have any specific interest in it. He seemed to be just enjoying retirement."

"As well he could on an Admiral's pension. Sounds like a favor thing then," said Herbert, visibly not impressed.

"That's exactly what Harry said." Sabine chimed in.

"Oh, really, Harry! How is that grumpy old bastard? Still propping up the bar every day at noon is he?"

"And doing it very well by all accounts," said Sabine.

"Well, Harry and I don't agree on much but we do agree on the pretentious bullcrap that frequents the bloody Honours List!"

"Herbert! Language! Really!" Molly said, as she brought in the tray with tea.

"Ahh, but it's true, it's poppycock," said Herbert, trying to enjoy one more minor expletive before being reprimanded again.

"Excuse my husband Sabine. He gets no better with age."

"Do any of them?" Sabine said, looking over to James and winking.

"Not that I've heard lass. Not that I've heard." Molly seemed resigned to the fact that men just continually get more cranky with age and there's nothing the world can or will ever do to change it.

"Thanks for your help Herbert. I'd appreciate anything you can find out." James said.

"Certainly. It'll give me a break from these," Herbert said, pointing to a stack of used books on the shelf. "Just received them the other day. All on the Burma Campaign. Imphal, Kohima and such. A little research before my next attempt at a book."

"Silchar Track?" Said James.

"Yes. That's right. You know it?" Herbert said, impressed that a relative youngster would know anything of the subject.

"Slightly. My uncle was killed during the fighting for the Dome. I chatted to a few old soldiers about it some time ago, just out of interest." James explained.

"I see. Northamptons were apart of that if I remember?"

"Yes. He was in 1st Battalion." James said.

"What a rotten place to fight a war."

"Yes it was." James said, and room fell quiet for a moment, as if a silent tribute was being paid. "Well, we must go. Thank you very much for the tea Mrs. Shipworth. And thanks for the help Herbert. I look forward to hearing what you find."

"I'll do what I can. Can't promise anything, but you never know. Take care you two. And good to see you again Sabine!"

"Goodbye. Thanks for letting us intrude… and the tea. It was good to see you both again." Sabine said.

Molly steered them both toward the door and they stepped out into glorious sunshine. It was freezing but the sun shone brilliantly, sitting low on the horizon between the two hills. But in a short while it would be dark again. Midwinter dark. On the way back the fields by the river were already bathed in mist, the ponies only visible when they raised their heads or flicked their tails. The river flowed black and gentle, almost enticing someone or something foolish to test its icy waters. At this time of year it was barren of insects and birds and yet a solitary fish could sometimes be seen breaking its surface, creating ripples to disturb its mirrored sheen.

Sheila was glad to get home. On entering the door she went straight to the hearth and slumped down on the rug. Within a minute she was snoring.

"Tea? Coffee? James?"

"No thanks, I'm all caffein'd out today." James said.

"Scotch?"

"Humm? How did you guess?" James said, smiling.

"Intuition. Experience." Sabine said, pouring James a stiff one and adding an equal amount of water. "Do you really think there's something in this thing with Harrison? You haven't spoken to him in 20 years have you?"

"No. I thought it wise to leave them well alone after the last time. Have to be honest, when I heard that they had been murdered it scared the shit out of me. I immediately thought that I was responsible; for digging up something that I shouldn't have been. That's really the moment when I decided to leave it all alone and just get on with my life." James said.

"But they hadn't been murdered. And you wouldn't have been responsible even if they had been." Sabine said. "All you did was pay them a visit."

"Yes. I suppose I knew that deep down. But when something like that happens you have to question yourself, and your motives. And you have a moral duty to protect other people. Besides, it wasn't going anywhere so I decided to leave it well alone."

"So why bring it back now." Sabine asked.

"Coincidences. Too many coincidences. And the fact that I feel I owe Sean something. Feel like I should as least look into what drove him, and why he continued to be so rigorous in his pursuit." James explained. "And why he was killed."

"His death had nothing to do with this. He was simply in Iraq." Sabine said.

"Yes. I know. But it was convenient to someone wasn't it?"

"What the fuck are you saying? That Sean was murdered?"

"No. No. I don't know." James stumbled. "No I'm not. I'm just saying that his death was convenient. That's all. Especially since reading those documents he sent. They meant something to him. There's something in them that he wanted to preserve otherwise he wouldn't have sent them in such an underhand way."

"If you knew him growing up you wouldn't think it underhanded. We used to do that all the time." Sabine explained. "It was probably just his idea of a joke."

"Yes, I know you did. But that was a long time ago, and these papers were important to him. And he's dead now." James said. "I feel guilty that he's dead now. I have a gut feeling that something I know somehow caused his death. And I don't know why. I've been wracking my brain for weeks. But I just don't know why. There's something. I just don't know what it is. I wish I had seen Sean that time back in '82, when everything seemed to be coming to a head. But I didn't. I got scared off, and was desperate to get on with my life after that, concentrate on other things. I wasn't paying attention. Then we never broached the subject again. Sean must have assumed I was no longer interested."

"We've both been all through those documents and we found nothing." Sabine said. "They're just old documents relating to the salvage he was working on. That's all. Nothing incriminating in them at all. They don't even mention what the salvage was."

"They don't even mention what the salvage was." James repeated, already on his way to the desk. He opened the manila envelope again and placed the selection of papers all over the desk, put on his reading glasses and leant over them, reading them quickly one at a time. When he finished one he placed it on the corner of the desk and fetched another until they were all in the corner pile. "They don't even mention what the salvage was." James said, once again, looking straight at Sabine.

They both understood. They had missed the obvious. If the papers had been redacted it would have been obvious. But they hadn't been. There was no reason to redact them because there was nothing incriminating in them at all. So why would something so devoid of information be protected for so long? The documents were valueless; not incriminating or damning in any way. So why would Sean have sent them? None of it made sense.

"Maybe this was his way of telling us he was finally laying it to rest." Sabine suggested, casually picking up a rumpled piece of paper. "This is most unlike Sean. He never wrote poems, certainly never read them. I didn't think he ever even liked them." [*]

---

[*] Politico's War (p. 281). Came to the author anonymously in 2011.

Chapter Twenty Four

Civilian police in the Green Zone, Iraq / February 2004

I don't think we handled the aftermath of the fall of Baghdad as well as we might have. But that's now history.

– Colin Powell

INSIDE THE ONCE OPULENT PALACES of Saddam Hussein strode hundreds of khaki-clad soldiers, contractors, political and technical advisors and civilian administrators. This administrative periphery was, as usual, basking in the glory that had been hard won by the grunts, and many of the white collar desk jockeys were dressed as if they'd won the war by themselves. Desert camouflage was everywhere, as if it had just become a must have fashion accessory. A sick fashion, but a fashion nevertheless. Even Paul Bremer, the State Department's chief administrator in Iraq, was strutting around in a suit and tie accessorized with desert boots. Many wore low-slung pistols as though they were in a Clint Eastwood western, even though the Green Zone was considered safer than most American cities. Indeed, many of its inhabitants would not have been there had it been otherwise.

Departments had hurriedly formed themselves into little cohesive units wherever they could find room, and before anyone could question the validity of them being there. They were all trying to justify their presence by either actually doing something worthwhile or pretending to. To the trained eye it wasn't hard to determine who was doing what and whether it was worth it. But money was no object and no one wanted to rock the boat lest someone else had more clout than they did, and at this stage most of the 'trained eyes' had either left or were elsewhere in Iraq.

In one corner a small team of American civilian policeman, assembled from all over the country, were setting up a rough looking office space. They had a couple of broken tables that had been strapped together and an assortment of stools hastily built from scraps of wood that Iraqi looters had not thought worth stealing. A draped parachute provided them some semblance of privacy. Sometime in the coming days their real office was supposed to arrive, and when it did they would be reassigned another location, so there was no point in expending too much energy on getting comfortable. Again, to the untrained eye the quality of their surroundings made them look particularly amateur when compared to the other groups. But they were far from it. Of all the groups assembled in that chaotic space these few men probably had, collectively, more experience in their field than anyone else. Although that alone wouldn't help when they butted against the burgeoning bureaucracy that was installing itself in every crevice – like a massive bulwark protecting the haphazard organization from reality and common sense.

The policemens' mission was a little ambiguous and they soon realized that their ability to do very much was hampered by their location; there was nothing going on inside the Green Zone. Everything that was going on was going on outside of it, in the greater city of Baghdad, where they were not allowed to venture due to the increasing level of violence that had erupted because of gross political incompetence in not preparing for the obvious.

In order to determine what was happening outside the safety of the Zone they were forced to employ a motley crew of civilians desperate to earn some money. Eventually, ex-Iraqi policemen would show up when they became desperate enough, but for now they were staying away from the Americans in case they got labeled as traitors by one of Iraq's competing factions.

There was no possibility of these American policemen making any dent whatsoever in the escalating crime epidemic that was now endemic, violent and indiscriminate, not in the foreseeable future anyway. Besides, those who committed a crime today might very well be dead tomorrow so what was the point. They felt at a loss. That their presence was a futile experiment, and that they were there solely to instill the impression of something being done. Like it or not, part of the biggest bullshit brigade in history.

The only communication they'd had so far was when a soldier dropped off several black plastic garbage bags. "We don't have any forensics yet, so I guess this stuff is yours," said the soldier, before walking away without saying another word.

So, over the past few days, a couple of them had sifted through an assortment of rubbish. For that's all it was, rubbish. There was the occasional broken watch but nothing of value and nothing that would help them with anything, because they didn't know from even where the items had originated since nothing was tagged. Nevertheless, they sorted each piece into a clothing, rubbish and an everything else pile. The 'everything else' pile was, so far, completely empty.

"I feel like I'm working for the Sally Ann, sorting clothing for the bums on First Ave." Doug, the older of the two, said.

"So why not? Why don't we do that? This stuff is going to waste as it is, there's nothing to link any of it to anything, so why shouldn't someone get some benefit out of it?" Chris, explained.

Being the younger, leaner, and more ambitious member of the group, Chris was still very much ideological. His fewer years of experience hadn't yet squelched a desire to always try and do the right thing. Whereas Doug, having spent what seemed a lifetime in the same role, had learned that doing the right thing often ended up with him in the shit. Although Doug wouldn't have said it was learned, more like beaten into him, and even a dog learns to avoid the unnecessary.

"Because it's crap. Not worth a shit. Look at it," Doug said, raising what looked like a table cloth. "Who the fuck wants this?"

"What's crap to you might be a prize to these people." Chris said. "Anyway, at least we'll be rid of it. It stinks anyway. There must be an NGO around here that'd know what to do with it."

"I know what I'd do with it. But okay. Go for it. Consider that your task for the day." Doug said. "See, we're actually doing something; earning Uncle Sam's money." The others laughed.

In the distance an explosion rocked the air. Then a few seconds later another. The Jordanian militant Zarqawi seemed to be getting his wish and stirring up sectarian violence in an attempt to trigger a civil war. This latest attack was, as usual, against a Shia neighborhood and the coordinated explosions by his Sunni insurgents had all the signs of al-Qaeda – a group not seen in Iraq prior to the invasion and only now present to parasitically exploit an already bad situation by exacerbating Iraq's instability.

"I think I can be happy sorting through this." Chris said, after the concussion wave shook the windows.

"Those poor bastards." Doug said, looking out at the plume of smoke. "This story's not going to be over for very long time."

Chris was going through a few of the coats that were at his feet. Not caring too much for putting his hands in any of the pockets he just held them upside down and waited to see if anything fell out. If nothing did, he threw the coat onto a pile.

On picking up a brown cotton jacket he thought it slightly too heavy on one side. Looking into the pocket he saw nothing, and yet there was clearly something there. He carefully peered into the pocket so as not to get stuck by a needle and saw the hole, and then felt around for an object within the lining.

"Well won't you look at that. The first thing we've seen worth anything."

"It's broke, otherwise it've been stolen by now." Doug said.

Chris pulled open the cover and looked through its viewfinder. The telltale light was still functioning. He pointed it at a nervous Doug and clicked. A second later a whirring sound came from the machine and it started to vibrate. Chris dropped it like a hot rock and jumped backwards.

"Get back. It's gonna blow!" Doug said, kidding him.

"Shit. Those damn bangs got me jittery." Chris said, picking up the camera from the pile of clothes at his feet. He opened the back and pried out the rewound film. "Know if anyone around here develops these?" He asked, looking around.

"Dunno. Gotta be someone." Doug said.

"I'll be back in a while."

Chris stepped through the parachute and out into the cluster that was the Green Zone. He knew there had to be a military intelligence group somewhere, and they always had access to darkrooms. It took him a while but eventually he found a team of British Army green hats that agreed to develop the film for him. After an hour of conversation with people hard to understand he had a stack of photos.

"What you get?" Doug asked on his return.

"Nothing much. Just bad pictures of a shop in some neighborhood by the look of it." Chris said, quickly going through the stack. "Except for this one. Look at this."

In the middle of the photo were two men sitting together in a shop. One of the men was white, the other Iraqi. They were sitting close together, almost leaning in to each other, both were smiling, as were a couple of older men in the periphery of the shot. But the edge of the shot was the interesting part. In an alley across the street a man among a group of masked men was pointing directly towards the camera. In their hands were an assortment of weapons from AK-47s to rocket propelled grenades. One of the grenades was pointing directly toward the camera.

"Christ!" Doug said. "Puts it all into perspective doesn't it?"

Chris put the photo down onto the makeshift desk and looked at the next one. "Not as much as this one does. Shit!"

The photo was blurred, as if it had been taken in a hurry, and the street was full of dust from the convoy of Humvees rushing past in the background. But it was still very obvious that something was tearing its way between two vehicles and heading straight toward whoever was taking the picture. And in the alley other men were firing up at the soldiers atop the vehicles either side of the projectile.

"Well it's obvious what the target wasn't." Doug said. "If they had wanted the convoy they'd have taken out the first or second vehicle, but this one here is at least the third, if not the fourth. Look at those people looking up. They're looking up at a vehicle that's already gone past this point, before the one that we see, meaning that this one here is at least the third. And from that range they wouldn't have missed. They wanted the shop. Or someone in it. But they made it look like an attack on a convoy."

"Shit." Chris said. "What do we do with it?"

"We finally get to earn our money and find out who this whitey is." Doug said, somewhat pleased with himself.

"And pray tell how the fuck do we do that?"

"Old fashioned police work. We ask around, and if we don't find, we ask some more. Can your friends in high places get us more copies of this picture? Bigger pictures? Cropped down to individual faces?" Doug said.

"I'm on it."

Chris returned an hour later with another stack of photos, larger ones that concentrated on all the faces in the original photo. "Here's the friendlies and here are the others, but their faces are covered. But here's some clips of the people further down the street taken from the earlier shots, maybe they'll be able to tell us what went on that day." Chris said.

"Nice." Doug said. "I finally feel like I'm worth something again. Let's see if we can't get these pictures out there into people land, then once we know the location we can organize some security, get out there, and have a chat with some of these locals. The location shouldn't be too hard to figure out. I've seen a board around here somewhere detailing all the attacks."

Chris went searching for the attack board while Doug assembled his motley crew of volunteers to go over the pictures to see if they recognized the street, or the people. None of them claimed to know anything, however, which Doug thought extremely unlikely. If it had been Chicago he'd have known exactly where it was. Clearly this wasn't the most trustworthy group he'd ever worked with.

"And Chris…" Doug shouted after him. "Take some copies of this white guy around to the NGOs. They'll be the only ones with folks like this on the streets."

"Sure thing. But what about the spooks, they're out there too? Or journalists?" Chris asked.

"If he was a spook we wouldn't have this camera and those fuckers would likely be dead already." Doug said. "And if he was a journalist we'd have read about it. No, he's a volunteer. Some poor sap who got himself in the wrong place at the wrong time."

Chris nodded in agreement and continued through the slit in the parachute. Instead of going round to the different 30 to 40 NGO offices, which were spread far and wide, he found a print/copy/scan/fax machine and started sending the pictures out to all the numbers he could find. He then made digital copies of all the photos so that he could email them around to anyone else they thought of. Once that was done he went off searching for the attack board, but after being unsuccessful he asked a well-armed marine at the door where he thought it might have been moved to.

"Sir. It's online now, sir. Get onto the network, you'll find it easy from the portal page. The brass thought the board was bad for morale, sir. Too visible, so they had it removed. Too many journalists wandering round these days I guess." The marine said.

"Thanks, I'll do that." Chris said, impressed by the young marine's professionalism.

Once back behind their Ripstop nylon wall, Chris sent scores of emails to all the NGOs on his list, hoping they wouldn't end up in a slew of junk folders. He then went through the pile of papers they had been given when they arrived, describing pretty much everything that civilians working in the Green Zone should know. Somewhere in the pile was documentation on how to connect to the local Intranet. Chris hated this stuff. Why couldn't he access it from their normal account?

Doug came back with two mugs of coffee. "How's it going?"

"I've faxed and emailed photos to all the NGOs we know about. If I don't hear back from any of them I'll be surprised. But if I don't, I'll get in contact with the ones that have since left and are now in Jordan, Kuwait, or wherever. I'm now trying to get onto the network to access this super-secret attack board of theirs." Chris explained.

"Better you than me." Doug said. "You'll have jump through some hoops to get in there. In fact, if you start now you might get in by... about... Friday. Next week."

Doug picked up the phone and asked to be connected to a Liaison Officer for the 1st Armored Division. After a brief chat Doug had the exact coordinates for the attack in the photos. The battalion officer he was forwarded to remembered it easily because the convoy had thought themselves extremely lucky not to have sustained more casualties that day. He assumed the attack had been performed by an ad-hoc collection of untrained or inexperienced insurgents not closely aligned to any specific group, which would explain their exceptionally poor shooting abilities. But once Doug mentioned the photos the officer realized his soldiers might not have been the intended target after all. The officer then requested copies so that he could see for himself.

"Police work." Doug said, rather smugly, pointing to a location in a Shia neighborhood. "That's where we need to go."

"Could get a little sporty. Want me to arrange security?"

"I'd sooner stay away from the trigger-happy, gun-toting cowboys. And I don't much want to show up in a convoy of blacked out SUVs. It'd attract too much attention and scare everyone away." Doug said.

With that the phone rang. It was the battalion officer again.

"If you guys want to get to that neighborhood we're getting a patrol organized. You could tag along if you like." The officer explained. "After seeing those photos our CO wants to know what happened that day too."

"Excellent. Just let me know where and when."

"Tomorrow morning. 07:00. We'll have a driver pick you up. Vests, helmets and boots are required. And if you want to talk to the locals more easily don't have any visible weapons or wear any patriotic insignia. And... oh yes, remove your shades when you talk to them. It's polite, and they might respect that."

Doug hung up the phone. "Do we have helmets?" He asked.

"Hell no. But we can borrow or steal a couple. There's people here who will never leave this place and won't miss them." Chris said. "I'll go see what I can steal."

"We'll need an interpreter as well. I don't trust any of our guys. Maybe your intel friends will know someone." Doug said.

"I'll go ask them." Chris said, leaving once again.

On his way through the mass of organized chaos that was the palace these days he started to think of what it might be like outside the safety of the Green Zone. He'd heard some pretty frightening first-hand accounts and he'd certainly seen the news reports. But he still didn't know what it was actually like to be outside; what it felt like, smelt like, how nervous he would be, or, more importantly, what every man fears, how he would react if something went terribly wrong. He wasn't sure that he was much looking forward to it. And he wasn't about to tell his wife, Sue, who was already at home worrying about him while trying to take care of their baby. She hadn't wanted him to go, but they needed the extra money in order to get out of the cramped apartment and into a house.

Like most Americans trying to live the dream and conform to society, they didn't think they could be a family until they owned their own piece of real estate, and they were willing to mortgage their safety and sanity, and even the very sanctity of their marriage, in order to achieve that goal.

Chapter Twenty Five

Visitors, Oxfordshire, England / February 2004

Violence does, in truth, recoil upon the violent, and the schemer falls into the pit which he digs for another.

– Arthur Conan Doyle

I'M SORRY JAMES, IT TOOK ME far too long to get back to you. It was harder than I thought to find anything on this navy chap of yours, this Harrison fella." Herbert said.

"That's fine Herbert." James said. "Thanks for spending so much time on it. I really didn't want…"

"No, no. No trouble at all. It wasn't that I was fully involved with it, I just had to wait for others to get back to me. And they took their time, obviously." Herbert said.

It was noon, Harry strode into the pub like he owned it and hoisted himself onto his regular stool. "Aha, I thought you might be dead b'now," he said, leaning forward to look past James at Herbert. "We haven't seen you for so long."

"Nice to see you too Harry. How's the missus?" Herbert said, looking straight ahead.

"Aye, she fine, thanks. Well she is now that I'm here, I'm sure." Harry said. "What are you two up to? You look like a couple of kids, all huddled over and whispering. Or d'you just fancy each other?"

"Hello Harry. Herbert is just helping me out with some research. Nothing special." James explained.

"It's about that Harrison fella isn't it? That knob who just got a government gong." Harry said.

"Yes, it is Harry. You're right." James said. "Frank, can we get another round please. Harry too. And one for yourself."

"Thanks lad, don't mind if I do. I'll have a half," said Frank, already pulling Harry's beer.

Herbert went on to explain to his new audience that no one he'd contacted had the slightest notion of why Harrison had received a CBE. They all came to the same conclusion that he must have done somebody very important a favor, a very big favor. But there was no inclination anywhere as to what it might have been. The decision to award Harrison a CBE had clearly come from the very top. And the very top was usually nothing less than the Cabinet, or Number Ten.

"And it took you a month to figure this out." Harry said. "Seriously? A month?"

"I like to make certain. Making certain takes time." Herbert responded. "All my contacts looked into this quite deeply and they are all, to a man, as perplexed about this as we are, even though they are still connected to the workings of government. Still in the loop, as it were."

"I agree we all thought the same when I mentioned it before. But I'm still indebted to Herbert for looking into it and clarifying it, and for spending so much time on it. Thank you Herbert," said James, raising his glass, trying to quell the rising animosity.

"You're very welcome James. Cheers!" Herbert said.

"So what are you going to do with this brilliant piece of deduction Sherlock?" Harry asked.

"I have no idea." James said, honestly.

"Brilliant. Just brilliant. You're like a couple of bleeding Watsons." Harry said, soaking down a quarter of his pint and staring at the wall in disbelief. "Hey, I've got an idea. Why don't you just bloody go and ask this fella straight up?"

"I might have to." James admitted.

"He'll either have a good answer, for which there's nothing to worry about, or he'll dance around the question and feed you a string of bullshit." Harry said. "You can recognize bullshit can't you lad?"

"Yes, I think I can manage to do that." James said.

"Well there you go then. Problem solved," said Harry.

James had no option but to take Harry's advice and two days later he was pulling off the A38 and heading toward Bovey in Sabine's old Jaguar. The tree-lined avenue on Bovey Straight was bare of leaves but the densely curled branches completely overhanging the road shut out much of the winter light and created the impression of driving through a tall tunnel. On the right was Bovey Heath, the historic civil war battlefield, badly neglected and used for off-roading and illegal dumping of construction rubbish. James didn't understand how the local council could allow that to happen to such an historic area. It seemed to be an insult to all the Englishman who'd fought there, on either side.

Before reaching the town, James turned off and headed up toward the moor, first along Haytor Road and then forking right toward Manaton. A further few hundred yards he turned down a barely used, very narrow, single track lane with grass growing in the middle where countless horses had dropped manure over the decades. The lane soon turned very steep and he had trouble stopping in time outside the Harrison's house, still with its perfectly manicured lawns, hedges and flower beds.

There was no obvious movement anywhere as James went up to knock on the old wooden door. But then he thought he saw a curtain move out of the corner of his eye, but couldn't be sure. He knocked again. About to leave, he heard shuffling inside and the latch being released. The door opened to an elderly lady who clearly had trouble getting around.

"Yes? Can I help you?" She asked.

"Mrs. Harrison? It's James. James Devlin. Do you remember me?"

"Devlin? No. What do you want?"

"I'd like to speak to Walter... Mr. Harrison if I could. We met many many years ago."

"Oh, I don't think so. Walter is not very well currently. Is it important? Does he know you?"

"I'm sorry to hear that Mrs. Harrison. But yes, Walter does know me. I came by many years ago to ask him about his time in the navy. Do you remember? I wanted to congratulate him on his CBE. I was surprised... pleasantly surprised to hear that Walter was in the Honours List." James explained, hoping the compliment would get him past Mrs. Harrison, who had obviously turned into the household gatekeeper.

"Walter doesn't like to talk about that to strangers."

"I see. But could you possibly tell me for what specifically he received it?"

"Services to the nation." Mrs. Harrison explained very curtly. "Now if you'll excuse me I have to go and check on Walter. He's not very well currently."

There seemed little point in continuing so James passed on his thanks and left. As he did, he noticed definite movement this time of an upstairs curtain. "Not bed bound then," he murmured.

He opened the heavy Jaguar door and casually glanced back before getting inside. There was something fishy going on, he just knew it. He turned on the ignition and the old inline six cylinder engine purred to life. It was no longer considered a fast car by any standards but it was solid, with an old-fashioned luxuriousness, and with its weight it still possessed a bit of old world shuffle. He shoved the gear stick forward and headed back up the steep incline to the Manaton Road, being careful not to scratch the bodywork on the overgrown brambles either side of the lane. Sabine would not be pleased.

He stopped for lunch in Bovey, at the Dolphin. Enjoying a whole, freshly battered cod and chips with lashings of vinegar. An hour later James was accelerating down the slip road to get back onto the A38, with the sun dipping behind him.

Sabine's old Jag was a pleasure to drive and his mind began to roam as the two lane A38 turned into three and then into the M5. As the car slid smoothly along the newly laid tarmac at 75mph the interior warmth and smell of old leather reminded him of childhood trips to the country. The only thing missing was his mother's subtle wafting perfume mixed with the sweet smokiness of his father's favorite pipe tobacco. It was a pleasant smell even as a child. It made him feel safe, comfortable, and he remembered the pleasure of inhaling the air as he leant against the window, watching lush green fields full of red and white cows roll by mile after mile. James, reminiscing, looked down at the ashtray and could almost see his father's pipe balancing delicately on the narrow ledge, his mother always wary of it falling onto the carpet while going around a corner, but his father casually picking it up, always at exactly the right moment before it fell. Even then James knew that his father was just teasing.

The realization hit James like a brick: Pipe smoke. His old CO never smoked and few people were of senior enough rank at the Admiralty to be allowed to smoke inside in those days. Harrison must have been in the CO's office just prior to James requesting permission to go to the States. It must also have been Harrison who had alerted the policeman, Killian, who had questioned him. Had Harrison been playing him all this time?

James was concentrating too much and trying to remember what had happened all those years ago at the Admiralty. Then with the increased traffic at Bristol he hadn't noticed the grey Vauxhall racing down the slip road to take up position a few cars behind.

He still hadn't noticed when he left the M5, joined the M4, and left the motorway at Swindon. But once on the smaller road and heading north toward Burford the car became obvious. Not for being right behind him. Completely the opposite, in fact. It was staying back a long way, not getting any further behind and not getting any closer. All the other cars were either gaining, racing past him, or making turns off the road. Those that he passed he never saw again. This one just hung there, even when he slowed down to go through the small villages it never got closer. It was only obvious because it was trying hard not to be.

James decided to see one way or the another if he was right, or if he was just paranoid. After going through one of the villages at a sedate 30mph he immediately sped up, hauling the Jag up to 80mph on the gently curving road. The car handled well, just lolling a little on some of the tighter bends but its wide tires stuck to the surface like glue. Once he knew he was out of sight he waited to see a road sign warning of a junction ahead and slowed quickly, without skidding, in order to make the tight right turn cleanly. He floored the accelerator again and the car belted up the narrow lane, staying hidden from view behind the tall hedges. Once over a hill he found an opening to a field, turned the car around and cruised back up to the reverse side of the hill so that he could see the main road a hundred yards away.

He shut off the engine and wound down the window. In the distance he could hear the repeated high pitched whine of a powerful turbocharged motor as it was threaded up through the gears. A few seconds later the Vauxhall passed the junction in front of him in a flash of grey, throwing up road debris in its wake. When he heard the angry engine disappear into the next valley he restarted the Jag and headed back toward Swindon, now being more aware of everything around him and driving the car forcefully but not illegally – he wanted no excuse to be stopped.

If it were the authorities after him they'd be able to track him using the overhead cameras on the bridges so he needed to ditch the Jag as soon as possible. He reversed his tracks and drove back down the M4, leaving the motorway this time at Bristol.

He hated driving to Bristol Airport from this direction but it couldn't be helped. He needed to park the car safely and get another, and the airport provided the best option. Once through the city he was only a few miles from the airport when he noticed in his rear-view mirror a dark car gaining on him unusually quickly, passing other vehicles with ease. Then he heard the siren and saw the flashing blue lights in the grill. An unmarked police car.

There was nowhere for him to go at this point. There were no intersections on this piece of road until the airport and he knew that will have been cordoned off. All the cars behind him were pulling over to the side of the road and letting the police car past. Four hundred yards. Three hundred. Two. A hundred yards. James resigned himself and steered the Jag to the left, took a deep breath and waited.

The police car surged past him without a thought and everyone started to get back onto the road. James sighed relief but knew he was still not out of trouble. Maybe they were waiting for him ahead. Maybe the person watching the overhead cameras had picked him up already and knew where he was going. "Enough maybes," he thought to himself, and continued toward the airport, worried that he was, indeed, fast becoming paranoid.

Once there he parked the Jag in the long term lot and strode casually into the terminal. Buying a cheap baseball cap he then went upstairs to the bar and ordered a whiskey before sitting down with a view over the concourse below. From here he could see if anyone was either looking out for him or watching him. He picked up a paper from a vacant seat and made it look as though he was reading. An hour later he decided that he had worried enough, unnecessarily, and returned downstairs to rent a car.

James was soon back on the M5 and heading north toward Cheltenham in a nondescript green Honda. Before reaching Cheltenham he left the motorway and drove across country to join the A40 at Shipton. Every once in a while turning off the road or waiting in a lay-by to check see if anyone was following.

Arriving at Burford he forked off onto Sheep Street without slowing and parked outside the Lamb.

"Can I use your phone Frank?" James asked.

"Sure lad, here you go. Need a beer?"

"Whiskey would be great, thanks!" James said.

There was no answer at Sabine's and the message system was off. The message system was never switched off.

"Has anyone seen Sabine?" James asked.

Everyone looked to each other and shook their heads.

"Something up James? You two had a fight or something?" Harry asked.

"No. Nothing like that. It's just... I've had a strange day... someone was following me. Cops, spooks, someone, I don't know, but I think they might be here. I'm a little worried about Sabine if she's not answering the phone." James explained.

"Well that's different. Who'd you say followed you?" Harry's ire was up. "Spooks you say? You mean our spooks, MI5, or someone else's spooks? What've you been up to lad?"

"I went to see Harrison like you suggested. On the way back I noticed a car following me back up to Burford from Swindon. But I lost them, doubled back, ditched the Jag and got another car."

"Sabine's Jag? Oh shit lad! She's not going to be chuffed with you." Frank said.

"No, no. It's fine. It's at the airport. But Sabine... I'm worried about Sabine since they must know whose Jag it was." James said.

"Yes! You're right. We should go up to the house and see." Frank said.

"Not so fast. If something's not right up there you don't want to just waltz on in." Harry said. "Tell you what, no one knows me, I'll take a stroll over there and see what's gong on, casual like, like a local yokel. What sort of car was following you?"

"Grey. A bigger Vauxhall or something. Powerful motor, had a turbo. Maybe I should come with you?" James said.

"No lad, you stay put. I'm just going to have a little looksee. Like I was walking the dog." Harry said.

"Okay. Thanks Harry."

Harry picked up his stick and strode out the door like a marine on a mission, his old hobnail boots crushing the pavement every smart step. Such boots still weren't out of place among the old retirees of Burford and few thought anything of the sound of an army platoon marching down the street past their windows.

Reaching Sabine's house, Harry walked up to the door full of confidence and knocked.

Nothing.

He knocked again, louder this time.

There was no sound from inside the house so he peered through the small window but could see nothing. Harry turned and walked back down the path to the garage, prying open the door just enough to see inside. Sabine's Jag was obviously not there, but the car in its place was grey. Harry pried open the door a little more and the squeak of the hinge masked the sound of the dull thud he felt on his head before collapsing to the ground like sack of potatoes.

He didn't know how long he'd been out but when he came to he was sitting in a chair, his upper arms tied to the Aga behind him and being confronted by two men. One of them very large and unbelievably ugly.

"Where's Devlin?" The ugly one said.

"Who? What's going on?" Harry said, still trying to make sense of the situation.

"Where's Devlin? We won't ask you again nicely."

"I don't know. I thought he was here," Harry answered.

The fist slamming against his jaw was something Harry had not experienced in a long time. But he instantly remembered the feeling, or lack of it. For some reason, even as a kid, he'd never been too bothered about being punched in the face, so long as his nose wasn't broken. But he made it look like it did and let out a yell, and groaned for effect.

"Where's Devlin?" The larger man said again.

"I just told you. I don't fuckin' know. I though he was here, that's why I came here." Harry said, spitting out a little blood from the inside of his mouth.

This time Harry saw the punch coming, turned his head a little and stiffened his chin. There was a slight crack as the fist made contact with the edge of his jaw. Harry knew that it wasn't his jaw, so the man must have cracked a finger, but he wasn't letting on.

"Where the fuck is Devlin?"

"We could go on like this all night. I just told you. I don't fucking know."

This time the punch came on the other side of his face. And he spat out a little more blood.

"Maybe the old codger doesn't know," the other man said.

"He knows."

Another not so crisp left hander planted itself against his upper cheek and Harry could feel blood start to trickle down from a cut beneath his eye, caused by the ring on the man's finger.

Spitting out some more blood and feeling his eye start to close, he said, "If I knew don't you think I'd tell you. I haven't had a beating like this in my life!" He lied. Harry'd had many beatings in his younger years. Never shy about being vocal in the wrong company often invited it. Although he'd always said that even when losing the other guy had never much enjoyed winning.

"You've got the face of a boxer you old fool. And if you hadn't looked in the garage you might have been able to see it again. But since you did, we can't just let you go walking out of here can we," the large man said, picking out a knife from the cutlery drawer.

Harry was starting to get seriously nervous now, fisticuffs was one thing, knives were different. Events were surpassing a simple beating and from his one good eye he could see the man start to expertly sharpen the blade on the kitchen steel. Rather too expertly for Harry's liking.

"Last chance. Where's Devlin?" The man said.

"I don't know. I seriously fucking don't know. Who are you guys?" Harry said, clearly getting nervous.

"Your choice," the man said, approaching with the knife.

The blast from the shotgun inside the enclosed stone kitchen was like an explosion. Everyone was immediately stunned and deafened for a few seconds as they each looked around to see where it had come from and where it had gone. Everyone who was there was still there, except there was now an extra. Sabine was standing in the corner, having just emerged from the hidden kitchen staircase that all the old local houses had. In her hands was an old double-barreled English shotgun, into which she had just replaced the expended shell with surprising dexterity.

"That was birdshot. These next two are not." Sabine said, almost too calmly while pulling back the hammers. "Cut him loose. And remember, if you slip, this thing will take your fucking head off." She said, bringing the long gun up to her shoulder and pointing it towards the ugly man's head.

Harry's ropes were cut and he stumbled from the chair, rubbing the side of his face. "Nice timing. I thought I was about to be kebabbed." He said. "You know these guests of yours?"

"Nope. But we're about to find out." Sabine said seriously. "Sit down you two, over there," pointing to the other side of the large kitchen table. "Hands on the table." Then, looking to see that Harry was okay: "Search them Harry."

"Nothing, not even a driving license. Real incognito couple of fellas we got here. Apparently no one will miss 'em." Harry said. "We could slot them, dump them in the river and no one would ever know. And we'd inherit a nice car in the process."

Harry looked down at the ugly man's right hand. One of the man's knuckles was starting to swell. "Just do that on me did yer? You should learn how to throw a punch if you're gonna be in this line of work."

With that Harry clenched his old farmhand fist and landed a colossal haymaker that rocked the man's brain and put him out cold, leaving him slumped motionless on the floor. "Kind of like that." Harry said, smiling to himself.

"Well done Harry, he's going to be sleeping for a while and not answering any questions." Sabine said, looking cross. "Please be a little more subtle with the other one." Sabine had never before seen this side of Harry but she had always suspected it might be there, hiding deep under the surface just ready to emerge once something, or someone, got his ire up.

"Looks like the tables have turned, eh fella? What's this all about? Who sent you? And why are you looking for Mr. Devlin?" Harry said, looking down at the smaller man who was clearly very nervous now that he'd seen his larger friend put down with so little effort.

"You'd have to ask him." The man said, nodding toward his fallen comrade. "He got the info, I'm just here backing him up."

"And how'd that work out for him? You 'backing him up' I mean?" Harry said, mocking the man.

"Not so well by the look of it." Sabine chimed in, looking at the motionless lump on the floor.

"Not by a long shot." Harry said. "So, what's it to be, the easy way or the hard way? Either way is okay with me. I could do with the practice."

"We got a call to scare Devlin off. Rough him up a bit. That's all." The man said.

"Who from?" Harry said.

"We don't know. It's a contract. We're told where to go and what to do, and we do it. We don't know what it's for or who it's for. We don't need to know, and don't want to know."

"You seriously expect me to believe this crap," Harry said.

"It's the truth."

"Point that thing at his foot." Harry said to Sabine. "And if I get to five, pull the damn trigger."

"You can't be serious? No one was supposed to get hurt." And then looking at Harry's face, the man said, "Not really hurt."

"One. Two. Three." Harry nodded to Sabine, who grabbed the gun tighter. "Four…"

"Okay! Okay! I heard a name. Harrison. That's all I know."

"So, this Harrison called you all by himself?" Sabine asked, still pointing the barrel at the man's foot and enjoying it.

"No. I don't know who set this up. All I know is that it's for Harrison. Someone doesn't want him bothered. Said he was being harassed and wants it stopped."

The man on the floor started to move and Harry placed his foot on the swollen finger, causing him to yell. "So, awake are we? How 'bout you tell me who called you?"

"Fuck you." The man said, trying unsuccessfully to remove his hand from beneath Harry's hobnail boots.

"Wrong answer." Harry put all his weight on one foot and there was a distinct crack. "All I have to do is grind my foot into the ground and you'll lose the use of your hand for a month." Harry explained. "Hobnails are good for that."

"Okay! Okay." The man shouted in pain. "All we have is a phone number. No name, nothing else. It's in my pocket."

"Using your other hand, get it out and put it on the table," Harry said, being careful not to allow the man any leverage.

Reaching across to his offside coin pocket, he said, "Here, that's all we know."

Harry looked at Sabine and nodded again. She stepped back, still covering the two men. "Get the fuck out of here." Harry said. "But remember, if I smell you around again I'll turn you both into pig food. Understand? Your fault, nobody's fault. If I see you…"

With that, Sabine handed the shotgun to Harry and grabbed her camera. "Smile gentlemen," she said. "Your holiday snaps are going round to the local pubs, just to make sure your faces are known. And if you come around here again you'll be lucky if all we do is give copies to the police. There's a big slurry pit just waiting for the likes of you. So, bye bye now."

The smaller man helped his friend off the floor and out the door. His right eye was completely closed and his hand was a broken mess. He wouldn't be hitting anyone for quite a while.

As they were leaving Harry told them: "Now don't go telling tales out of school. You might get to keep your wages if your employer thinks you were successful. And we won't tell a soul."

The grey Vauxhall emerged slowly from the garage and headed off down the narrow lane.

"Think they'll come back?" Sabine asked.

"I wouldn't have let them go if I thought they'd be back." Harry said, quite sincerely. So sincerely, in fact, that Sabine felt a shiver go up her spine. "But what you and James need to do is find somewhere else to stay for a while, just in case. Someone is getting very serious and there's no telling where this might lead."

That idea had already been on Sabine's mind and she started to shake a little as the realization of what she had just done sank in.

Grabbing a couple of glasses and a bottle of Jameson from the counter, Harry poured them both a stiff whiskey. "Drink this lass. You'll be alright, you did great. You saved my sorry ass! James is one lucky fella!"

Chapter Twenty Six

Streets of Baghdad, Iraq / February 2004

God has given such brave soldiers to this Crown that, if they do not frighten our neighbours, at least they prevent us from being frightened by them.

– Queen Elizabeth I

THE HEAT INSIDE THE HUMVEE was incredible and their body armor just compounded the misery as they approached the gate to the Green Zone. In a few seconds they would be on the outside. Doing what thousands of young soldiers had been doing, and would be doing for many more years to come. Driving through the streets in convoy most Iraqis seemed to just ignore them. But now and again, whether it was Chris's imagination or not, he caught the occasional glimpse of pure hatred staring back at him. It was chilling. One man in particular seemed to be very interested in their journey and as Chris looked behind him the man dialed a number and started talking.

"Don't worry about him," the young sergeant said, seeing Chris do a double-take. "The ones you need to worry about are on the roofs, watching everything we do and letting others know where we're going, and then trying to make something happen when we get to where they think we're going. But we don't take direct routes and we have an eye in the sky watching for possible traffic jams. Plus we try not to stay on the grid too long unless we've got a protective cordon. Today we've got some heavies watching the area, so we should be okay. It takes the insurgents time to set something up as well, they've learned that lesson the hard way, they can't compete against our firepower. So we use that, and our eyes in the sky can spot if traffic is merging toward us, because they're usually in a hurry too."

Chris felt mildly comforted. Not so much for what the young man said, but for the sergeant's professional demeanor, and seemingly, as much as possible given his surroundings, being in control of the situation. The sergeant reminded him of those young lads he'd seen in movies, storming ashore on some foreign land, and having the wrinkled expressionless experience of someone twice their age. Chris knew it was just ingrained, trained, military competence, but it was, nevertheless, nicely reassuring to hear while he was sweating buckets and being buffeted backwards and forwards inside an armored can that was being driven aggressively over the dusty pockmarked streets.

"I'll take your word for that." Chris said.

The sergeant showed the merest flicker of a smile before regaining his hardened, stoic face, but in that instant Chris realized just how young this boy was. Probably not a day past 22. He looked around and saw the other soldiers were probably even younger, their faces though hardened and obscured by helmets and sporty sunglasses. Any expression of boyish youth was hidden behind an element of cautious fear that was itself cloaked. These were, indeed, brave young lads to be doing this job day in and day out for months on end.

Chris had to admit to himself that despite his obvious trepidation there was a certain thrill in being part of this convoy. The projected power was considerable and the heftiness of the vehicle provided some sense of safety, even if it wasn't completely warranted. The thrill, though, Chris decided, was not so much the vehicle, the convoy, or the projection of power, but being among the soldiers. Soldiers in a real situation. Moreover, he realized, by simple fortune of birth he'd been lucky to have been born on this side of the fight, with the power and might, and not on the other, with the hope of a decent future dwindling daily.

Looking out from the small armored windows of the Humvee Chris could see what living on the unfortunate other side meant. For instance, there was more technology and wealth inside Chris's vehicle than most of the people mingling outside in the streets would ever possess in their lifetimes. It was surreal and he felt somewhat guilty. Guilty that all the wealth inside their rugged, sand-colored vehicle was designed solely for fighting, and killing, in a voluntary war. Whereas the miniscule wealth the people on the streets possessed was reserved solely for basic survival in a world not of their making and in a country arbitrarily sliced from a lost empire.

Chris hadn't noticed the mule cart emerging from an alley, but the driver had. He accelerated to cut it off before it had a chance to block the street and cause their convoy to concertina into a possible killing zone. The mule reared backwards in fear at the oncoming vehicle and turned to run, twisting the shafts of the cart and spilling all its contents, leaving the owner in two minds whether to first tend his mule or the contents that were now strewn across the road.

The quick acceleration had caught the second driver unawares and there was now a larger gap between the two vehicles, a gap large enough for a small passenger bus to unwittingly merge with the convoy. A few rounds fired from the gunner on top into the road directly in front of the bus quickly dissuaded its driver from continuing and it pulled off the road immediately.

But that little action in the space of a hundred yards, albeit in self-preservation, had upset the whole neighborhood. Chris could see an obvious change in people's expressions; there were now hard cold stares, shouts and waved fists. Then the inevitable rocks thrown by unemployed youths hitting the armored glass, having little effect and thereby making the youths even more brazen.

"Welcome to the neighborhood." The sergeant said.

"Feels like freaking LA," a voice said.

"It'll quiet down once we get away from here, but it's limited our time on the ground. We've pissed off some people and they'll be trying to set something up." The young sergeant said.

"How much further?" Chris asked.

"Five minutes, seven most." Said the sergeant. "The armor is already in place and we've got air support. Once we get there you two do what you need, our guys will look after you. But if any of us says move, you move with us immediately, no questions, and stick to us like glue."

"Got it." Chris said.

A short while later after taking several obscuring turns they arrived outside of what used to be the corner teahouse. The walls had been hastily rebuilt and the space merged with the neighboring shop, now used for storing an assortment of household electrical items. There was nothing any longer that resembled a tea shop.

Chris looked over the street and saw the alley from where the rocket had been fired. In it was standing a soldier nervously watching the rooftops, his rifle at the ready. Behind him two more soldiers were at the far end of the alley, where an iron gate led to the small courtyard of a house. Chris and Doug walked across the street and went up the alley. Two more soldiers followed.

"Where does this lead?" Chris asked.

"A private residence, more money than most of the others around here. We had it checked out right after the attack, and a team arrived to question the occupants but they found nothing. We figure the attackers probably hopped over the wall and made their way to a waiting vehicle on the next street." One of the soldiers said. "The house is empty now. The neighbors over here said the occupants just moved out a few days ago. Probably left the country like everyone else is doing. And like I'd like to do."

"Were the occupants questioned?" Doug asked.

"You'd have to ask the Lieutenant sir."

"I will." Doug said.

"Why would they hop over the wall when they could go right through the house onto the next street?" Chris asked.

"That's what I was thinking." Doug said.

They returned to the corner shop and attempted to ask some of the other storekeepers if they remembered seeing anything, but were met with the usual protective ignorance. No one was about to risk their lives, and the lives of their family for that matter, by inadvertently or otherwise saying the wrong thing and ratting on a local insurgent. The locals knew when to keep their mouths shut.

"We're done here," the sergeant said. "Let's load up. We're past our sell-by-date in this location."

Chris and Doug were manhandled back to the Humvee. As everyone crawled inside and rearranged their weapons, backpacks and armor before sitting down the interior quickly filled with fine dust. Sweat was pouring from everyone, creating little rivulets down everyone's faces. One soldier removed his helmet to grab a piece of material to daub his sweat before the sergeant reprimanded the carelessness.

"That's when you get hit! Replace it soldier!" He said. "Don't tempt fate when you're fucking sitting next to me!" The soldier duly complied, briefly looking sheepish for being chastised in front of his comrades. But no one cared, they each gave it and each took it. Everyone knew the drill.

Once back inside the safety of the Green Zone Chris and Doug began to relax. Neither of them had fully realized how tense they had become. Adrenaline had taken hold and now that it was wearing off they became tired. It was a relief to finally be able to remove the body armor and they dumped it unceremoniously on the floor in their little corner of the building before chugging down a quart of water each. Their t-shirts were drenched with sweat and it felt as though their boots were full of water. "How those guys do it and keep it up I'll never know," Doug said.

"Youth." Chris replied. "Did you see how young that sergeant was? He couldn't have been twenty-two. And in charge of a group barely out of school."

"Responsibility comes quick these days, I guess." Doug said. "That's war."

Chris didn't reply. He was already staring at the computer screen and deep in thought. The question on his mind was who had questioned the owners of the house? It seemed to be the only logical way out of the alley. And yet there was no report anywhere in the records. Not even in the platoon logs of the soldiers after the attack had taken place. He picked up the phone.

"We weren't involved in that. For some reason the Brits sent a team down." The battalion officer explained.

"So we don't share records with our allies?" Chris asked.

"We do, but it takes time for information to trickle down to the right department."

"No wonder it's a fucking cluster. The left hand doesn't know what the right's doing." Chris said.

"That about sums it up. Anything else?" The officer asked, obviously busy with more pressing matters.

"Yes. The regiment that might have been used for this?"

"Oh, these folks weren't part of a regular regiment. No cap badges. No rank insignia."

"SAS?" Chris asked.

"I doubt it. They're too busy elsewhere for that kind of work. Basra for instance. Security services more likely. MI6 maybe."

"You're shitting me! That stuff'll be in wraps for years. It's like pulling teeth getting anything from those limeys. Unless, of course, they're trying to sell a fucking war." Chris said cynically.

"Well, that's your job. If there's nothing else I've got reports of my own to write."

"No, thanks. I'll let you know if I find anything." Chris said, rather hopefully. "Someone's got to share the damn information." And put the phone down.

"No luck then?" Doug asked.

"Not a lot, no. But why would the Brits use security services to perform a simple interview?" Chris said, not really expecting an answer.

"Because the guy who died was a Brit," Doug said, passing over a photo of Sean O'Connor.

"Where'd you get this?" Chris asked.

"It was sitting right here. Someone left it here while we were out. No message though. Just the photo with the name on the back. But it's the same guy as in the photos isn't it."

"Sure looks like it."

"Well at least we now have a name." Doug said. "Why wasn't it in the papers? Someone had to have known and the guy's family must have been informed. But it's still not MI6 stuff. That's way beneath their pay grade."

"Unless it wasn't beneath their pay grade." Chris said. "From the photos we're going on the idea that the shop was the target, or at least someone inside the shop. If it was a simple assassination, by one side or the other, they're never usually worried about deception. Instead, they brag about their actions because their murders are meant as warnings. And they either use indiscriminate bombs, kidnapping and decapitation, or a bullet to the head while walking down the street. This was conducted to make it look like an attack on a convoy, but it wasn't. Neither the Shia nor the Sunni's do that. There's no reason for them to."

"But," Doug said. "There's no way they could have known the army would be in the area. Not at the same time as their target, and they must have been following him pretty closely in order to get this set up in the time that he stayed in one place."

"Yes, you're right. There was no way for them to know about the convoy. But they used it. It would have been safer for them just to have waited another minute or so for the army to pass on by. What they did was instinctual. Whoever they are saw and utilized an opportunity, like pros," Chris explained.

"If you're right, this might prove to be above our pay grade." Doug said.

"That's what worries me," said Chris.

Chapter Twenty Seven

Sabine and James, Nakskov, Denmark / July 2004

By repetition, each lie becomes an irreversible fact upon which other lies are constructed.

– John le Carré

JAMES SEEMED AS IF HE WAS SLEEPING, but beneath his sunglasses his eyes were wide open. In the distance a beautiful woman, clad only in a skimpy white bikini, was emerging from the gentle Baltic surf. The sun, low and off to the west, accentuated every curve of her body as she walked casually, but purposefully, from the water. She shook her head and the water cascaded around her as she ran her fingers through her hair; being more blonde than usual from days in the northern sun.

James thought himself lucky. This wonderful woman was walking directly towards him. Her legs, fit and taut from thrice weekly runs, merged at that marvelous triangle of light just beneath the crotch. She was full of confidence and strutting across the sand as the evening sun glistened on her wet skin, tanned to the perfect shade. Only a few yards away now, she turned, faced the water and bent over to pick up a towel.

"Like what you see?" She asked.

"The scenery is spectacular. I think I might love you." James replied.

"After last night you'd better," she said.

Sabine walked closer and bent down to kiss him. Her skin smelled of sun and salt water and the pretty little freckles on her nose were in full bloom. James grabbed her buttocks and pulled her closer. "God I do love you." He said.

"Like I said, you'd better, because I adore you too. Are we ready for dinner?"

"Yes we are!" James said, before packing up the chairs.

Sabine removed her wet bikini, unconcerned for anyone who might be watching, or maybe because someone might be watching, and put on a pair of tight shorts and a long t-shirt. Picking up the towels she walked alongside James to the beach exit near Langholm, where their car was parked.

James and Sabine had spent the last few months living in Nakskov, on the western side of the island, in a friends house. No one knew where they had gone after the kitchen incident and that's exactly what they wanted. Sabine had been scared by it. Not so much by the men, but scared by what she found herself capable of doing and, moreover, what she had so desperately wanted to do. She had wanted to kill them both for invading her house, and when she had held the shotgun the temptation to pull the trigger was more than she could bear. That's what had scared her; the physical ease with which to take a life, unconcerned, in that moment, for the repercussions of that action.

James explained that it was perfectly natural for her to feel that way. Vengeance being a true, basic, human emotion that has only recently been harnessed while living in civilized society. But when civility is lost, and the need to protect oneself is paramount in a desperate situation, then the ultimate deterrent is sometimes seen as the only option. But she only saw it as an ugly side to her and was having difficulty coming to terms with the experience.

So when they saw a man sitting in a car, who was obviously waiting for them, they both knew that Sabine's memory would either return to the black days of guilt or rekindle the hate that caused it.

"Let him make the first move." James said, opening the back of the car. "Act normally, dry your hair or something while I put the things away."

James slid the beach chairs forward, closed the hatch and bent to place their bag on the back seat, taking the opportunity to see what the man was doing. He removed the 9mm Sig that Harry had given them from the armrest and pulled the slide before wrapping it in a towel.

"Maybe he's just waiting for someone." Sabine said.

"And maybe he's just a murderer waiting to bury a body," said James. "Either way, I don't like him."

The driver door opened and a fit looking man dressed in jeans with a light leather jacket approached them. James knew what the leather jacket meant on a hot day. He released the safety on the Sig with a slight click.

"Miss O'Connor? Miss Sabine O'Connor?" The man asked, holding out an identity card in front of him.

"That's far enough." Sabine said. "Who are you?"

"David Jeffries. I'm from the British Government. I'm afraid we have some bad news." He said, reaching forward to give his ID to Sabine.

"What's this? Security Services? You guys carry ID? How do we know this is real?"

"Sign of the times I'm afraid. When you get home, call the security services in London, tell them who you are and they'll verify the name on that card. They'll ask you a few security questions beforehand and then verify my location. Then call this number," Jeffries said, reaching forward again to give Sabine a piece of paper and retrieve his ID.

"Bad news?" Sabine asked.

"Call the number. Oh, and Mr. Devlin, you can put the safety on now please." Jeffries said, waving to someone behind them.

James didn't. But he turned on hearing a noise behind him and saw another man walking from the long grass toward the other car. He was carrying a silenced Heckler like he knew how to use it. James felt a chill go up his spine, realizing that he had probably been in that man's sights the whole time.

"Remember Miss O'Connor, call me later this evening. Have dinner, relax, then call me." Jeffries said, walking back to the car.

"Shit! Five minutes ago I was relaxed without a care in the world. Now I'm strung up like a banjo. Did you notice that other guy?" James asked.

Shaking her head, Sabine said: "We knew this would end sometime. Good things never last forever."

Not wanting to wait until after dinner Sabine confirmed the numbers Jeffries had given her were genuine and, when James was in the shower, gave him a call. As Sabine listened she started to go as white as a sheet, and had to sit down. The words reverberated in her brain and instantly brought back the pain of first hearing about how Sean had died. When James entered the room she was sitting on the side of the bed with her head in her hands, trembling.

"What is it?" James asked.

"Those fuckers. Those fucking fuckers," she said angrily, tears streaming down her face.

James sat beside her, not saying anything. She would tell him when she was ready. He put his arm around her until the crying subsided. When it did, the anger was apparent.

"Sean was murdered." Sabine said after a few minutes.

"What? How…?" James was at a loss for words.

"In Iraq. It wasn't an accident. He was murdered. Jeffries has proof." Sabine said.

"MI6 has proof Sean was murdered?" James said, realizing he was pretty much just repeating everything Sabine was saying, and knowing how annoying it was. "Because of those documents? Because of Harrison?"

"MI5. Jeffries is MI5. And Harrison died a few weeks ago." Sabine said, without really thinking.

"Guess that was on the cards." James said.

"Jeffries is coming over right now. Said he would explain the rest." Sabine said.

With that there was a knock at the door, and for the next couple of hours Jeffries ran through everything that the security services knew about why Sean might have been murdered. He explained that "Harrison had spent years protecting Fletcher, James's old Admiralty CO. The documents Harrison had in his possession were not so much about the gold, the salvage, or the secrets surrounding them, but about protecting Fletcher from scrutiny. Fletcher was a spy. He'd been passing information to the Russians, or the Soviets, as they were then known, for years. Which was why he never amounted to anything in the navy, always being landlocked, as it were, and only ever given a minor promotion to keep him around in case we needed him again. In any other situation he should have retired years ago."

"You've got to be kidding! Fletcher? He was always riding my ass and trying to stop me doing things. He was no spy."

"What did he ever stop you from doing?" Jeffries asked.

James thought for a moment and then realized Fletcher hadn't actually stopped him from ever doing anything, he had just constantly made a fuss over everything James wanted to do. But James had done it anyway. "I guess nothing," James said, seeing his error. "So Harrison was also a spy then?"

"No. We got Harrison all wrong." Sabine said, feeling somewhat guilty.

"No. Like Miss O'Connor said, Harrison was protecting Fletcher because MI5 didn't want Fletcher's cover blown. The security services knew Fletcher was giving away secrets, or what he thought were secrets. MI5 knew for years because of the gold. Philby, one of the infamous Cambridge Five working in the British Embassy in Washington, D.C., at the time, had heard rumors about the gold and requested the Soviets confirm the rumor. It was Fletcher who confirmed the fact after the war, albeit unwittingly it's thought, to another of the Five, probably Blunt, that the gold Churchill sent to Roosevelt had never really existed. MI5 then immediately knew where the information had originated because we had just reeled in a questionable Soviet defector who was giving us low level information of little value, except for this." Jeffries explained.

"Just because Fletcher messed up once doesn't make him a spy." James said.

"Once Fletcher realized his mistake he apparently tried to make amends. But we think he was probably blackmailed, because Blunt, or someone else, had squirreled some money away in a bank account with Fletcher's name on it."

"Did he, then, pass on more information?" James asked.

"Oh yes, lots. We made sure of that."

"You made sure of that!" James said, confused.

"Once we knew that he had been used and that he knew it and didn't inform the security services, we started feeding him information that we wanted the Soviets to have; false information mostly, about naval exercises and submarine locations, but interspersed with the occasional truth. We used him as an unwitting conduit for years."

"Even now?" James asked.

"No. He passed his use-by-date a long time ago thanks most probably to Kuzichkin, a KGB defector, who thought he was doing us a favor but, instead, brought the whole operation to an abrupt end. It was good while it lasted, though. For a time we had the Soviets chasing their tails, or rather we had them chasing non-existent submarines all over the Atlantic." Jeffries explained.

"So while I was working at the admiralty he wasn't being used any longer?"

"No. His final few years at the admiralty were spent limiting his exposure to anything and everything, and trying to hide what he did in order to keep his pension. For instance, he couldn't have really stopped you from going to Sean's salvage operation without drawing undue attention to himself. And everyone knows that story by now – or, at least, the governments that matter do. It's no longer a secret."

"What about Harrison. What's his angle in this?"

"Harrison knew that Fletcher was an unknowing asset for us and wanted to protect him, mainly because it was Harrison who had first been interested in finding the facts behind what was being called Churchill's Gold. Due to Harrison's naval career, when he was involved in some pretty hairy clandestine operations during the war, he became friends with Roger Hollis, MI5's Director General in the '60s. When Hollis heard about Harrison's interest in the gold, and not wanting him to spill the beans, Hollis told him what was going on, knowing that someone of Harrison's caliber was beyond reproach."

"Hence the late knighthood?" Sabine suggested.

"Exactly."

"I really got him wrong. I feel bad about that now." James said. "But if Fletcher was of no use after the '80s, as you say, why was Harrison still protecting him?"

"Harrison didn't know. Once Hollis left the service in '65 the whole trust level changed. Hell, there was even a time when senior people thought the Director himself was the Fifth Man, thereby tarnishing all Hollis's friends by association. When Hollis died in 1973 that was the end of it; Harrison was left out in the cold, as it were, ignorant to everything that had since transpired. And, of course, no one thought about telling the poor sod. Bureaucracy has a tendency to do that." Jeffries said.

"What does this all have to do with Sean?" James asked.

Jeffries tried to explain: "Sean was suspicious of Harrison, just as you were, and someone at the admiralty, not you because you were obviously no longer there, but someone, passed Sean documents suggesting that Fletcher was a spy. Sean had probably followed Harrison to the admiralty one day. Harrison hadn't been there in years and for some reason had a sudden urge to visit. Who knows why? Maybe after James here, sparked an interest, or perhaps a worry. Anyway, it looks as if Sean suspected that both Harrison and Fletcher were in cahoots, that both had something to do with the gold, and were going to make it known for their own reasons. The documents Sean sent you, which we intercepted by the way, specifically named Fletcher. Although it was old news, we can't have documents like those on the loose; after all, there's no telling who that might affect if such information got out, even now. And the Official Secrets Act still does apply you know."

"So I've been told, repeatedly," James said. "Which explains why we found nothing incriminating in the documents when they arrived. But what about Sean?"

"Sean was unfortunately playing a game in which he didn't know all the players. While he didn't much like the government and how it goes about doing things, he clearly disliked traitors even more and, to him, both Harrison and Fletcher were traitors. What he completely forgot to take into account was the other side; the Soviets. Or the Russians as we now call them. Cats, spots and all that."

"But this was so long ago. Fletcher has had nothing to do with them since the '80s!" James said.

"This is true. But what we now believe is that either the Russians still believe Fletcher to be an asset, even after all this time, or they have another source or handler that could somehow be linked back to Fletcher. He might have even been tied in with John Walker, the U.S. Navy spy, who was doing the exact same thing. The only difference, of course, was that we knew about Fletcher and the Americans had no clue about Walker. In this game everything is connected, like a web, so we suspect the Russians are still trying to protect a handler who might have replaced Fletcher with someone we don't yet know of, and that they're trying their damnedest to protect this new asset at all costs." Jeffries said.

"The Russians killed Sean? In 2004 we're still playing cat and mouse spy games with the bloody Russians, and people are still dying?" Sabine said incredulously, cutting in, having been quietly absorbing everything.

"That's what we're thinking, and that's only by accident. Two American cops in Iraq stumbled onto it by chance and delved a little deeper, but soon realized that they were, in their words, 'above their pay grade,' and asked British Army Intelligence for help, just because they happened to be in the same building. The army green hats, in turn, passed it all on to us and we put the pieces together, because we had more of them. The pieces, that is." Jeffries said.

"It would seem that if you, the security services, had let a few of those pieces loose earlier none of this would have happened." Sabine said. "I would still have a brother and Harrison wouldn't have had to live with a non-existent secret until he died." Then, remembering the knighthood, Sabine suggested: "Is that why

Harrison only recently received his award, because no one knew, or cared to know, about his lifelong effort to keep a state secret?"

"I can't say," Jeffries said, ignoring the first question. "But by all accounts Harrison should have received recognition of some sort sooner, if only for his wartime exploits. Clearly someone felt guilty later when they read about him in Sean's documents."

"In Sean's documents?" Sabine repeated.

"Yes. It wasn't until Harrison's name came up, relating to Fletcher, in those old documents, that we understood the part that Harrison had been playing all these years."

"Efficiency not a trait at MI5?" Sabine said, sarcastically.

"I'll be first to accept that. But one has to remember that everything MI5 has ever received or done, every scrap of information, has been written down and stored somewhere. That adds up to a lot of paperwork and we're not funded well enough, despite the political brilliance of the War on Terror, to digitize all that old stuff. Especially since most of it is completely redundant by now." Jeffries explained.

"Redundant? Ask Sean what's fucking redundant." Sabine snapped.

"Wrong word. I'm sorry." Jeffries said.

"But why are you telling us all this now?" James asked.

"Not obvious to you? Why did you come here, to a little quiet corner of Denmark?"

"You think that because the Russians might have killed my brother, they're after us now?" Sabine said.

"That's the obvious assumption. Your brother sent you documents. The Russians don't know that you didn't get the real ones. And they don't know what they contain, apart from something incriminating to do with a specific admiralty office and some missing wartime gold, both details of which were in the charge of one of their assets." Jeffries said. "There's more than a few within Russian intelligence who are still bitter about America's successful '80s Afghan insurgency and the later dissolution of the Soviet Union. They'd like to turn the tables and see the same thing happen to the Americans now that they're the ones fighting in Afghanistan. And the Brits also, for that matter. We rather suspect that a few rogue Russians might be instigating trouble; providing weapons and money, via a third party of course, to the nastier elements within the Sunni insurgency. And even though we have contacts in the Russian security services, and we've come a long way since the Cold War, they're not about to answer questions about a possible rogue group of spies, because that itself would be an admission of failure within the organization, something the Russians will never do, especially when they have their own Islamic problem going on. Knowing the mentality, though, it's certainly not beneath certain individuals to use one enemy to thwart another. We do it."

"Christ! How many enemies do we have?" James said.

"We'll always have enemies. Trying to discern which are the real ones, the more dangerous ones, is our job. These Russians, however, are playing a very dangerous game. Because unless Russia's geopolitical stance regarding extremism changes, and no one can foresee that, these archaic troublemakers are a bit like trapped rats. And trapped rats are especially vicious. They'll do anything to protect themselves, and if that means killing a few more innocents if they perceive a risk, they'll do it."

"Do you know for a fact that we will be targeted? Do you have definite information?" James asked.

"Wish that everything we did was that easy." Jeffries said. "What we do think is that the team that killed your brother were probably killed themselves very soon afterwards. Not that that's any consolation. These Russians would never allow the fact that killing Sean was a specific assassination to get out, or allow themselves to be blackmailed by those who carried it out. They probably spent $500 to get some out of work Iraqis to do it. And then killed them when they showed up to collect the other half of their wages. We're also assuming that these Russians got particularly nervous because Sean was in Iraq. Even though Sean was there, we believe, working quite legitimately for a relief organization. But everyone also knows that those organizations are often used, wittingly or otherwise, as fronts for governments. As yet, we have no information on anything they might be planning for you, but it remains a distinct possibility. And I found you quite easily."

"How exactly?" Sabine asked.

"We collect the comings and goings of everyone interesting. And we can access credit card data within minutes if we need it." Jeffries said. "Don't expect the Russians not to have the same tricks, albeit that it might take their rogue element a tad longer."

"I think Sabine might have already met the Russians," James said, telling the story of the two men at Sabine's house.

"No, those two wankers were Irish. The Russians used them as reconnaissance to see what you knew. They just picked a couple of bitter, anti-English amateurs who, fortunately for you, came face-to-face with an old soldier with whole lot less sympathy and a whole lot more ambition." Jeffries said.

"You knew?" Sabine asked.

"Yes, we were there. We couldn't tip our hand, but would have if it got out of hand." Jeffries said.

"I wonder what Harry would think." James said, remembering the afternoon he saw Harry's swollen but cheerful face. "And what about the police? The ones who picked me up, drove me around to get me lost and then told me the Harrisons had been murdered?"

"Yes, well, that was a long time ago and I'm afraid we slipped up there, there was nothing solid on the radar then. Those really were Russians. But since you apparently knew nothing at that point they let you go. Presumably they hoped that you might do their work for them, knowing that they could grab you at their leisure later for a more meaningful discussion." Jeffries said.

"What are you suggesting we do then? Preferably before that happens." James said. "Because as pleasant as it is, we can't stay here forever."

"Well, that brings me to why I'm really here," Jeffries said, reseating himself more upright in the chair.

"I can't wait for this bit," Sabine said, suspecting what was to follow. "Methinks this gentleman wishes us bait."

Jeffries didn't have to say anything, his expression said it all.

Chapter Twenty Eight

The Russians, London, England / August 2004

Russia is a riddle wrapped in a mystery inside an enigma.
– Winston Churchill

BEFORE JEFFRIES TRAVELLED TO THE idyllic, southern Danish island of Lolland the seed had already been sown. A few days after Harrison's death the *Daily Telegraph* published an account of his life in its respected, and oft read, military naval obituary. Everything was laid bare and honor was given where it was deserved, which in Harrison's case was long overdue. His wartime exploits were prominent in the article, in final, respectful recognition of services tended to a grateful nation. Then followed a short, deliberately obtuse paragraph, fitting for the security services, about his longstanding effort to protect people and national secrets. To further grab attention, the old, worn out phrase Churchill's Gold was used, but it was obvious, even to the uninformed, that there was another, deeper, reason as to why Harrison had been awarded a knighthood so late in life. It was somewhat explained, in roundabout terms, that spies do not usually receive honors whilst still in service, only when their service is both accomplished and completed. The great irony to that exception, of course, as anyone with an interest knows, was Anthony Blunt, who had been Fletcher's one time handler. Sadly then, as is so often still true in life even now, the lying traitor had received, and accepted, the honor before the honest patriot. While the patriot had instead been put out to pasture and forgotten.

It was subtly suggested that because of Harrison's death the mantle of secrecy had now passed to another; to someone of equal ardor who was also keen to protect the nation's interests. Even in death Harrison was proving useful. No sooner had the early morning print made its way to the Russian Embassy and calls were being made. When those bright little lights lit up on a computer screen Britain's Secret Service knew immediately that they had attracted someone's attention. Now it was just a matter of old fashioned leg work; in seeing where they went and watching who they met.

The streets of London are, as if designed to be, a labyrinth of deception, and many a foreign operative has, in the decades since the service's beginning, been overly confident in their ability to either blend or hide in the great city. But Britain's MI5 has eyes, ears and valued old contacts everywhere. During two vicious world wars, untold foreign insurgencies, a long and dirty cold war, the Troubles, and modern-day Islamic terrorism, MI5's expanding assets are an integral part of London's survival mechanism. After 100 years there is barely a nook, stump, bench, rock or cranny that hadn't been used before. And even spies have their routines.

Within half an hour of those phone calls three separate surveillance teams were following three Russians. One, the Russian Ambassador himself, was on his way to meet Britain's Home Secretary to discuss closer ties between their respective departments. It was mostly empty rhetoric, of course, but diplomacy meant that teams of civil servants had to go through the rigors anyway – even if it was fraught with twists and turns and destined to be all for naught.

Another, possibly a clerk, looked as though she was simply stepping out for coffee, but she was followed anyway and anyone who came close to her was photographed repeatedly before themselves being followed. The third, clearly a high ranking diplomat, was being chauffeured quickly to Heathrow Airport, and, under Diplomatic Immunity, paying no attention whatsoever to bus or cycle lanes. For him the team used a few of the thousands of CCTV cameras that have, in the last two decades, successfully turned London into a rendition of Orwell's *Nineteen Eighty-Four*.

Not unusually, the least of the three proved to be the most of the three. The bustling coffee shop proved the easiest to crack when, after the clerk had left with her cardboard crate of lattes, a barista surreptitiously also left. No one would have especially noticed except for the fit young man sitting in the corner who had made a mental note of all the employees and customers within the first minute of sitting down, and then noticing one of the baristas missing soon after the female clerk left. He was better at remembering the females and they were all still present. So, going through the photos he had discreetly taken with his phone while the clerk was at the counter, he realized that the man who had served her was the one no longer there. He quickly emailed the photo to the other officers on the surveillance team and went to check the bathrooms. They were both empty. He then approached the counter and asked to speak to the gentleman who had served him earlier, and was told that he was outside making a phone call and would be back in a minute. Not waiting, he walked through the kitchen and out the back door, just in time to see a figure in the distance jogging down the back alley and onto the street. He spoke into his sleeve mic and informed another officer to be on lookout for someone emerging from the alley. But they had already noticed the man and were preparing to follow him; the coincidence that a worker would leave at exactly the same time as the clerk was too great to ignore. The fact that he also appeared to be in a hurry was a dead give away.

On leaving the alley he stopped jogging and tried to fit in with the pace of the commuting public, but stood out from the crowd because he seemed unduly concerned about something, and it wasn't about catching the bus. Crossing the street, he went to a small newspaper stand and bought a *Daily Express* before heading toward Notting Hill Gate Underground Station.

The District Line train trundled its way to Earl's Court where the man disembarked and headed underground to meet the Piccadilly Line, which took him west across London. Before reaching Acton Town the man folded his newspaper and stood up, waiting for the doors to open. He didn't seem too concerned of his surroundings and was clearly unaware of anyone following.

Emerging from the station he turned left down Gunnersbury Lane, casually dodged the traffic on the busy avenue and entered the park, finding himself a bench on the edge of the old boating pond (not for the first time had this particular bench been used for espionage). There he waited. And continued to wait an hour later. The only others around the pond were an elderly lady and her grandson feeding the ducks, but they had left within half an hour of his arrival. Now there was no one of interest, just a few folks walking by on the main path and an officer of the surveillance team well hidden in the shadow of some trees. The other was sitting on a bench by the museum having a cup of coffee.

Suddenly the man stood up, threw his newspaper into the bin, strolled out of the park and went back to the station, having done absolutely nothing. One of the team waited by the pond to see if anyone would arrive to retrieve the newspaper while the other followed the man all the way back to the coffee shop, where he received an immediate bollocking for being absent. But which he shrugged off with a certain amount of unconcerned disdain.

No one arrived to retrieve the newspaper and later, after having it examined, they decided it was just that, a newspaper.

Nowhere along the way did he ever leave anything or even remotely have contact with anyone else. Jeffries' support team summoned the security camera footage from inside the coffee shop, examined it, but saw nothing untoward. It looked as though either the barista had been used as a decoy or the simple act of throwing the newspaper in the bin was a signal, which was a stretch since an unobtrusive coffee cup in the window would have sufficed. Something, though, was going on and Jeffries was not pleased with the results of the day, especially given the number of assets he had personally requisitioned for the task. It was not looked upon as a benefit to squander assets. Worse, it was not generally deemed proper to use two members of the public as bait and then botch the surveillance. He was wondering what he would tell Sabine and James when they arrived back in Burford the following day, at his request.

Despite his worries, Jeffries was convinced that he shouldn't bring in the barista for questioning. That would tip his hand. Also, there was a good chance that the young man was completely innocent since it was common practice for security services the world over to use impressionable, or gullible, members of the ordinary public for decoy operations, with the promise of either financial or sexual reward for performing something simple; like taking a newspaper to a park bin.

What both teams had failed to spot, however, was the tiny ceramic magnet the female clerk had deftly attached to the underside of the stainless steel door handle on entering the coffee shop. The next customer, entering the shop a few seconds later, had retrieved it just as adeptly with not a soul noticing. It was a classic, well practiced, old-fashioned drop, performed right under the eyes of the security services.

On the back of the magnet was a simple, stick on, matrix bar code, not much different than any ordinary QR Code found in a shop, which would attract no undue suspicion if lost. When scanned, however, using a normal smart phone with a keypad initiated decrypt application, it provided the user with, in this case, a flight number and, by automatically linking the phone to a secure server, photographs of those arriving – the code for which was also encrypted. The one-time-use decrypt algorithm, triggered by specific Unicode characters in a timestamp, was virtually unbreakable. The process from start to finish was very quick. The tiny QR Code could be printed within seconds and decrypted even quicker. For small amounts of completely untraceable data QR Codes were proving ideal.

The section chief summoned Jeffries into his secure meeting room for an update and afterwards ordered that a fresh team be tasked to look at the available information. New eyes can often see things instantly that tired ones looking at a screen for hours on end cannot. He also ordered a protection team to meet James and Sabine at the airport and take them to a safe house, although he made it perfectly clear that he wasn't pleased to be using further resources. Resources, for which, he was presently strapped due to the Home Secretary's request for his department to be seen to have more congenial relations with the Russians. "Don't say a word, Jeffries! I know it's bullshit. But we'll do it for as long as needed." The chief said, seeing Jeffries' expression of disbelief.

"Yes, sir." Jeffries said, portraying thespian understanding.

On leaving the office one of the officers assigned to examine the video footage from the coffee shop was eagerly waiting. "Sir, we have something for you to see," the officer said. "We think we've discovered how they did it."

"Show me." Jeffries said, not expecting much.

Jeffries followed the officer into the lab, where a couple of people were watching a high definition display looping though the same bit of tape. On another screen a man's photo was undergoing facial recognition. Despite what people assume, it was actually a slow and laborious process, demanding intense concentration from the operator once one of many matches had been made.

"Here you are sir," the officer said, allowing Jeffries to sit down before playing the video. Describing what they were looking at the officer continued: "This is the clerk entering. See how she opens the door, using two hands. Now watch this chap. Notice anything unusual?"

"Some girls struggle to open a door and use both hands, even switching hands sometimes. Nothing too much unusual there."

"True, but watch this chap again." The officer said, rewinding the video. "He enters immediately after our clerk. Watch where he puts his hand. He deliberately turned his hand upwards to grab the base, and not the more obvious portion of the handle, the upright."

"Yes, that's an unusual grip. Are you suggesting…?"

"The girl attached something to the underside of the handle, probably a magnetic capsule or something, and this chap simply snatched it back. No one opens a door like that." The officer said.

"I suppose no one saw where he went?" Jeffries asked.

"Nope. We were all too busy tracking the decoy." The officer said sheepishly, as if it was his fault.

"How'bout facial recognition. We got anything on that?"

"Not yet sir," the young girl watching the screen said. "We're triaging. All we can say is he's not Russian. At least no Russian we've seen before. But we're waiting to get information back from the Americans, they've got more resources to deal with this stuff."

"Not much help so far then. But keep at it and let me know." Jeffries said, trying to reinstill the girl with confidence in a highly competitive environment where success was the only option and failure always taken personally – even when underserved.

Chapter Twenty Nine

Boris Khorkov, London, England / August 2004

And that is called paying the Dane-geld; but we've proved it again and again, that if once you have paid him the Dane-geld you never get rid of the Dane.

– Rudyard Kipling

WHEN THE RUSSIAN AMBASSADOR returned to his embassy after meeting Britain's Home Secretary he had one simple request: To reel in the disgruntled elements that were operating in the UK. He didn't care who did it or how, he just wanted it done immediately.

"The British are sniffing around." He said. "They know we have a few embittered ex-KGB agents and they're on the lookout. I don't want them linked to us by association. We've spent years convincing these Brits that we're no longer the old order and this is no time to have another expulsion order thrown at us."

Thirty years hadn't dulled the humiliation of Operation *FOOT* and it was still firmly on the ambassador's mind.[*] September 1971 had been an embarrassing time for Soviet espionage and the world had congratulated Britain for its fortitude in both expelling and refusing visas to a total of 105 Soviet agents. This unprecedented

---

[*] Oleg Lyalin, a defector recruited into MI5 in 1971, sparked the operation by informing MI5 that KGB agents were planning terrorist activities in several western nations, including Britain.

action caught the Soviets completely off-guard, and immediately broke up a series of deeply embedded spy rings. Although afterwards the Soviets continued to recruit spies from their satellite countries, who were not on the list, and managed to keep up their numbers in that way, the damage had been done and other countries began to follow Britain's lead, which eventually resulted in the Soviets losing an array of capabilities all over the world. To put the damage in perspective: It was thought that during the war and afterwards, certainly up to the expulsions in 1971, the Soviets were successful in stealing so many western secrets that a full seventy percent of the design of their weapons hardware, especially in nuclear and aircraft manufacture, was of western origin – predominately British and American design – thanks to a steady stream of Soviet recruited ideologues. Some fostered by the notion of communism, others, more shamefully, by base greed.

It was no surprise, then, when Jeffries heard rumors that even the Russian Ambassador had issued instructions to rein in the more disenchanted elements they had working in Britain. Maybe there was to be a more congenial meeting of the security services after all. Although he doubted it; government agencies the world over are all inherently self-serving, by nature and mandate, and he expected this act of contrition to be no different. But whatever the reason, if Russia was truly going to recall some of its more undisciplined operatives to Moscow, Jeffries' work load might be lessened for a while, giving him time to clean up his desk.

That was to be a pipe-dream, however, for while a few of Russia's peripheral agents were being escorted from Britain, by their own countrymen no less, another far more dangerous one was arriving. As had been the purpose of the clerk, who, attracting little suspicion in her menial desk job, was playing a dual role inside the embassy; one as a normal embassy secretary, showing little concern for anything apart from the proper use of grammar; the other as a courier, delivering clandestine information to the rogue SVR groups operating in relative freedom right under the noses of embassy officials, without official sanction, of course, and amidst the diplomatically protected environment of the Russian Embassy itself. Groups that were hell-bent on restoring the status, prestige, and many would say brutality, of old Soviet Russia by any means necessary – including assassination.

Hence the arrival of Boris Khorkov, a specialist in leaving little or no trace while performing his murderous occupation. Boris had come to prominence while serving in the army during the First Chechen War, where he amassed a substantial body count that led to him being recruited by Russia's Secret Service and taught more intricate skills before being used in Eastern Europe and again in Chechnya during the Second Chechen War. But he had since fallen foul of the restrictions imposed upon him by a new government that he no longer believed in, however, and set himself up as an independent contractor, where the money and freedom to do as he pleased were insurmountably better – even though he worked for the same people, making him a bit of a priceless hypocrite. Despite that, he prided himself on a job well done and his Swiss bank account, as well as his already inflated ego, grew accordingly, even though he was a classic psychopath devoid of any normal human compassion whatsoever. In daily life he was completely lost and acted almost like an automaton; unsmiling, factual to a fault and stern to the brink of rudeness, but never truly meaning to be rude even though his words were always construed as such. But then no one ever argued with him. At a very impressive and muscular six-foot four he portrayed a powerful presence wherever he went. And his impeccable suits placed him in a category for which there was no real description. Many would have said champion boxer, except that his face was untouched but for a solitary scar on his forehead, over his right eye. The result of being too close to a grenade in

Chechnya that, except for the actions of a onetime friend, would have shredded him on the spot.

As it was, Boris spent several months in hospital and emerged with a steel plate where part of his skull used to be. His army friends hadn't recognized the person who returned to them; any soldierly compassion that he'd had previously had vanished. Now he seemed to actually enjoy the killing, looked forward to it even, whereas before it had solely been a soldier's duty in protecting himself, his friends, and his beloved unit.

Unable to get along with his old friends any longer, Boris was eventually forced to leave the unit and find an occupation that better rewarded him for his unique talents. But soon, even Russia's Secret Service realized that he was a bit strange, devoid of concern for anyone whatsoever, even those on his own side, and decided to let him go, or rather let him stagnate without any meaningful work, thereby inevitably enabling the ex-KGB rogue element to pick up this dangerous oddity. As was often the progression for such men.

Boris was sporting a deep tan when he arrived at the airport and the immigration official checking his U.S. passport placed him as just another big American celebrity sportsman. No matter though, because a camera had already taken his picture and within fifteen minutes a flag had gone up on a screen at MI5. The computer was programmed to pick up a variety of facial recognition matches. If they were met a height and weight match was automatically initiated. Boris met all three criteria, his statistics having only recently been placed on the massive U.S. Watch List after leaving Iraq a few weeks earlier, his second such visit there in six months. Boris's major flaw was that he was not a person who could easily hide in plain sight. Size and ego precluded any notion of him as a grey man, and a massive terrorist database, along with modern software, both shared among western nations, had, inside a very few years, created a technical world somewhat beyond his cocksure, hands-on comprehension.

The technology had done its work, and performed brilliantly. All that mattered now was for a human to realize the connection. For no matter how quickly or how efficiently modern technology performed its duties in collecting vast amounts of data, human beings still had to disseminate it, make sense of minute portions of it, and forward meaningful stuff to the correct actionable person. As with all feats of engineering, the human, while being the supreme strength and brains behind it, was often also the weak link in front of it. Or, as in this case, when not around at all.

That weak link had enabled Boris to leave the airport along with everyone else; quietly and unmolested. With only carry-on luggage even alert customs agents were unconcerned. Meaning that, so far, only a network of computers knew that one of the most dangerous men in the world had entered Britain like a tourist.

The Russians, however, were a little less-reliant on modern technology, preferring to keep tabs on their, and others', people of interest more personally; by using good old-fashioned manpower. They'd also had a little more time to determine where Boris was heading and what he might be up to, thanks, in no small part, to a severe lapse in allied communication procedures. The Green Zone in Iraq was, especially in early days, considered relatively secure from national espionage. They did, after all, have many other things on their mind, not least persuading a rightly cynical world that they were doing everything right, when they so clearly were not. It was never envisaged that elements of the old Cold War would want to tap into day-to-day allied transmissions, or that those usually mundane inter-departmental transmissions would in any way be advantageous to anyone else.

If Boris Khorkov had not been in Iraq those transmissions would indeed have remained secure. But since Boris was there his old bosses within Russia's SVR had been entrusted to keep tabs on him, and were intercepting all allied communications, both radio and network, knowing that if anything happened in Iraq those communications would be used. What sparked an immediate Russian interest, apart from Boris's presence, was the transmission of a solitary photograph to all of Iraq's NGOs: A photo taken from a young boy's camera the instant before he and his father had been killed by a rocket-propelled grenade.

If that photo bad been put through MI5's facial recognition software it would have come up with absolutely nothing, except, of course, for Sean O'Connor, who was thought to be of no interest. MI5's brilliant software had no way of knowing who a solitary boot belonged to. But a human, a Russian operative based in London, did. Several years ago he had trained alongside that boot while in the army and would likely never forget it, or the person to whom it belonged. While examining the remarkably clear photo under the magnifying glass his blood had gone cold. There was only one pair of handmade boots like that in the world. The built-in, thick leather ankle-braces, tightened with old-fashioned side buckles, were there to protect the weak ankles, the Achilles if you will, of a big man; Boris Khorkov. The only visible part of Boris was his boot, sticking out carelessly from behind a wall while someone in front of him pointed a long skinny bulbous projectile.

Boris was an immensely powerful man. Yet all men have a weakness and Boris's had always been a constant embarrassment. His massive frame, and the power that it generated, from years of training, were completely reliant on a pair of unusually thin and weak ankles. While training as an army recruit he had suffered numerous sprains that had put him back several classes, always embarrassing him in front of what he considered to be inferior people. Ironically, one of those lesser, inferior soldiers suggested that he get specialist boots made. Thereafter, he wore them on all operations, and the ruggedly built, heavy leather boots seemed to personify his outward strength – even though they only existed to protect his inherent inner weakness.

The operative inside the embassy had only ever trained with Boris, but knew well of Boris's history and was determined to never again meet the man. So, from that moment, using all assets at his disposal, he had started to keep tabs on Boris's whereabouts. One of those assets had, only hours earlier, informed him that Boris was on a flight to London. It was unlikely a coincidence that his arrival was timed to coincide exactly with the Ambassador's expulsion order. That Boris had now been implicated on a recent hit in Iraq also proved that he was still very much active, and not in forced retirement as they had been led to believe.

As the operative delved deeper, names such as O'Connor, Fletcher, Blunt and Kuzichkin seemed to merge. Two of the names were instantly recognizable. They were, each in their own right and in their respective countries, infamous. Fletcher's name came up only in old files, and there had been nothing new from him since the eighties, exactly when the spy John Walker of the U.S.A. had been discovered doing the same thing. O'Connor had to have been associated to Fletcher otherwise he'd have been known already. While the players and their positions within the game became apparent the purpose of the game did not. Not least why a high profile character like Boris Khorkov would be involved in assassinating a low-level British subject with no previous history or links to espionage or subversion.

In the old days of the KGB, when money was no object, even minor subversives were subsidized, coached and encouraged to pursue leftist tendencies, often by proxy through the Communist Party of Great Britain (CPGB). While others, those in more useful occupations such as trade unions, were tempted more directly by power, money and sex. Or were simply blackmailed. Times had changed, however, and these days were different. Besides, Sean O'Connor had never been tagged as a lefty. He was just someone trying to get the peoples' attention, and the only reason his name was known to the security service was because he had knocked on the wrong door, as it were, or indeed too many doors.

No matter. O'Connor had a sister and whether she was an active player or a simple bystander she was a link. The following morning two Russian SVR teams were assigned to find Sabine O'Connor, if only for her own safety.

At the same time, and because his plan to sniff out a Russian had failed, Jeffries assigned a protection team to Sabine and James; picking them up from the airport and moving them to a safe house on the Cornish coast.

While each country's secret service was involved with Sabine O'Connor, the Russian Ambassador was having a difficult time assuring the Home Secretary that he had, in fact, removed all the rogue elements from Britain, and trying to explain the reason why such people had been there in the first place. He was desperate for the high profile meetings to continue and was livid when the Home Secretary called about suspected rogue elements operating within the U.K. The ambassador didn't mention Boris Khorkov because he was not supposed to know of Boris's arrival; the female clerk had been deliberately lax in passing that information on, mixing it with low priority paperwork of little timely significance. No doubt she would be sent back to Moscow if her indiscretions were ever discovered. But for now she thought she was holding her own and key to the safety and progress of Boris's mission.

But that was a mistake. To persuade the Russian Ambassador that Britain's Secret Service indeed knew about their troublesome people, the Home Secretary was forced to explain how they knew – in the best intentions of cordiality, of course. Jeffries had earlier sent a courier to the Russian Embassy with CCTV footage of a swift dead drop, with instructions that it be delivered directly into the ambassador's hands. British Russian cordiality was breaking boundaries and a few old spies were likely turning in their graves.

But not everything was forthcoming by fact of necessity. The ambassador couldn't show his hand for risk of losing the chance to permanently eliminate the rogue network. He therefore needed to keep the clerk working, but under limited surveillance arousing no suspicion. But by doing that he was also willing to gamble that his people would reach Boris before he could carry out his mission, and do so before the British Secret Service found out about either.

The problem being, in the time that it had taken the Home Secretary to gain a partial admission of guilt from the ambassador, Jeffries had learned the identity of the mysterious big man who had just yesterday entered the country as an American tourist. From that moment it hadn't taken long to determine his purpose for being there, given that the only risk with which they were currently involved was that of Sabine O'Connor and James. The fact that the ambassador had given a promise to the Home Secretary, indeed only that very morning, that all rogue operatives were out of the country, leant Jeffries to the inescapable conclusion that Boris's presence in Britain had been officially sanctioned. Thus setting a precedent for the relatively new SVR. With that in mind Jeffries immediately requested more assets, and was happy to be provided two teams from the Special Air Service currently at home doing counter-terror refresher training in Hereford, along with their equally talented American counterparts. The secluded old stone hotel above the cliffs on the south Cornish coast was soon to be the most protected piece of property in the land – although few would ever notice.

Chapter Thirty

On Secret Service, Cornwall, England / August 2004

In a battle all you need to make you fight is a little hot blood and the knowledge that it's more dangerous to lose than to win.
– George Bernard Shaw

FROM THEIR WINDOW IN THE WEST wing of the hotel James and Sabine had an unobstructed view of the coastline from east to west. The sun was streaming through the west-facing window in the early evening, casting a yellow glow on the lush hills above the rocky cliffs to the east. Below them a few pre-dinner holiday makers were making the most of the sunset and enjoying a quiet stroll along the beach, now empty of screaming children playing in the surf. A few anglers stood at the edge of the water, casually pointing their long hopeful poles toward the ocean. Off to the east the long green fairways stretched above them and golfers were finishing the last few holes, no doubt before ending their day in the hotel bar, known to all as the Nineteenth hole. The refreshment stand in the car park directly beneath them was closing up and the attendant collecting the day's rubbish. It was classic English summertime, the height of summer, barely four sun-filled weeks before school would once again start. The Cornish Riviera was bustling with activity.

Two floors beneath them dinner was being served and, being England, everyone was dressing appropriately. Sabine was ready and just waiting for James to finish tying his tie.

"It's usually the man who waits for the woman," she said.

"If you hadn't spent so much time in the bathroom I'd be ready," James snapped back. "I have no idea what you do in there for so long."

"I make myself beautiful, for you dear." Sabine said.

"Yes you do. And it's well-worth it. You look fantastic, as always." James said.

"Why thank you sir!" Sabine said, enjoying the compliment. "Shall we go down?"

James smiled at her, turned to open the door and came face-to-face with a tall, well-dressed gentleman who stopped him in his tracks. His heart raced.

"Sir, your dinner is on the way up. Please do not leave the room." The man said.

"Seriously? We can't leave the room?" Sabine asked, upset at spending so much time getting ready for no purpose.

"We're awaiting another team and we'll evaluate the situation when they arrive. Until then we'd prefer that you remain here. Mr. Jeffries' instructions." The man said, in a way that warranted and expected no argument.

"That's fine. No problem. Thanks for your concern." James said, forestalling a quip he sensed was on Sabine's lips.

"Thanks for your understanding sir. I'll be sure to let you know if anything changes." The man said, before closing the door.

"He's just doing his job." James said.

"I know. I'm grateful, really. It's just…"

"What?"

"Never mind." Sabine said, picking up a book and making her way to a chair by the window.

A few moments later a knock on the door brought dinner, with a note attached to a bottle of wine, which read: "Sorry to keep you prisoners. Maybe this will help. Jeffries."

Jeffries was downstairs in a room he'd commandeered from the hotel. He was concerned because the Russians had disgorged a lot of personnel in the previous couple of hours. Not only from their embassy, which was under constant CCTV surveillance, but from other locations around the city. In all, he figured about thirty Russians were on the move, so something serious was going on.

He also knew the Russians would have been watching his team's movements, possibly even the movements at Hereford. And while his teams had staggered their departures, initially used different modes of travel and gone in different directions, he knew the Russians would be as concerned about his movements as he was about theirs. It was difficult moving large numbers of people around right under the nose of a competing secret service without being noticed. The only thing he could do was disguise where they were going.

In that, Jeffries was entirely unsuccessful, but it wasn't for lack of trying. The Russians had had in place, for a long time now, a very efficient air tracking system that completely covered the U.K. There wasn't an aircraft that took off that they didn't know about and, with Britain's Armed Forces stretched to the hilt in both Iraq and Afghanistan, the military personnel at home were strapped for resources. Meaning they had little opportunity to disguise their direction of travel while in the air by using decoys. Also, on the ground, the Russians possessed a quiet and little used network of informers who still kept track of military movements. It was an archaic network from the old days, had its gaps, but still functioned. So when a grey Chinook was seen traveling southwest over the Bristol Channel someone in the Russian Embassy knew about it. When it passed over the north Devon coast and didn't head towards the training ground on Dartmoor, or land near the marine's barracks at Plymouth, the Russians knew their quarry was probably in Cornwall.

Once the Chinook discharged its passengers a couple of miles west of the hotel, in a sloped field hidden from view from further inland, it headed north a few miles to find a secure flat spot in which to hunker down. The soldiers assembled their gear and sat down to relax. They weren't going anywhere until darkness fell.

There are only three main roads into Cornwall, though there are many small ones, most of them single lane with high hedges and occasional passing spots, much like the bocage country in Normandy that was so troublesome to the armies after D-Day. Farm tractors abound during the summer making traveling along the smaller roads incredibly frustrating and time consuming. It's also easy to get lost and GPS has left many a motorist stuck and confused when confronted with a dead-end or a cliff with no way to turn around.

Jeffries knew that anyone finding Sabine's whereabouts would have to travel on the main roads, and they were literally littered with CCTV cameras. Then, even if someone managed to get close, the secluded hotel, its beach and golf course, were well-off the main roads and limited to hotel guests only. And every guest currently in the hotel was a member of a family, all of them had children. Anyone walking around without a child nearby would be recognizable in an instant.

Jeffries' team and the military personnel on hand had studied photographs of all the hotel guests and workers, knew exactly in which rooms they were staying and knew who the vehicles in the parking lot belonged to. Such things were normal procedure.

A couple of hours after sunset the soldiers began to arrive in twos and took up their predetermined positions after having studied the hotel and its grounds. Snipers were placed on the higher ground overlooking the hotel and others on the roof of the hotel itself. With the night vision equipment available to them, and movement detection software installed on computers attached to digital cameras, there was little chance of anyone penetrating the perimeter unseen.

The hotel, however, was not in lockdown. Guests were unaware of the human perimeter and were allowed to come and go as they pleased. But with only one narrow hedge bound road down to the cove, keeping tabs on the cars and their occupants was straightforward. People were counted out and counted back in, and checked when they emerged from their vehicles under the lights of the car park. Cameras at all entrances of the hotel recorded the coming and going of everyone, guests and workers alike – even the hotel's friendly Great Dane.

Jeffries was happy. Or as happy as he could be given the situation. Nothing is totally secure, but in this case even the old sewers were being electronically monitored. And the old grates that used to feed the sewage into the sea had been welded shut years ago.

It was then, while Jeffries was searching his brain over a cup of coffee, that he wondered why the Russians were putting so much effort into Sabine and James. They had to know the security services were protecting them, and if that was the case one had to presume that all that could be told had already been told. So why the hit? Jeffries' got a sinking feeling in his stomach. He knew the Russians were already in Cornwall en masse, he'd seen the CCTV footage from the bridge cameras. What, then, were they after? Was their purpose to hit his section. Was MI5 the real target? Had Russia's SVR returned to their KGB roots? He asked for another situation report from all sectors. Everything was fine, everyone checked in.

Three people inside the perimeter did not check in, however. Three Russians had already penetrated the cordon by following a gully down from the road to the cliff edge. They had just managed to get inside the cordon a few minutes before it was secured, although they were almost spotted by a couple of late golfers when a ball landed a few feet away from them. But were fortunate because the golfers had obviously started in on the nineteenth before reaching the sixteenth, and were already a little soused. The three were now ensconced under a thick gorse bush, with one taking notes of movement to pinpoint possible security positions, one reporting back using digital burst transmissions, and the other watching out for the team. It was nothing more than they had been trained to do and, indeed, had done numerous times in far more dangerous places, where, being lucky, they would have immediately been shot if caught. Whereas here, in the pleasant British countryside, they understood that their gentlemanly counterparts would never resort to such overt brutality. At least that is what they hoped. For there is never a guarantee and accidents do often happen.

But they didn't know Jim and Terry. Jim was barely six feet away from the closest Russian. So close he could smell the stale smoke on the man's breath in the otherwise fresh sea air. Jim already had his knife out and could have taken the man's life inside a couple of seconds. Terry had the other two covered with his silenced Heckler. All they were waiting for was word about what to do with these three jokers who had stumbled unknowingly almost right on top of Jim's position.

Terry wanted to laugh at the irony, but was concentrating on his breathing because the night was starting to get a chill and he could already make out the translucent steamy breath of the Russians in the evening air. He didn't want to do the same and be the one to start the firefight.

"We've got Russians in the east sector, just above the cliffs," the radio operator said.

"Already? Damn, that was quick." Jeffries said.

"Too quick. They almost landed right on top one of our teams. They're so close our guys are tapping out Morse on their mics," the operator said. "They want to know what to do."

"Nothing. Hold tight and monitor. We don't want to start World War Three here in Cornwall if we can help it." Jeffries said.

"The others are still outside the perimeter?"

"Looks that way... Hell, now we've got lights over the water. Looks like a helicopter." The operator said.

"Shit! The hotel's not expecting company is it? Maybe it's going over." Jeffries barked.

"What if it's not." The operator said, stating the obvious.

"Do we have anything to handle a chopper?"

"We got that capability. But we'd better be damn sure." The army captain said. "Where exactly is it, and on what heading?"

"Looks to be about three miles out, heading north – straight towards us." The operator said.

"Get air traffic and see if they have a flight plan." The captain said. "And get Starstreak up and running. Just in case. But Jesus, I hope not."

To the west, in the field where the troops had been dropped, a soldier bolted upright. The only words from his mouth were: "Shit! Is this for fucking real?" Before doing another quick check of the device and designating the only target in the sky. He'd only ever fired a simulated training round and hoped to God he didn't bollox it up. He rechecked the procedure over and over in his head, like an athlete visualizing his event, and waited for the order.

"Starstreak's ready to go." The operator said. "No flight plans filed for this area."

"Do I have authority to loose this thing?" Jeffries asked, only now realizing the full repercussions if things went wrong.

"I don't know about you, sir. But I do." The captain said. "Those are my troops. I'll take responsibility."

"Brave lad." Jeffries thought.

Jim still had the Russian within reach and was coiled ready to lunge if the helicopter did anything. He wasn't going to wait for orders. He was going to take the Russian out. Terry could feel the anticipation in the air, and his partner's eagerness. His adrenaline was surging. This was no ordinary surveillance operation. This was real and it was a hair's breadth away from getting dirty.

"Still coming…" the operator said.

"Within range?" Jeffries asked.

"It's been there ever since we first saw it." The captain said.

"No, their range, are we within their range?" Jeffries corrected himself.

"We are now." The captain said. "It could be a decoy for the Russians to act. Everyone within half a mile is no doubt watching that chopper."

That thought had already occurred to Jeffries. "Your choice."

"Take out the chopper." The captain ordered.

"Wait!" Jeffries said. "None of this makes sense. Why would the Russians want to start this? And why are all these people in Cornwall? Abort the missile. I'll take responsibility."

"Two air-to-grounds can destroy this hotel, and all the people in it. That's a lot of lives. You want that. You willing to risk that?" The captain said.

"Abort the missile. None of this is right. Snatch the three Russians. Alive dammit!" Jeffries said.

As the helicopter roared overhead Jim took the opportunity to pounce and clouted the closest Russian on the temple with the butt end of his knife, knocking him briefly senseless. Terry jumped up and loosed a series of rounds into the dirt in front of the other two, just for effect.

The Russians were completely stunned. They couldn't hide the gut wrenching fear that engulfed them in an instant. Men! Coming from absolutely nowhere! How could these men get so close without them knowing? They were shocked beyond belief.

With Terry covering them they were forced to lay prone while Jim tied their wrists with twist ties and searched them. Two of the snipers on the hotel roof were also taking a bead on the situation, and were first to relay that the three Russians had been secured. Other snipers were watching the surroundings, making sure there were no other threats while the helicopter flew overhead.

"Okay Ivan. On yer fookin' feet. War's over for you." Jim said, lifting them up one by one and pushing the three down the cliff trail towards the hotel.

"I want the details on that fucking helicopter. Find out where it goes and interview the pilot." Jeffries said. "What about those three Russians?"

"On their way," the operator said.

"Good. Maybe we'll get some sense out of this clusterfuck. Is everything else still secure?"

"As houses." The captain said.

"That's something." Jeffries said, visibly relieved.

"What about the other Russians?"

"No movement as far as we can see. They seem to be as confused as us, and not willing to commit." The operator relayed.

"Good." Jeffries said. "It's time to finish the game. Let's start getting those two out of here. Bring the vehicles around."

Two black Range Rovers and an Audi S8 appeared. The two Rovers drove around the fountain in the middle of the car park and waited as the Audi backed down the alley to the kitchen entrance.

"Is the road clear?" Jeffries asked.

"We've got the road blocked half a mile in both directions from the intersection." The captain said.

"Okay. Let's do it." Jeffries said, leaving the room along with the captain to take up their seats in their respective Rovers.

Two people were bundled into the back of the Audi and it took off immediately, taking its place neatly between the two Rovers as they raced up the narrow lane toward the main road. At the intersection they didn't stop, but took the opportunity to go even faster on the wider 'B' road.

They knew the Russians would have people placed at all the likely intersections because, in reality, there were only a couple of ways out. But once the cars were on the larger A road the two main intersections were each quickly blocked with very large tractors, trapping the Russians in a box and giving the Audi plenty of time to leave the area. With the convoy safe, Jeffries stepped out of the Rover and waited for the inevitable arrival of the Russian commander.

To say the Russians were upset would be an understatement. They were furious at being so easily outmaneuvered. But that's why Jeffries had specifically picked the location; he knew it well, and was long ago aware of all the oddities of the area, having grown up there as a child. The Russians would have some explaining to do before being allowed to go on their way – diplomatic immunity being damned for a couple of hours – which further ruffled their feathers.

"Tractors? How did they get here?" Jeffries said to a very upset Russian, not mentioning that they belonged to his uncle. And then asking: "What brings you lot to this sunny part of the world? Team building exercise? How about it Ivan, you willing to let us in on your little secret?"

"We are missing three men. You cannot hold our people."

"Your men are fine Ivan. They're probably having a cup of tea in the kitchen as we speak. Which is a lot different to the outcome of your intention by the look of it." Jeffries stated.

"Yes. We need to talk. This almost got out of hand. But you have to keep this to yourself. For the time being. Please."

"By all means. I'm all ears." Jeffries said, waiting.

"I think you are here for the same reason as we." Ivan said. "Is this correct?"

"I don't know. We're here protecting two of Her Majesty's Subjects. We have reason to believe you, or someone you know, wishes them harm."

"Not us. I can assure you, not us. We are not the KGB, we do not hurt civilians. But we believe that someone…"

"Someone you know?"

"Yes, someone we know. We have intelligence that someone intended to, intends to, hurt your people." Ivan said.

"You have intelligence, or you have facts?"

"What is the difference?"

"Analysis. One is an assumption based on information. The other needs no assumption."

"Okay. We know." Ivan finally admitted.

"So do we. Boris Khorkov was one of yours. Some say he still is. When he arrives in a country people tend to end up in boxes. We don't take that lightly. And we don't take it lightly when a foreign power either sends, or hides the presence of, people like Mr. Khorkov. Which is it? Sends or hides?" Jeffries asked.

"It's delicate."

"I'll bet it's fucking delicate." Jeffries said. "When you want to tell me something, let me know. In the meantime I've got an operation to run. So why don't you have your boss call my boss?"

"I can't do that. I've told you too much already. If you want my help tracking down Khorkov it has to be done quietly. Just you and I. We also have an ongoing operation and its success will not only be advantageous to us, but to your country also."

"So, Boris has gone rogue has he?" Jeffries said, expecting as much. "He's embarrassing for you."

"Yes. This is true. We cannot let anyone know he's in the country because we're trying to close his network down. If he knows we know... if he knows you know, he'll disappear again."

"He's getting most of his information from your embassy. Don't you think he already knows that you know, which is why we're all here on a wild goose chase? Try being honest with us." Jeffries said. "From what I know, Boris doesn't give a damn if people know of his whereabouts. Because by the time people find out exactly where he is, it's always too late."

"Yes, that's right, of course." Ivan admitted.

"So where is he?" Jeffries asked.

"We don't know, we thought he would be here, to finish what he started in Iraq."

"Brilliant." Jeffries said. "Together we almost started World War Three because, thanks to you not notifying us, we thought Boris was sanctioned and you were here to help him."

"Those were our instructions, from the top." Ivan said. "I should not be telling you this, but it would seem to be for the best."

"This whole thing stinks. The deeper we get the less sense any of it makes. Do you get the impression that we've both been had... that this whole thing has been a setup from the very beginning, a decoy?" Jeffries asked.

"What do you suppose is Boris's target then?" Ivan asked.

"He's your boy, you should know Ivan." Jeffries said.

"Wish that I did." Ivan said.

"Well, if you're using something as a decoy you've usually got bigger fish to catch. So look for something bigger, closer to home possibly." Jeffries said.

"There's a move to eradicate people like Boris. They're too much of an embarrassment. That comes from the top."

"The Ambassador?" Jeffries asked.

"Higher than that, but he's the one responsible for seeing it carried out in Britain."

"Could he be the target? You've emptied the embassy of active staff; sent them to the other side of the country. Who've you got left in London?" Jeffries asked.

"Skeleton crew. Administrators mostly, apart from the embassy's main security."

"Are they all trustworthy?"

"Yes, all of them. Spetsnaz. All loyal." Ivan said, and then, "God I hope so."

"In God We Trust doesn't always work Ivan." Jeffries said. "You need to get your people back to London. Although I fear it might be too late. Wait here."

Jeffries walked away a few paces to get some privacy and called his section chief.

"Russians on one of our ships? Are you sure?" The section chief said incredulously.

"Yes sir. We've got seats for 36, but we can get everyone in if we have to. It's imperative that we get everyone to London. In the meantime, the Russian Embassy needs extra security, all you can spare, good people, armed." Jeffries explained.

"Alright. Do what you have to. I'll let the Home Secretary know. You'd better be right or it'll be porridge for the duration."

"Fine sir. We'll get organized." Jeffries said, beckoning the Russian over.

"Okay, Ivan. We'll give you a ride to London, get everyone over to the green." Jeffries said, before calling in the Chinook.

Chapter Thirty One

Russian Embassy, London, England / August 2004

'Evil men have no songs.' How is it that the Russians have songs?
– Friedrich Nietzsche

BORIS WAS INWARDLY LAUGHING at the stupidity as he studied the outside of the Embassy. Looking at his watch he had plenty of time before his accomplice would overfly the hotel and try to initiate a firefight between the two competing security services. If successful, it would be a bonus and both sides would blame each other indefinitely, eliminating any cross-service protocol for years to come, perhaps even decades. Such a hope was a long shot, however, but even if it failed he had lost little, he still had time on his hands. The drive back from Cornwall was long, even when the roads were empty. So he had time enough to enter the embassy and time enough to rid the world of the new order taking shape within the service, that which now made his country look weak and subservient, an insult to the memory of its glorious past.

A flicker of light came from a window and he walked forward, knowing the cameras would no longer be recording his movements and that a door would open on his arrival. How easy it had all been; one trusted clerk had managed to arrange everything. She had been well trained indeed, a product of true Russia.

The door ajar, he slid in, removing a silenced Beretta – the west knew how to make weapons, reliable accurate weapons, another sad indictment to the Soviet Empire. It had been a while since he'd been in the building but little had changed. Thanks to the clerk he knew exactly where the security team were located, knew where the Ambassador would be resting undisturbed, knew where to hide and knew his escape. Everything had been planned to the closest detail, as always, it was his signature.

The old servant stairways were as he remembered; cold and a little damp, even in August. The lighting had been improved but there was still no carpeting on the stone steps, worn uneven over years of use. But his soft soled boots didn't make a sound as he made his way to the second floor before positioning himself in the small closet down the hall from the Ambassador's bedroom. Once inside, with the door slightly ajar, he watched to see if the telltale red light of the camera would kick in again, the clerk having managed to temporarily turn them off while the security officer went to the bathroom, after enjoying too much of her company and drinking too much of her coffee. It didn't. He waited a little longer but still nothing.

The girl was usually better than this. He'd watched her through her training, mentored her, molded her to his wishes. She was disciplined and unquestionably loyal to the cause, and besides, she knew what would happen to her family if she strayed. But still the camera was not back on. He thought about aborting the mission because something was clearly not right. Maybe she was letting him know that something was wrong.

He looked out and started to make his way back down the stairwell, walking beneath the camera as he went. He stopped, looked up at it and stared in confusion. Reaching up he tore off a small piece of black electrician's tape. The light was on!

In the operations room the ambassador said: "Hello Boris," to the screen just before it was splattered with spots of blood. "Goodbye Boris."

The two rounds caught Boris smack in the back of his head and the big body crumpled to the floor a corpse. There was nothing dramatic about the incident, the trooper was positioned at the end of the hallway, squatting in the bay window behind the curtain. He took his first opportunity and completed the task at hand, professionally, no questions, no emotion, then secured his weapon and walked away. Someone else would clean up the mess.

Two floors below, the ambassador left the operations room, stepped around the body of a woman in the hall and entered his office to pour himself a celebratory whiskey. Vodka was good for getting drunk, whiskey was for pleasure, and for reward.

A minute later the trooper arrived to be congratulated as requested, his weapon slung across his chest. But before entering the office the ambassador's personal bodyguards disarmed him, which he took as an insult to his loyalty since he had just saved the ambassador's life. Such was the life of a soldier.

On leaving the ambassador three of the embassy guards were helping the stirring woman to her feet and dragging her away. He wouldn't want to be in her shoes. While times might have changed since the heady days of the KGB, treachery still meant months of interrogation followed by a lengthy incarceration. Her days in London, one of the great cities of the world, with all its opportunities and culture, were over. All for a cause that was foisted onto her while barely out of adolescence; gullible, naïve, impressionable and malleable. A pretty, simple girl, now lost to the world because of a fanatic, a psychopathic lunatic intent on dragging the world back to what never existed. That delusion born from a grenade in yet another of the world's brutal wars of independence, creating more ripples of violence.

Chapter Thirty Two

Sabine and James, Oxforshire, England / September 2004

It is a curious sensation: the sort of pain that goes mercifully beyond our powers of feeling. When your heart is broken, your boats are burned: nothing matters any more. It is the end of happiness and the beginning of peace.

– George Bernard Shaw

BY THE TIME SO19 FROM THE Metropolitan Police arrived everything was over. The ambassador thanked them profusely and called the Home Secretary to inform him that the problem had been taken care of. The secretary knew well enough not to ask for specifics. Protocol was one thing, being nosey was another, and the embassy was, for all intents and purposes, Russian soil, so better to leave it at that.

The Chinook, almost full to the brim with the two countries' secret service teams, was diverted back to Hereford. After which, to placate the eyes of a world that is now always watching, the whole thing was described as a successful joint counter-terrorism training exercise. Even though it had come barely a hair's breadth away from becoming a disaster of epic proportions.

The pilot of the chopper had his license revoked by the Civil Aviation Authority for not filing a flight plan. The excuse that he had been physically coerced into performing the flight by one of Boris's accomplices, but who had conveniently not been aboard the flight, because he didn't trust Boris and didn't believe that the chopper wouldn't be shot down, was not itself believed, and MI5 did nothing to alter that decision. The accomplice disappeared completely and was, no doubt, very relieved to discover that Boris would never be after him, or indeed anyone else within the rogue group, which had been successfully rounded up once back on Russian soil, where it was easier to do so.

James and Sabine were back at home, enjoying late summer in the Cotswolds. Harry and the rest carried on as though nothing had happened. Well, to them, I suppose, nothing really had. They had just been along for the ride, on the periphery.

The end of summer was calm and relaxing. Fields were cut of hay, wheat and barley had been harvested and tourists were heading home. It was a pleasant time of year; days were warm and the nights were slowly cooling, perfect for two people finally getting to know each other. They had been together, explored each other, loved each other, but only now could they truly discover what it was like to actually live with each other. Share each day, the good and the bad, knowing what they now knew of the world.

It is a truism that ignorance is bliss. What they now both knew was hard to understand and at times they were each found staring into space, wondering, trying to make sense of it all. Did anyone know how to make sense of it all? Is there ever anyone who knows all the intricacies of their plots, with all the twists and turns, each designed by competing entities in order to dominate the game, gain the upper hand? Or do the people in charge, the powers that be, even the players themselves, just pretend to know, but are, in all truthfulness, just as lost as anyone else? Once the reality of those answers set in, the more difficult bit of trying not to be too cynical began. They both knew time would heal, though not completely, never completely, even as the memories slowly migrated to the recesses of the brain. They each looked forward to that moment in time, in the hope of getting back to an ordinary life, seeking for nothing more than those around them always had. But time they didn't have.

A month later, during a delightfully balmy Indian Summer, exactly the kind for which we wish before winter strikes, James was standing beneath a canopy of rusty, cathedral-like oaks and yellowing birch, next to an old late-Medieval church in a secluded Oxfordshire valley. Beside him, sitting obediently still and quiet, leaning slightly against James's leg for comfort, was Sheila, Sean's loyal canine companion, who seemed to sense the sadness of the occasion. Flickering through the gradually thinning branches the sun was winter bright, accentuating the brilliance and color of the autumn leaves, falling one by one, as if in homage, onto the quiet, respectful, somber scene below. The newly laid headstone read: "Sabine O'Connor. The beauty and the love that was my life."

She never told him. Never mentioned what the doctor had told her, not until it was too late, after the cancer had fully taken hold and it was obvious that something was seriously wrong. James had thought those days, seeing Sabine deteriorate before his very eyes, the worst in his life. But they weren't. These days were the worst in his life. This day. This moment.

Sitting on the bench in the park he reached into his pocket for the pistol Harry had given him not many months before. It would be easy, relief from the torment, relief from failure, relief from the loss he could no longer bear. Sabine's face emerged from behind his tears and the steel felt suddenly uncomfortable. The horrid guilt insurmountable. Sheila nudged him and placed a heavy head on his leg. Her sad old dog eyes, full of endless hope, and yet endeared with canine confusion, unknowing why all her people had left her, looked up as if to say: "Don't do it. I need you."

Afterword

Missoula, Montana, U.S.A / August 2012

The misfortune of a young man who returns to his native land after years away is that he finds his native land foreign; whereas the lands he left behind remain for ever like a mirage in his mind.
However, misfortune can itself sow seeds of creativity.
– Brian Aldiss

AFTER APPALLING PROSCRASTINATION for eight years about documenting the conversation I had with someone I did not know in a London park – a casual meeting solely by chance since I no longer lived there – it is hard now to perfectly remember every detail of his story. In this attempt, for which I hope he's still around to read it, and hopefully finds his approval, and instead of always calling the man 'he' or 'him' throughout, I have named 'him' James Devlin. I sincerely hope 'James' does not mind the choice, nor is offended by the presumption, for names become us, they are intrinsically personal. But from what I remember of him I think the name suits.

It does, however, I'm sure you will agree, beg the question as to why I never inquired after this gentleman's name? I can only surmise, after all this time, that I found his story so fascinating and compelling that I simply forgot. That, at least, is the answer I shall give. My wife, though, would suggest that I was simply foolish, as with many other foolish things I have done. Another reason perhaps, is that I have a rather old fashioned social flaw in that I rarely inquire after people's names if they are not forthcoming. I do not like to intrude and presume that people will introduce themselves if so inclined, and will not when not so, and who am I to judge one way or the other.

Despite my errant foolishness in regards to the absence of a name, the rest I do remember quite well: This man stands out in my mind as if it were yesterday, more than a causal acquaintance he now appears like a friend, a ghost, an angel even; arrived to protect my thoughts, like a soldier guarding them in close order so that I should never make the same mistake. That image remains as clear as looking into a mirror, as vivid as the Montana mountains I see from my window, as crisp as the chill autumn breeze coming in through the window.

In this I hope I have done him justice, for he deserves no less. My thoughts are forever with him, and the loss which, hopefully, he still endures. That is not to say I wish upon him sadness, for on the contrary, not wishing to be trite, I wish him a long and happy life. Just that I hope the life he lives and the losses of which he no doubt still endures have finally found, through time, a sense of balance, perhaps of reserved contentment.

My tardiness and foolishness now explained, as well as, I hope, my respect, not only for him but for other players, and statesman, for whom he also had respect, the following is the last he told me and I place it here simply because I could not find suitable space enough in the final chapter without ruining the flow, the feeling and the sentiment of the story, which, since I was there watching, was both a deeply emotional and worrying experience for me. Thanks to our conversation, though, I left the park to stroll quietly along Parliament Square, feeling relieved and assured, but, at the same time, hoping that his dog, Sheila (its real name), lived forever. For it was very clearly this wonderfully loyal companion which was keeping Mr. Devlin alive.

This, then, is the final piece of the story, written like the former:

> *As if by a soldier who is no writer, to a reader who is no soldier.*
> – Ambrose Bierce.

IT WAS A SHOCK WHEN JEFFRIES approached James and Sabine a few days after everything was over to debrief and explain to them that the whole conspiracy theory was untrue, a falsehood, not initially by design but by basic error. Just someone assembling the pieces in the wrong order by mistake. A riddle hidden in a cocoon of truth. The gold, that which had started everything, reached America just as Churchill promised it would, just not by the route specified in the conspiracy. Churchill wasn't about to sacrifice the friendship of an industrious swathe of the English Speaking Peoples for a few pieces of precious metal, not least of which because he was himself half American.

The sinking of the merchant ship *Albatross* by the British submarine *Sturgeon* had simply been an elaborate exercise to show the Americans how easy it would be for German U-boats to sink shipping up and down the eastern seaboard. With no blackout in effect in towns along America's coastline every vessel was starkly silhouetted against the illuminated skyline, making each and every one a perfect target. The torpedo Larry's father had dragged up in his nets years afterwards had either gone wide, run too deep or was a dud. The gold-plated lead was simply a decoy – "attended by a bodyguard of lies" – and, once aboard *Albatross*, nothing more than basic ballast. The bodies washed up on shore or fished from the ocean were indeed German, as their underwear determined. They had been hurriedly buried at sea by a British destroyer a few days earlier, though obviously not well. Perhaps they had been too busy worrying about other things at the time to properly bury bodies who only an hour earlier had tried very hard to sink them. Who knows?

No one really knew who first started the theory, maybe even an unknown local like Larry, but it had somehow migrated into official channels whence it became false information given to Philby's office in Washington D.C. in order to flush out a spy, which it did, it flushed out Fletcher. From that moment Britain's SIS were bound to maintain the story's integrity. From which point it entered a life of its own, becoming the catalyst to every twist and turn for the next 60 years. Who could have known that such an obscure, mostly insignificant, and largely unbelievable story would have so many repercussions, and last so long?

\# \# \#

If I remember the story correctly, the following was related in confidence to James while Sabine was out of the room, and James thought it best never to tell her. So Sabine died never knowing exactly why her brother was murdered in Iraq, never knowing why she and James had also been targeted. Was this the best thing to do under the circumstances, to lessen the discomfort, now knowing that she was ill? I cannot be the judge. The certainty was that there had already been enough sadness and there was plenty more soon to come.

What follows, then, is the last of the last piece of this story:

\# \# \#

JEFFRIES TOLD JAMES PRIVATELY that Britain's Secret Service had got a lot of miles from the original deception. First and foremost, during the Cold War, using Fletcher, Britain successfully fed the Russians reams of false information that allowed British, French and American navies to better track Soviet submarines while they were, themselves, tracking ghosts. Dramatically helping to advance western anti-sonar capabilities and increase by volumes the Soviet Submarine Acoustic Signature Database by which the navy could specifically identify each Soviet sub, and hence each submarine commander – often the most valuable piece of information when playing dozens of simultaneous games of chess blindfold and underwater. Especially since, during this time, Soviet submarines were becoming far more advanced than anyone had previously thought, thanks to many years of successful Soviet spy recruiting in Europe and the United States. But the *Conqueror's* ability to sneak to within a few feet beneath the bow of a Soviet spy vessel – which was itself trailing a two-mile string of hypersensitive hydrophones on a three-inch thick steel cable, all designed to track and get a multi-directional fix on submarines, without the telltale ping of sonar – showed an astounding advance both in western submarine stealth technology and the training and caliber of the submariners who sailed these vessels. For the *Conqueror* to then actually steal this array, using General Dynamics designed pincers on its bow, is something more akin to a science fiction novel, and would never have been possible but for the many years of risky, though obviously successful, underwater sleuthing and surface subterfuge, such as that which followed for years the fiction of Churchill's Gold. Churchill would indeed have been proud.[*]

Secondly, thanks to Fletcher's amateur carelessness (only recently surmised to have been a guilt wish to be discovered), MI5 were able to identify several other spies, albeit low level ones, with close ties to the Communist Party of Great Britain and several of

---

[*] Indeed, *Conqueror's* sister ship, HMS *Churchill*, had already tried to steal the Soviet sonar array in the Mediterranean by steering through its cable, but got herself damaged in the attempt and was summarily depth charged by Soviet support vessels. She survived and was decommissioned in 1991.

the manual workers' unions, which in turn, it is thought, enabled the government to circumvent strike action and eventually formulate a strategy that resulted in Prime Minister Thatcher being able to break the back of the coal miner's strike in 1985.

Thirdly, it put an end, once and for all, to the longstanding conspiracy theory greatly enhanced by Peter Wright in his controversial and rather vindictive book *Spycatcher*, that Hollis had for years been a Soviet mole. This last tidbit came too late to exonerate Hollis, however, because he was already dead, but it did finally tie the knot in a loose end that had been dragged about for years, wasting countless effort. There is probably a fourth and even a fifth, but such is the skulduggerous nature of secret intelligence that it might take years to uncover more, if ever.

The Russians finally got wind of what might be happening, though, after Vladimir Kuzichkin defected to Britain's SIS station in Tehran in 1982, coincidently(?), during the same timeframe as Operation *Barmaid*, and were intent on plugging the conduit of loose information more than the theft of their toys obviously. Indeed, some disgruntled agents within the KGB sought immediate revenge; those who later became the more roguish element when the KGB rebranded itself the new and improved SVR. That was the conduit Harrison had spent a good part of his life protecting, and the one Sean uncovered but misinterpreted, to his eventual cost. Boris Khorkov, on his own volition it seems, then used the story both as cover and justification to further his own ambitions.

In essence, the whole drama, spanning 60 years, was based on a fiction, a brief filament, a misaligned spark in someone's brain during a distant war. It had all been based on a nothing, and yet it reaped tangible rewards but untold consequences. How are we to know what is true and what is not? What is real and what is not? And how much do we really want to know, now knowing the risks of such a venture, and the waste of a life in searching?

FOR THE FALLEN

by Laurence Binyon

With proud thanksgiving, a mother for her children,
England mourns for her dead across the sea.
Flesh of her flesh they were, spirit of her spirit,
Fallen in the cause of the free.

Solemn the drums thrill; Death august and royal
Sings sorrow up into immortal spheres,
There is music in the midst of desolation
And a glory that shines upon our tears.

They went with songs to the battle, they were young,
Straight of limb, true of eye, steady and aglow.
They were staunch to the end against odds uncounted;
They fell with their faces to the foe.

They shall grow not old, as we that are left grow old:
Age shall not weary them, nor the years contemn.
At the going down of the sun and in the morning
We will remember them.

They mingle not with their laughing comrades again;
They sit no more at familiar tables of home;
They have no lot in our labour of the day-time;
They sleep beyond England's foam.

But where our desires are and our hopes profound,
Felt as a well-spring that is hidden from sight,
To the innermost heart of their own land they are known
As the stars are known to the Night;

As the stars that shall be bright when we are dust,
Moving in marches upon the heavenly plain;
As the stars that are starry in the time of our darkness,
To the end, to the end, they remain.

TWELVE LITTLE *S*-BOATS

Based on Septimus Winner's 1870 nursery rhyme, *Ten Little Injuns*.

Twelve little *S*-boats "go to it" like Bevin,
Starfish goes a bit too far – then there were eleven.
Eleven watchful *S*-boats doing fine and then
Seahorse fails to answer – so there are ten.
Ten stocky *S*-boats in a ragged line,
Starlet drops and stops out – leaving us nine.
Nine plucky *S*-boats, all pursuing Fate,
Shark is overtaken – now we are eight.
Eight sturdy *S*-boats, men from Hants and Devon,
Salmon now is overdue – and so the number's seven.
Seven gallant *S*-boats, trying all their tricks,
Spearfish tries a newer one – down we come to six.
Six tireless *S*-boats fighting to survive,
No reply from Swordfish— so we tally five.
Five scrubby *S*-boats, patrolling close inshore,
Snapper takes a short cut – now we are four.
Four fearless *S*-boats, too far out to sea,
Sunfish bombed and scrap-heaped – we are only three.
Three threadbare *S*-boats patrolling o'er the blue,
…
Two ice-bound *S*-boats…
…
One lonely *S*-boat…

POLITICO'S WAR

by Sean O' Connor.

Politico's war; devoid of honor or stately good,
Striven to purpose, body and soul soundly given,
By willing poor, old, and young, man and woman.
Soldiers all, for agenda reigned, confidence supreme,
To fruition, lies designed, populace manipulated, and said,
Despite worldly experience opposed, held in contempt.
From egos want of historical place, came spit and crack,
Not shock and awe. From rock to sand and rich to poor,
All seemed misplaced in time and space.
With money spent, against grasp, to poor man's poverty,
And honorable truth no more. Spilt of nation's blood,
Ebbed in sand. Patriotism resounds in devious design.
Architects protected, rear of hefty lies and puppeteers,
Truth falls unquestioned upon wealthy apathetic ears.
Post motive's change in methods original of desire,
But slow discovery, for glorious account of blood's
Involuntary withdrawal must be found.
Nation's grievous past expounded, such to warrant intervention,
As others, such in want and need, wait vainly as death scours by.
Be stately good vanished? Honorable salvation dissolved?
When financial interests laid bare? No responsibility, for reasons,
Or actions lacking, towards another's earlier fare?
Be the politico safe in exodus, clasped of bible tight?
Whence nation's soldiers blooded and maimed return,
To realize no accounting and warrant denied.
The unwoven agenda alters perception against time,
Was this worth a trial of so powerful a fire?
That history's place beheld in so high esteem,
And by so inept a queue. History shall remember,
Though not for thought's original few.
History built, memories remain, always, in soldiers' face,
Awful visions etched by blood and limbs honorable waste.
Contrasting those who succumb to dubious regard,
And wealth, then fade. A name, a date,
And blame recalled, accountable, finally, for all deeds made,
Ego destroyed by history's pages, yet remain unread in future ages.
Monuments rise to glorious dead,
Less we forget the toil, violence, the glorious bled.
But for them, the politico is naught and dead.

BIBLIOGRAPHY

This brief and simple bibliography is not for any high scholarly appreciation, the author having been a glorified ditch digger most of his life precludes any such assumption, but is solely because the story instilled a fundamental desire to know more; not so much for the story itself, but for the much greater events on the periphery, those that 'Mr. Devlin' was also so interested in. In that regard I owe him a double debt; one for the story, the other for being inspirational in my desire to learn more about the world around me and how we humans, inclusive of ditch diggers and scholars, consistently muddle through to make the world as it is – warts and all.

While failure is integral to the process of learning, and one should never be too concerned for its imminent arrival, an oft-used excuse for repeated, or blindly obvious, failure is being unfortunate not to have been previously endowed with '20/20 hindsight'. However, we are fortunate in this time that we live, unlike previous generations, for not only do we have wonderful libraries from which to draw our knowledge, but we now have a colossal network of information available at our fingertips every minute of every day that was impossible for most to comprehend prior to the late 20th century.

Which begs the obvious question: Why don't more people, especially politicians, better utilize these vast resources?

The Great Boer War – A. Conan Doyle (1900)
The Second World War – Winston S. Churchill (six volumes - 1953)
War in the Shadows: The Guerrilla in History – Robert B. Asprey (1975)
The Battle for the Falklands – Max Hastings & Simon Jenkins (1984)
Ten Commando 1942 - 1945 – Ian Dear (1987)
Task Force: The Falklands War, 1982 – Martin Middlebrook (1987)
On the Psychology of Military Incompetence – Norman F. Dixon (1988)
Spy Catcher – Peter Wright (1988)
The Battle of Britain: The Greatest Air Battle of World War II
        — Richard Hough & Denis Richards (1989)
Signals of War – Lawrence Freedman & Virginia Gamba-Stonehouse (1990)
Seizing the Enigma – David Kahn (1991)
Churchill: A Life – Martin Gilbert (1992)

Afghanistan: Soviet Vietnam – Vladislav Tamarov (1992)
The Boer War – Thomas Packenham (1992)
Margaret Thatcher: The Downing Street Years – Margaret Thatcher (1993)
Strategic Deception in the Second World War: British Intelligence Operations Against the German High Command – Michael Howard (1995)
Hitler's U-Boat War – Clay Blair (two volumes - 1998)
Finest Hour – Tim Clayton & Phil Craig (1999)
Churchill and Secret Service – David Stafford (1999)
A History of the Twentieth Century – Martin Gilbert (three volumes -1999)
FDR: The War President 1940 – 1943 – Kenneth Davis (2000)
The War We Could Not Stop: The Real Story of the Battle for Iraq
    — Guardian Newspapers (2003)
Against All Enemies: Inside America's War on Terror – Richard A. Clark (2004)
Blowback – Chalmers Johnson (2004)
Secrets and Lies: Operation "Iraqi Freedom" and After – Dilip Hiro (2004)
The Puppet Masters: Spies, Traitors and the Real Forces Behind World Events
    — John Hughes-Wilson (2004)
Churchill and America – Martin Gilbert (2005)
One Christmas in Washington: Churchill and Roosevelt Forge the Grand Alliance
    — David J. Bercuson & Holger H. Herwig (2005)
The Dieppe Raid: The Story of the Disastrous 1942 Expedition
    — Robin Neillands (2006)
State of Denial: Bush at War Part III – Bob Woodward (2006)
Road to Suez: The Battle of the Canal Zone – Michael Thornhill (2006)
History of the Second World War – Sir Basil Liddell Hart (2007)
Fiasco: The American Military Adventure in Iraq, 2003 to 2005
    — Thomas E. Ricks (2007)
Cobra II : The Inside Story of the Invasion and Occupation of Iraq
    — Michael R. Gordon & Bernard E. Trainor (2007)
The Age of American Unreason – Susan Jacoby (2008)
Gandhi & Churchill: The Epic Rivalry that Destroyed an Empire and Forged Our Age
    — Arthur Herman (2009)
Defend the Realm: The Authorised History of MI5 – Christopher Andrew (2009)
A Fiery Peace in a Cold War: Bernard Shriver and the Ultimate Weapon
    — Neil Sheehan (2009)

A NOTE ON FOOTNOTES

Footnotes have occasionally been included for much the same reason as the bibliography, not to provide any academic source information for the material, but to maybe, hopefully, spur a casual desire among interested readers to delve a little deeper into the long, convoluted, often opinionated and sometimes changing history of our world. To see what is true and what is not. And because a very smart, very highly educated person once asked me, in all sincerity, "what good is history?" Whence, after first being utterly gobsmacked, I stood up from my chair, walked over to him and gave him a good solid swift kick in the shins. Sitting down again calmly, I asked: "Are you going to ask me that question again?" To which he instantly replied with some shock: "Hell no!"

Well, that's history!

If we learn from it, history has done its job. But it cannot do its job if we do not read it, question it, research it, add the perception of hindsight maybe, but try also, as we must, to understand the realities of the period, the hard truths of life at the time for which we often now harness a horror.

We must also thank the thousands of industrious, brilliant historians who have endeavored over centuries to provide the world with a record, from the early Greek writings of Herodotus through the propagandized peoples' plays of Shakespeare to popular historians like Keegan and Ambrose. But probably more so to the many impressive researchers who push out volume after volume – such as Gilbert has done for the 20th Century and Churchill – and, of course, all those thousands of authors in between and yet to come. Yes, even those who attempt to write history in their own image (in effect, "a riddle hidden in a cocoon of truth"). For that, too, is history, and often a more telling history because we are forced to question the reason for it. As we must question everything.

But we must also thank those wonderful friends who recommend, lend and give us these books. You know who you are.

ABOUT THE AUTHOR

Capt. Vasili Borodin: I will live in Montana. And I will marry a round American woman and raise rabbits, and she will cook them for me. And I will have a pickup truck... maybe even a 'recreational vehicle.' And drive from state to state. Do they let you do that?
– Tom Clancy, The Hunt for Red October.

Robert D. Hubble grew up to be a farmer, leaving his London school at the first opportunity to do so. Immediately after college, however, when life forced a change, as it so often does, Robert became a Sapper and served as a Combat Engineer in Britain's renowned Corps of Royal Engineers. Then, still with a desire to farm, he left England to help run a mid-west dairy farm among the frozen lakes of northern Minnesota. A life changing experience then led Robert to the wilds of central Idaho where he immediately fell in love with the magnificent mountains and the dirty physical work of fighting forest fires. A job which eventually enabled him to experience many wonderful years as a U.S. Smokejumper in the Rocky Mountains of Montana. Where he now lives with his American wife Christina, who, she "suggests" the author mention, "is not round and does not raise rabbits."

ALSO BY ROBERT D. HUBBLE

Inside The Great Game

The Great Game continues. In its long and bloody history there have been periods of relative peace and tremendous violence. Through all, the subtle intrigue has remained, often coming violently to the fore when national interests are at stake. As is the case now, with one major superpower vying for influence against many smaller nations, rich and poor, for the only truly valuable commodity left in the world. Oil.

For this, countries still send their soldiers. But now under the guise of consultants and advisors, instead of travelers and tradesmen. The present struggle is no longer limited to the mountains of Central Asia, but is fought worldwide. And neither is it fought solely by nations. Individuals drawn into this fight are still abandoned by fickle national and corporate policy and few are ever remembered for their efforts. When the instigators give up and wash their hands soldiers die. All so their masters can have a continued role in the Great Game.

The Independent, January 24th 1994 – British Mercenaries for Azeri War.
Tim Kelsey reports:

"The Government has given tacit support to an illegal scheme to supply Azerbaijan with military backing in its war with Armenia, according to a British peer who has admitted his own involvement.

"It is understood that negotiations are still not complete, but private chartered Russian aircraft have been put on standby to fly mercenaries into the area. The first phase of the scheme is to provide British military trainers.

"An American Oil company is reported to have provided training for Azeri soldiers by former members of the US armed forces in breach of American embargoes. The US State Department is investigating the allegations, which were made by foreign diplomats based in Baku, the Azeri capital."

Printed in Great Britain
by Amazon